The Savage Valley

D1452753

by

James Penny

Grosvenor House
Publishing Limited

James Penny is hereby identified as author of this
work in accordance with Section 77 of the Copyright, Designs
and Patents Act 1988

The book cover picture is the copyright of the artist, Don Troiani

This book is published by
Grosvenor House Publishing Ltd
28-30 High Street, Guildford, Surrey, GU1 3HY.
www.grosvenorhousepublishing.co.uk

A CIP record for this book
is available from the British Library

ISBN 978-1-906210-99-1

Foreword

Wherever there are great natural barriers, nature has ever provided some path through them that allows the movement of men. No grand design. Merely the random chance dictated by the movement of the earth's surface in its last great upheaval and the power of water to erode in the millions of years following.

Like water, men would find that path which offered the least resistance to their efforts. Once found they became the migratory routes, the trade routes, and of course, the routes of invasion. Fortifications mark their way, old and ruined or of more modern construction, guarding against the easy passage of armies.

There is such a route in the eastern United States. Much later than some in becoming of strategic importance, but one that was fought over as bitterly as any.

In the North it begins where the Richelieu River flows into the broad St Lawrence some miles downstream from Montreal. Follow this river upstream through low-lying featureless farmland and it opens out into an imposing body of water that stretches one hundred and fifty miles to the southward. Lake Champlain shaped like an arrowhead, broad and islanded in the north, tapering to its apex in a wooded creek a mere twelve miles from the great River Hudson and separated from it by a narrow strip of land. Lake George stretches parallel to Lake Champlain linked by a short river and affording an alternative route for the last third of Champlain's length Two hundred miles downstream lies the Atlantic Ocean.

Bisecting the then British colonies, later the embryonic United States, the valleys of Champlain and the Hudson were a highway into their heartland. As such, it saw the movement of armies, colliding in set piece battles or in the vicious skirmishes that is the small change of war.

On a fine spring morning in 1754, far to the south and west in the Ohio Valley, a group of Virginian militia under the command of a Lt Colonel George Washington attacked a party of Frenchmen, killing around a dozen of them. The shots fired that morning were to lead to a war that was to spread around the globe, waged wherever French and British influence clashed. A war that saw the true beginnings of a British Empire, but in its aftermath sowed the seeds of dissension that lead to the loss of Britain's oldest colonies

As the conflict grew, a Regiment sailed across the Atlantic to play their part.

It was a unique formation! The first of it's kind to take a place among the Regular Regiments of a British Army. Composed solely of Scottish Highlanders it was designated the 42nd Regiment of Foot, but to the Gaelic speaking people whose menfolk filled it's ranks it was known better by a nickname. *'Am Freiceadan Dubh.'* The Black Watch!

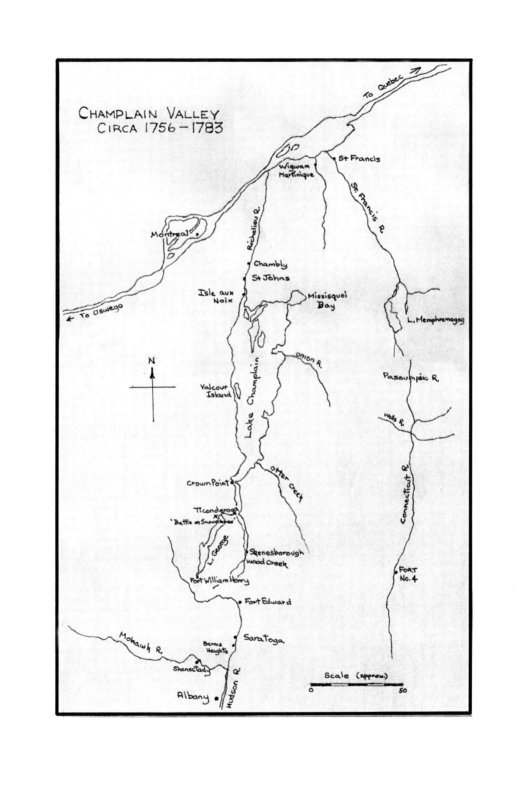

Chapter 1

The clang of the ship's bell and a patter of seamen's feet on the deck mere inches above his head woke him. He lay a while, listening to the now familiar sounds of the transport ship. There was the creaking of timbers, the slap and whisper of the sea on the hull and the night noises of the cramped troop deck where fifty hammocks swayed in unison to the slow roll of the vessel. In the next hammock Iain Mhor was snoring loudly and Jamie gave up any attempt to drift back into sleep. He slipped to the deck and bundling up his plaid moved in a crouch toward the faint light of the hatchway. As he passed under Iain Mhor, he spitefully punched upward at the bulge of canvas covered buttocks and grinned at the protesting grunt that was followed by another resonant snore. Reaching the main deck he paused and breathed deeply of the cool fresh air, clearing his head of the foetid atmosphere in the troop deck, then, draping his plaid over his head and shoulders made his way forward to the bow.

The seaman on lookout jumped in alarm as the shrouded figure appeared silently at the rail beside him.

'Soddin' hell, mate! Creepin' up on a man like that. Try coughin' or summat next time,' the seaman grunted indignantly. 'What's amiss? Couldn't sleep for thinking about all these Frenchies and their heathen mates what's waiting for ye?'

'Nothing like that. Just a friend that snores very loudly... and I'm sorry I startled you.'

'Ye speak a proper language then. Not that gibberish you all chatter away in. Whatcha call it again?'

'That would be the Gaelic,' Jamie answered, mildly.

The seaman sniffed and wandered off to the lee side to spit a stream of tobacco juice into the sea.

The sky behind them was lightening and Jamie could hear the clatter of utensils as the cook and his helpers prepared breakfast in the galley below where he stood. There was a belch of smoke from the galley funnel a few feet behind him.

'A rum lot you are,' the seaman remarked in a friendlier tone. 'Quietest trip I've made since we started carrying redcoats. Not one flogging since we left Cork.'

1

He chuckled. 'We carried some of Braddock's lads a year back. Now them were real redcoats. Fighting and cursing and hardly a day without one of them havin' his back scratched with the lash. Poor buggers! Wonder how many of them are left. You heard did you?'

'We heard!' Jamie answered, shortly.

The rumours had spread quickly through the army after Braddock's defeat the previous year. Rumours of a new type of warfare in the Americas. Of an enemy that no longer stood upright in line and exchanged volleys, but lurked among the trees and presented no target. A litany of horrific tales of the French's savage allies who took no prisoners and tore the scalp hair from living and dead alike. Painted naked warriors who did not stand to receive a bayonet charge like civilised men, but who melted away into the woods… then returned to shoot men down from a distance. Of a British army tumbling back in rout, carrying with them their dying general.

The light from the east was fast overtaking them and Jamie could make out the dark bulk of the nearest ship to them, a glimmer of phosphorescence in its bow wave and wake. Further off, all around them, the twinkling stern lights marked other ships in the convoy carrying part of a new and stronger army to the war in the Americas.

'Not long now. Likely we'll sight land come full light.' the seaman remarked.

'You think so? How can you tell?'

'The old barkie's movin' different. Shallower water d'ye see. Besides, ye can smell the land.'

Jamie lifted his head and sniffed hard, holding the air in his nostrils. He closed his eyes and there it was…the faintest of scents, but distinct from the salt air, tar, and bilge odours he had become accustomed to in the last six weeks. A hint of pine resin and greenery.

'Why, so I can,' he said, softly.

The seaman glanced at the young man beside him. In the strengthening light, he could make out his features. A lean face, dark of visage with a slight hook to the nose, his crow black hair long and clubbed at the nape. Tall, and from what he could make of his body under the draped plaid, well built.

'Here! You're the lad what plays the fiddle. Played it a treat too.' The seaman laughed and clapped Jamie on the shoulder. 'Showed up that bloody old scraper we've got. Five years I've sailed with him and never known him to play more than the same three tunes.'

There was the thud of cannon as the naval escorts signalled to the merchant ships in their charge to increase sail. Seaman scampered up the rigging to loose the main courses, the custom being to reduce sail at night to avoid the ships becoming too dispersed. A

2

naval frigate glided past toward the rear of the convoy, in its never-ending task of chivvying the wallowing transports into a semblance of order and gathering up the inevitable stragglers. A hail from the masthead made Jamie look up.

'Deck there! Land! Land... two points off the starboard bow.'

'Told ye so, son,' the seaman chuckled. 'America... and if they're navigation's right that should be Long Island, off the mouth of the Hudson. A couple of days should see us berthed in New York...and God knows what them Dutchies are going to make of ye when they see your hairy shanks. Give all the girls the vapours, so ye will.'

The ship's bell struck. 'That's me off watch then. Good luck to you, lad. You take care o' them Frenchies for me.' With a grin and a long stream of tobacco juice over the side, he slipped off the forecastle and disappeared onto the now crowded main deck.

'Jamie Campbell!' He heard Iain Mhor's bull roar and looking round spotted him a few feet up the main shrouds. He was clad only in his shirt, uncaring that the wind was blowing the tails up. When Jamie reached the deck below him, Iain bent over to say something. The man hanging on the ratlines next to him complained plaintively.

'It's America I want to see, Munro... so will you get your great hairy arse out of my face?'

'Ach! Away wi' you, McPhee. It's a good match. Your face and my arse,' Iain retorted and swung clumsily to the deck.

'Can't see a thing and bedamned if I'm climbing higher. Where have you been?'

'Away from your snoring. I smelt it, Iain. Smelt America.'

'Did you now? Well, all I can smell is food, or what goes by its name on this tub. God, I never thought I'd miss Army rations.' Food, being one of Iain's favourite subjects, he rambled on. 'A sailor was telling me they have a way of baking hams where we're going. They mix honey and mustard and glaze the ham with it... and they make a sort of fish stew they call chowder with fresh cream. Aye... and there's these beans they cook with pork. They sound good....'

'Munro! Black shame on ye! Will ye go and make yourself decent before some of these seafaring men start having improper thoughts.'

The loud voice of Sergeant McIvor put a stop to Iain's itinerary of succulent dishes and sent him scurrying below.

In the same draft to join the Regiment in Ireland, they had gone through the recruit training together. Although the opposites in temperament and looks they had in that time formed a strong friendship. Jamie, dark and lean, quiet spoken and apt to take life seriously at times. Iain, a careless bull of a man with hair the colour of wheat chaff, was noisy, irrepressible, and universally popular in the company. Both tall, they should by rights have gone to the Grenadier Company, but Jamie's uncle, Captain Alexander Campbell, ensured they both served under him. Family and name still played their part in the make up of the 42nd Regiment of Foot, the muster rolls full of Campbell's, Munro's, McKays and Grant's. In the company, there were no less than two sets of brothers and a father and son serving.

Alexander had been granted a commission in the Campbell militia during the hectic days of Prince Charles Edward Stuart's bid to restore his father to the throne. He had fought from behind the dry stone dyke on the left flank of Cumberland's line at Drummossie Moor, and he had fought well, as the clansmen charged forward to their death and the destruction of a way of life on the bayonets of King George's redcoats.

A restless fellow in the days before the rebellion, he had had little interest in the thriving carpentry shop his father had left to him and his elder brother James, near Kenmore on the banks of Loch Tay.

Jamie's father, ten years older, was on the other hand, a craftsman. His furniture, of fine quality, was greatly in demand by the gentry of Perthshire. A gentle man with quiet ways, he was a lover of music, and used his skill in the shaping of wood to produce fiddles that were sought after by other musicians. It was a love and a skill he passed on to his two sons, Jamie and Callum, by patient teaching.

The day Alex returned after the militia disbanded stood out in Jamie's memory. The two boys, taking turns to stagger around brandishing his weighty broadsword, bombarded him with questions on his adventures, which he laughingly fended off, until their mother shooed them off to bed. They crept back out onto the stair landing and listened to the adults talk.

'So Alex...how was it? We heard some disturbing stories,' they heard their father say.

'It was a strange thing James. God knows I have little regard for those who let themselves be led by that strutting idiot of a Prince, and none at all for their cause. Yet, at the onset, I was proud of them. Aye, even as we shot them down, I was proud of them. And when it was over, I felt angry... and sad that they had died for men who were unworthy of them.'

'The stories we heard were of the aftermath of the battle.'

'I'll not talk of that.' Alex had said, abruptly.

'They were true then?'

Alex gave no answer and there was a long silence, then he remarked 'You know that this madness has yet to run its course. The Highlands are to be tamed, once and for all. The prescriptions they are bringing in are to apply to all the clans whether they were loyal to the government or not. The belted plaids, the carrying of arms, even the pipes are to be proscribed. They are set, as they see it, to civilise us, James.'

'I rarely wear the philamhor, have no arms but a fowling piece and though I would sorely miss the pipes I am as civilised as any man.'

'As am I! But try to explain that to some fool in London who has never set foot in Scotland. They think the place fair leaping with Jacobites, yet near half the men who fought in Cumberland's army were Scots. The rebels could raise but six thousand men, most of them unwilling. Only their chiefs threatening to burn the roofs over their head brought them out. Argyll has but to whistle and he can raise five thousand Campbell broadswords for the Government cause. Yet we are all to suffer for the folly of the few. Charlie Stuart has much to answer for.'

'Perhaps it will not turn out as badly as you fear Alex. Perhaps they will lift these restrictions when all has quietened down.' they heard the soft voice of their mother say. 'What of yourself? Has this past year finally rid you of that wild streak? Ready to settle down?'

'Ach, Kirstie! Forever trying to tame me and tie me up with a wife and bairns,' Alex laughed. 'Not yet I fear and my future depends on you, James. My Colonel thought well of me. He thought I had an aptitude for soldiering and truth to tell I have acquired a taste for it. It satisfies something in me. He said if I wished to serve in a King's regiment, he would use his influence... but I need money to purchase a commission. Would you consider advancing that money for my share of the workshop? An unfair bargain for I have done little to make it more profitable.'

'I would prefer not to. Poor carpenter you may be, but I'd rather see you ruining good wood than leading the chancy life of a soldier,' James said quietly. 'But if that is what you want, I shall. We'll call it a loan, though. If Army life begins to pall there is always a place for you here, and I will not deprive you of your share.'

'You're a good brother James.... But I think I've found what suits me. Come.... Raise your glasses and we'll drink to my new life.' Then to the boys' consternation he added with a grin. 'Kirstie, two glasses of well watered wine for the eavesdroppers on the stairhead to drink a toast to their uncle.'

His visits were infrequent over the years as the boys grew to young manhood His arrivals were usually unannounced and were always an occasion for great excitement in the household.

Whenever he appeared, resplendent in his regimentals of red coat and kilted plaid in the dark government tartan, the officer's gorget hanging bright on his chest, all work would cease and the family would gather round him to listen as he related his latest travels and stories of the life he led. He spoke of the campaign in Flanders shortly after he had joined and of his time spent in England and Ireland. Describing people and places, he spawned a desire in his nephews to see the wider world he spoke of and to travel as he had done, venturing out from the limited horizons of the loch and the mountains surrounding it. For one of them it was Alex's talk of his regiment and the men he served alongside that fascinated the most.

Chapter 2

A few days past his eighteenth birthday, Jamie heard the news over supper that a recruiting party of his uncle's regiment was staying at the inn at Kenmore. His father had mentioned it and suggested to his mother that they could perhaps invite the officer to a meal and find out if he had some news of Alex.

Jamie slept badly that night. The urge to taste the life of a soldier fighting with the fear of making a commitment that would change the whole course of his settled existence. He agonised over the pain he would cause his mother and the bitter disappointment his father would feel, but try as he could to erase it, that longing persisted.

He arose while it was still dark and stole out of the house quietly. Walking the two miles to the village he told himself it was curiosity that brought him out at this hour. A need to find out more. To merely talk with soldiers.

It was early when he reached Kenmore, the houses quiet and the village street deserted. He heard the clank of the pump outside the inn and saw a man swilling his face in the horse trough.

As he approached the man looked up and gave him a broad cheerful grin. 'A good morning to you,' then nodded at the pump handle. 'I'd be obliged if you'd give it a stroke or two.'

Jamie obediently pumped the handle and the man stuck his blond head under the stream of water snorting and spluttering, then stepped back, shaking himself like a dog. He stood up to his full height and Jamie blinked at the size of him. A full three inches taller than Jamie with a bulkiness in the chest and shoulders that made his hips and legs look thin by comparison, he was around Jamie's age. Dressed only in a pair of patched breeches, raw hide brogans, and a shirt that had seen better days, he set about wringing the water from his long hair.

'A dram too much last night,' he laughed. 'You're up bright and early. From the village are you?'

'From nearby. I heard there was a recruiting party staying at the inn?'

'There is, but they are all still abed. Looking to enlist?'

Jamie shook his head emphatically. 'No! I have a kinsman in their regiment. I thought they might have some word of him. And you?'

7

'I took the shilling ten days ago. I'd just helped drive a herd of black cattle from Glen Shee to the market in Perth and man, was I sick of seeing the dung-covered rumps o' the beasts. I decided this war they were all talking about might be more entertaining than prodding cows arses,' he stuck out his hand. 'Iain Munro is the name, although folk in our glen tend to call me Iain Mhor, so as not to confuse me with my first cousin who they call Iain Beg because he's a good handbreadth shorter than myself.'

Jamie laughed and shook Iain's hand. 'Have they enlisted many?' he asked.

'A round dozen of us so far. The rest are snoring away in the stables. The lieutenant is very particular who he takes. Are you sure you don't want to enlist? Just think…three years away from damned cows and sheep or whatever it is you do for a living.'

'Three years? I thought you had to enlist for twenty-one?'

'You still can, but there's new enlistment regulations on account of the war. Three years or until hostilities end, whichever is the longer. They're fair desperate for men. Why, Perth is full of recruiters for the breeched regiments, which is why the lieutenant didn't linger there.'

'Three years,' Jamie thought. 'I could be a soldier for three years.'

Iain read the expression on his face. 'Ha! That has you thinking about it,' he chuckled.

A figure in belted plaid, the end draped over his shoulders came out of the inn door, stretching and yawning, then made his way round the side toward a privy.

'That's Sergeant McNabb that is,' Iain said admiringly. 'Fought at a place called Fontenoy in the last French war he told us. Told us they took one look at the broadswords and run like rabbits, the French did.'

The Sergeant came back, washed his face at the trough and dried himself with his plaid. He was short and broad shouldered, with a lined craggy face, his hair neatly clubbed, but streaked with grey.

He looked over at them and eyed Jamie appraisingly.

'Good morning lad! Thinking of joining us, are you?' he said in a kindly voice.

'He's not sure, Sergeant.'

'Hush, Munro! Let him speak for himself,' the sergeant said with quiet authority. 'Well, lad?'

'I really only came to seek news about an uncle of mine. Captain Campbell?'

'If I recall correctly we have four Captain Campbell's serving,' the sergeant said, grinning. 'Archibald, Alexander and two Johns. I've long lost count of the Lieutenants and Ensigns of that name.'

'Its Alexander,' Jamie said hurriedly.

'Ah yes! A good officer and when I look at you I see the resemblance. I served in the same company when he was a lieutenant.' He stared at Jamie steadily, causing him to flush, then slipped smoothly into his recruiting sergeant role

'Now why would a strapping lad like you, with kinfolk already serving, be unsure about enlisting. I'd have thought your uncle would have told you what a fine body of men he commands. Highlanders all, officers and men alike. Would you not be proud to wear the garb of your race. To be a member of the only regiment to wear the belted plaid in the Army of King George the Second, may God preserve him. To shoulder a musket and march to war behind the pipes, with a broadsword hanging by your side. Why, I was but a lad like you when we first mustered not ten miles away on the banks of the Tay at Aberfeldy, and a brave sight we were. A thousand strong, and every man a hero. Proud I was then and even prouder today, and in all these years I have never regretted a moment of them. It's an honour and a privilege to serve in the 42nd Regiment of Foot and we take only the best and boldest. I remember after Fontenoy, when we cut the heads off Frenchmen like bairns' wheeching the tops off thistles with a bit stick, the Colonel coming up and saying to me, personal like, 'McNabb! You're a dab hand with the broadsword, but ye must learn to leave some for us officers.'

He was getting into his stride when an amused voice broke in.

'Good morning, Sergeant McNabb. You've started early today.'

An officer stood at the inn door, his red coat bright against the dark room behind him.

'Good morning to you sir, and begging your pardon, but you've completely made me lose the thread of what I was saying,' the Sergeant replied, looking slightly aggrieved.

'Sorry, Sergeant! That was thoughtless of me. You can start again if you wish.'

McNabb snorted and went over to speak quietly to the lieutenant.

'He has a rare gift for speech making, has the sergeant,' Iain whispered hoarsely. 'He said much the same and more in Perth. Why, when he was into his full flow he had the crowd hanging on his every word. Mind you, normally he has the piper at his back and four men, the bonniest dancers I've seen, to entertain the folk when his throat got dry and he had to retire for a dram. They're still snoring away so you've missed the full entertainment.'

'Sergeant McNabb tells me you're kin to Captain Alexander Campbell,' the lieutenant said, strolling over to them. 'I know him well. I'm Lieutenant Ogilvy.'

He was older than McNabb but like the sergeant, brisk and upright.

'Good day to you, sir. My father was hoping you'd take a meal with us and give us what news you have of him.'

'Ah! I regret I must decline. We leave here in a few hours. The recruits need to be in Greenock soon to take ship for Ireland. She is due to sail in six days. Is it not a fine place Ireland, Sergeant McNabb?'

'It is indeed sir. A fine homely place to soldier in,' the sergeant agreed heartily.

'The Sergeant says you may be thinking of enlisting?'

'I'd dearly love to, sir. I've thought of it a long time. But...'

The Lieutenant said nothing, merely raised his eyebrows quizzically.

Jamie took a deep breath. 'Is it correct that I may enlist for only three years?'

'It is! Three years or the duration of the war. Whichever is the longer.'

'Then I shall enlist, sir.' As he said the words, he felt a sense of relief at having at last committed himself. Of making his first adult decision.

'Good man! Sergeant McNabb, give him the shilling.'

The sergeant groped in his purse and produced a silver shilling. Pressing it into Jamie's hand, he said, 'That seals your bargain with the King, lad. Welcome to *Am Freiceadan Dubh.*'

'You will wish to inform your family of your decision,' Lieutenant Ogilvy said after the formalities of signing attestation papers and swearing Jamie in were completed. 'I suggest you go home now, settle your affairs and collect what you may need. We march in two hours time so be ready to join us as we pass your house.' He paused and raised a finger in warning. 'I'm taking you on trust by allowing you this time. Don't let me down. Now, off with you.'

When he arrived home the reception was much as he had expected and dreaded when he told his parents. Tears from his mother, anger and words of disappointment from his father, initially. It took them some time to realise that there was no going back on his decision and his father, practical, as always, was the first to recover from the shock of the sudden news.

'I wish you had talked to me first and perhaps I could have dissuaded you by reasoned argument, but you are a man grown now and though I suspect this was done on impulse, as a man the choice was yours to make,' his father said resignedly. 'Callum! Fetch me ink and paper. I have a letter to write.'

Jamie collected spare stockings and a shirt from the room he shared with Callum and turning to his brother said, 'I'll have no use for more. The rest is yours.'

'I wish I was going with you,' Callum said enviously.

'No Callum! That would never do. I've caused enough grief to Mother and Father. To lose you as well would be too much for them to bear.' He ruffled his brother's hair affectionately. 'Forbye! You're not old enough yet. Promise me you'll stay with them until I get home again.'

Callum nodded, his face glum.

They gathered at the door of the house as the little column came marching up the lochside road, the sound of the piper preceding them.

'This is a letter for Uncle Alex,' his father said hurriedly. 'And some money never goes amiss.' He embraced his son. 'Keep safe, lad,'

Jamie held his mother close for a long minute, murmuring reassuring words that he knew would never console her, then anxious to end this pain of parting, eased from her clinging arms and walked to the roadside.

'Hush now Kirstie!' James murmured to his sobbing wife. 'The lad will be fine. He'll be serving with folk of his own kind. There's many a man of good family serves in the ranks of the 42nd. Forbye, Alex will be there to keep an eye on him.'

They watched as the column swung by, the officer raising his hand in acknowledgement to them as he passed.

They saw their son fall in beside a tall blond youth who grinned and clapped him on the back in welcome and as the column passed out of sight Jamie turned and waved his bonnet in farewell.

Chapter 3

'Do you think they may have brought us to the wrong place, Jamie?' Iain Mhor grumbled, his broad beefy face scarlet and moist with perspiration. 'I thought America to be cold.' He took off his bonnet and mopped his streaming brow, straw hair matted to his head.

'Quiet on parade, Munro,' the voice of Sergeant McIvor rumbled from behind them. 'And put your bonnet back on, you great pudden.'

Their half company was drawn up in ranks on a quayside in New York waiting for the other half to disembark. It was a wide and crowded thoroughfare with solid, brick built buildings overlooking wharves, busy with wagons and men loading or unloading cargo from the ships berthed the length of the waterfront.

A large crowd had gathered to watch and stare at these out-landishly garbed redcoats. Portly Dutch burghers in sombre black, their wives in pristine white aprons and starched bonnets, mingled with roughly dressed seamen and dockworkers. The usual loafers and a rowdier element of youths added to the throng of on-lookers.

The heat was stifling although only June. Jamie could feel the sweat trickling down his thighs under the thick wool of his kilted plaid and his shirt was sodden beneath the heavy serge of his red coat. Glanc-ing along the quay, he saw his uncle conferring with the two other officers of the company, a sheaf of papers in his hand. As he watched, the group broke up and Captain Alexander Campbell looked over to his men, a frown on his face. They were swaying as if still on ship-board and he knew they would be less than marching fit after the weeks of enforced idleness.

'Have the men pile arms and rest easy, Sergeant McIvor. We're likely to be here a fair while yet. Don't let them stray though,' he called, stalking off to where the other transport was moored, busy with baggage being unloaded and men disembarking.

Iain Mhor scuttled for the meagre shade of a baggage wagon and made room for Jamie on an upturned empty barrel. It was only marginally cooler but at least their heads were shielded from the hot sun.

He spotted a plump rosy-cheeked girl close by and caught her attention by waving his hands frantically, then made drinking motions, beaming hugely all the while. The girl giggled and disappeared, coming back a few minutes later with a jug of water. Drinking gratefully, they were about to thank her when an older woman stormed up, snatched the jug from them, and shooed the girl away scolding her in shrill Dutch, glowering suspiciously over her shoulder at the pair of them.

'Encouraging is it not,' Iain Mhor grinned. 'Same as Ireland. The lasses friendly enough... if you can catch them away from their mammies.'

They had enjoyed their sojourn in Ireland. The Gaelic-speaking Highlanders finding their relationship with the people less charged with the suspicion and dislike of redcoats held by the population in general. The ability to communicate was part of it, as was the common Celtic culture, but also the men carried out their duties of policing in a conciliatory manner. Never in a heavy-handed way. Many in the ranks had memories of the aftermath of the FortyFive rebellion and shied away from the sometimes harsher methods of other regiments.

That they were different from other regiments was obvious in more ways than their dress. Highlanders to a man they had a closer affinity with their officers, sharing names and in many cases kinship. Flogging was unknown, the discipline more relaxed and the men, although high spirited, were circumspect in their behaviour.

Soldiering had for long been regarded in Scotland as an honourable profession. A land poor in resources but rich in manpower, it had for centuries seen it's younger sons leave to follow a mercenary calling in Continental armies or serve as officers and other ranks in every regiment of the British Army. A son who had gone for a soldier brought no shame on his family.

The ranks of the 42nd were filled with the sons of tacksmen, the tenant farmers of the highlands, proud to be bearing arms and wearing the highland garb, both of which had been proscribed throughout Scotland since the Rebellion. The age-old clan feuds, which had bedevilled the highlands, lost their meaning when a man enlisted in the regiment. Pride in name was still there, but second only to pride in belonging.

Alex Campbell had been less than welcoming to his nephew on his arrival in Ireland.

Taking him out of earshot of the rest of the recruits, he had regarded him sourly.

'If you had written before you up and 'listed I would have given you some advice. There are other ways you could have gone about it. As a gentleman volunteer for one! You'd serve in the ranks but the way is open for a commission by merit. We'll be at war soon and the opportunities are to be had. By his letter your father seems to think I'll take you under my wing. Look after you! He has little idea of military life.'

He paused and taking in Jamie's crestfallen expression, sighed, and softened a little.

'Well, it's done now, so let me explain the rules between you and I. You're my nephew only when I say you are. I'm Captain Campbell and you'll address me as sir. I'll make sure you serve in my company. I owe your father at least that. But you'll receive no favours. You understand?'

Jamie flushed. 'I never expected to be favoured, sir.' He hesitated, then said tentatively. 'I have a friend, Iain Mhor Munro?'

'And you'd like to serve alongside him. Very well! Your first and last favour,' Alex laughed. 'I'll arrange it. Friends are precious things for a soldier. Dismiss Private Campbell.'

He watched as his nephew rejoined the recruit draft and grinned. 'Ach! He'll be fine,' he murmured.

Jamie and Iain watched in idle amusement as a youth, egged on by his friends, stealthily reached forward with a stick to raise up the rear of Private McPhee's kilt only to be thwarted by Sergeant McIvor's large brogue crushing down on his bare foot. The youth yelped and the Sergeant smiled benignly, wagged an admonishing finger at him, then ambled over to join them in the patch of shade, leaning on his halberd. Almost as big as Iain Mhor, he had a wicked sense of humour that belied his normally impassive face.

'Not long now, lads. Baggage is loaded. Then just a wee ten mile march to where we're to be camped'

He grinned at Iain Mhor's look of dismay. 'Now Munro, don't you be fretting. The Captain has kindly ordered packs to be carried on the wagons, so you'll be walking light as a feather.'

He saw the other half of the company marching up the quay to join them and bawled. 'Two company! On parade! Quickly now!

Iain swore as he retrieved his musket, the metal burning hot from the sun. He pawed at his leather cross belt settling his broadsword, then moved the waist belt with bayonet and cartridge box to a more comfortable position, muttering imprecations under his breath.

'Money in my purse and a rare looking place to be spending it.... And we're off to sit in some damned field. 'Taint fair Jamie!'

Captain Campbell viewed his men with a paternal eye. A mere ten miles in this heat would tax them. He planned to take it steady. The company's womenfolk and children were scrambling up the sides of the wagons to perch on top of the baggage The formidable Jenny McIvor, his senior sergeant's wife, chivvying along the gaggle of wives, mainly Irish girls lucky enough to be chosen by lot to accompany them

The company piper struck up a march as the column swung away and strangely, the crowd of onlookers, mainly silent and curious until then began to clap and cheer.

They cleared the environs of the town, the road following the river, passing neat and prosperous looking farms each with their orchards of apple, pear, and cherry trees, the boughs heavy with, as yet, unripe fruit. The crops in the fields grew tall and fat cattle and sheep grazed on the rich grass of the meadows. Every now and again some large imposing house would come into view.

'A land of plenty, Jamie,' Iain Mhor gloated, his good humour restored. 'Man! Did you ever see the like?'

Having marched about four miles they halted at a stretch of the road shaded by trees and broke ranks to rest on the verges. Within minutes a small crowd of men, women and children from nearby farms appeared to stare curiously at them.

Alex Campbell approached them, spoke to the men, then reached in his purse and produced coins. Women and children rushed off to return with flagons and jugs of cool well water and passed among the soldiers with them.

Their thirst quenched the men were forming up again when a women appeared assisting a frail looking but upright old man his eyes white with cataracts.

'My father,' she said to Alex, hesitantly. 'He heard the pipes. He's blind and his mind is confused these days but he must have remembered the sound for he begged me to lead him down to you. Could your piper play for him perhaps. It would make him happy.'

'It would be a pleasure ma'am,' Alex said, and signalled to the piper. 'How long has your father been in America?'

'These forty years past. He was transported here after some rebellion. He would talk of a battle he fought in. I cannot bring the name to mind.'

'Would it have been Sheriffmuir?' Alex suggested.

'Why, that's the very name. You've heard of it, sir?'

Alex nodded, smiling. 'Oh yes. I have heard of it.' Another failed Jacobite rebellion, he thought and another generation of lives changed because of it.

The old man stood quietly listening to the piper play a selection of tunes. His eyes were bright with tears.

When the piper had done and the company was stepping off the man spoke for the first time. He called loudly and firmly in the Gaelic.

'*Cuimhnich gniomhan ur sinnsearan!* Remember the deeds of your ancestors!'

Chapter 4

He threaded his way through the noisy bustle of the Albany wharves, heaped with supplies and teeming with work parties from the regiments whose tented camps surrounded the neat Dutch township with it's red brick houses and staid burghers. Harassed supply officers rushed around with bills of lading directing the loading of wagons and the allocation of stores. A group of cursing artillerymen struggled to wheel a recalcitrant four pounder cannon ashore up two narrow planks. Barges lay off in the river waiting for a vacant berth to unload more munitions of war.

Clear of the activity he followed a path that ran by the river, passing through the welcome shade of small copses of trees. Finding a convenient log in the deep shadows of a towering maple he sat, savouring the quiet coolness and the absence of human company. A string of barges passed him, carrying, by the men's lack of uniform clothing, more Provincials. It reminded him of his own journey up river from New York that had brought home to him the vastness of this land they had been brought to. Much of the river valley was extensively inhabited and cultivated, the river itself busy with boat traffic, but where a view of the distant horizon afforded itself he could see the dark green forests and high ridges of, as yet, untamed land.

The variety of trees fascinated him. Some he recognised, but many were of a species he had never seen. His carpenter's mind wondered how their wood looked when it was shaped, fashioned and polished.

The month the Regiment had spent on Manhattan Island as they recovered from the long voyage and prepared for the move north to join the army gathering in Albany had convinced Iain Mhor that a finer place to fight a war would be hard to find. Fresh food was plentiful. Sutlers booths had sprung up within days of their arrival selling a wide range of food and drink to those who had the money to purchase them.

'God's truth, Jamie, but this is how soldiering should be.' he commented one evening as they sat outside a booth clasping flagons of cider. He drained his mug and smacked his lips. 'Your turn to buy, McPhee.'

McPhee sighed, fingered the coins in his purse, and rose reluctantly.

'We're in the civilised parts, Iain. I doubt if we'll live so well in the north. It will be back to salt pork and mouldy biscuit no doubt,' Jamie said.

John Cameron, a carrot haired older man, who was known to have been out with the Prince during the rebellion, agreed. 'Aye! I hear it's wild country.'

'Nonsense! Its Albany we're headed for and she's a fine town I've been told. They'll have inns and plump young Dutch girls. It'll be rare I tell you,' Iain, ever the optimist, retorted.

John snorted. 'The colonists refuse to quarter us so there will be no cosy inns for you and me. And your Dutch girls will be locked away safely if their parents are wise. Half of King George's army is heading there. The place will be fairly swarming with redcoats.' He gulped the last of his cider and looked about. 'Was McPhee not off to buy some more?'

'He was!'

'Aye, well, I've just spotted him sneaking away to our lines.' He chuckled as Iain Mhor set off in pursuit.

Today Jamie had left Iain Mhor playing a noisy game of cards with McPhee and the others in their tent and set off in search of some solitude and to explore his new environment.

The sound of angry voices broke the quiet. Curious, he rose and moved toward the sound, pausing at the edge of the trees.

Two roughly dressed men stood with their backs to him. A few yards from them, his face mottled red with anger, stood a small compact man in a plain blue coat. His feet were spread apart, head, shoulders, and chest thrust forward aggressively, and he was waving a fist in the air. Behind him was a woman with a look of concern on her face holding on firmly to a slight, brown haired, heavily freckled young girl.

Thirteen year old Sarah McConnell hefted the piece of wood she had picked up and tried once again to range herself alongside her irate father and yet again her mother dragged her back behind her skirts. Her father had just been called an English poophead by the raucous pair of teamsters who confronted him and was working himself up into a rare temper.

'You dare call me English, ye pair o' colonial scuts,' he roared. 'Irish I am, through and through.' He brandished a light walking cane at them. 'Come ahead, ye great oxen!'

'Will you stop your nonsense, Martin,' her mother called pleadingly.

'I will not,' he snapped. 'I asked them politely to moderate their language in the presence of my womenfolk and all I get is abuse. I'll not have it.'

'In God's name.... We live with an army that curses most horribly. And I've heard worse from your own mouth.' She looked apprehensively at the two men, who were beginning to look surly and ripe to take up her husband's challenge. 'Please Martin! Come away!'

Sarah saw the tall figure of a Highlander emerge from the woods. He had his broadsword drawn and she gulped with excitement as he came up silently behind the unsuspecting men...only to be disappointed when he merely tapped one of them on the shoulder with its tip and spoke quietly to them. They moved back hastily when they saw the naked blade. The Highlander smiled pleasantly and gestured with his sword, whereupon the two turned and staggered off, stopping at a safe distance to shout some insult, then disappeared into a patch of woods.

'Too much rum in them. They fairly reeked of it,' the Highlander said, doffing his bonnet to her mother and herself.

'A terrible thing the drink,' her father sighed. Her mother snorted sarcastically. Ignoring his wife, her father continued. 'Thank you for your intervention. We are indebted to you. Martin McConnell, surgeons mate to His Majesty's Thirty Fifth Foot.'

'James Campbell, sir.'

'Of the 42nd. Stout Gaelic speaking gentlemen all. Well, James Campbell, the least we can do is offer you some refreshment. A dish of tea perhaps.... Or something stronger if you have a taste for it. I rarely touch it myself.' This, with a grin and a wink before turning up the hill to the tented lines of the Thirty Fifth.

'Sarah, darlin'! A few tunes from you to entertain our guest. She has a rare gift with the music has Sarah, Mr Campbell.'

They were seated with mugs of watered rum in the shade of an awning that extended over the front of the family's tent while Mrs McConnell busied herself at a campfire making a meal.

Sarah disappeared into the tent to emerge with a whistle, and, without any preliminary coyness she straightway went to playing a set of jigs. Jamie listened appreciatively. The girl was good. Finishing the jigs she played a slower air he recognised from his time in Ireland.

'That was an O'Carolan piece, was it not?' he asked when she had finished. She nodded shyly.

'You seem knowledgeable. Do you play an instrument yourself, Mr Campbell?' her father asked.

When Jamie told him, Martin dashed into the tent and reappeared with a fiddle and bow

'I bought it for Sarah, but she prefers flutes and whistles.'

Tuning the instrument to Sarah's whistle, Jamie thought for a moment then began to play an Irish reel he'd learnt. Sarah's brown eyes widened, and on the first repeat she slipped smoothly into the lively piece. Her father beamed with delight and leaned back in his seat, his foot tapping away to the rhythm.

The music attracted others and before long two other fiddlers and a fifer from the Regimental band had joined them. It soon became a lively affair with soldiers swinging the camp women into brisk step dances

'You're a rare fiddler, Mr Campbell,' Martin commented as they took a break to eat the meal prepared. 'I take it you can read the music?'

When Jamie said that he could, Martin went on. 'Sarah now, she's learnt by ear and I would dearly love her to be taught the reading of it. I thought of asking the band master, but the man's a drunken swine and no fit person to be teaching a young girl.'

'He drinks no more than yourself Martin McConnell and its only because he brought you down in a hurling match that you're set against him,' his wife interjected.

'It was a dirty foul, as well you know Bridget... and only what you would expect from a Donegal man.' Martin snorted. 'Whatever! The thing is Mr Campbell, the regiment is moving to Fort Edward shortly. There's a Dutch woman, a Mistress Yonge, who runs a school for young ladies in the town and she's agreed to board Sarah whilst we're there. Bridget and I have decided the fort will be no place for a young girl, and there's little point in screwing up your face and making sounds as if you're about to be sick, Sarah darlin'. It's settled! You'll study your penmanship, reading and such like a good girl. Now, Mr Campbell! On such a short acquaintance I hesitate to impose on you but I would be most grateful if you would consider calling by the school on occasion and teaching Sarah the reading of music...given of course, the exigencies of service and your duties.' he added hastily.

His wife sighed. 'Martin, for sheer, brazen effrontery, there's none can outmatch you. I'm sure Mr Campbell can find better things to do in his off duty time.'

'Not at all!' Jamie laughed. 'What better way to while away time than with music. If Sarah is willing I would be happy to do it. I doubt if she will need many lessons. She has a rare natural gift.'

Martin beamed. 'Well now, Sarah. Would you be happy to be taught by Mr Campbell?'

Sarah blushed and nodded. She rose, gave a quick curtsy, then fled into the tent.

'Ach! The darlin',' Martin chuckled. 'I'm thinking she's taken a wee shine to you Mr Campbell. And why not? A fine looking Scotch gentleman like yourself.'

'I can hear you, you know,' came a muffled plaintive voice from the tent.

'That is enough rum for you, Mr McConnell,' his wife said, severely. 'Embarrassing the girl like that in front of our guest.'

Martin looked suitably chastened for his wife's benefit, but grinned and winked at Jamie behind her back.

Jamie rose and thanked them both for their hospitality. 'I'd best be getting back to our lines. With your permission, sir, I'll call the next time I'm off duty and if you could find some sheet music, I'll make a start on teaching Sarah.'

'Tomorrow, gentlemen, we begin training,' Lt. Colonel Grant announced to his assembled officers. 'You will be aware there has been much thought and discussion at all levels of the Army as to how best to prepare our soldiers for the type of warfare we are about to embark upon. I know you have debated it yourselves. General Braddock's defeat last year tended to concentrate the mind somewhat as to the wisdom of adherence to formations and tactics best suited for a war in Europe. I have here a letter from John Campbell, the Lord Loudoun, in which he makes suggestions pertaining to the type of training most useful in the environment we find ourselves. Let me read some extracts from it.'

'Your regiment, consisting of men accustomed to the rough bounds, they being hardy, agile and fleet of foot, is particularly suited to the task of skirmishing with the enemy's irregulars,' he paused and looked up smiling. 'He obviously did not glimpse our quartermaster on his visit. Aye Donald?'

The quartermaster, plump, rosy cheeked, and with the buttons of his waistcoat straining, grinned good-naturedly. 'Quartermasters require only an agility of mind. We do not run or leap. We proceed in a stately manner,' he said, placidly

Colonel Grant inclined his head and grinned. 'Touché Donald! To continue! He recommends a regime of firing at the mark to improve the individuals accuracy, with practice loading and firing from behind cover in kneeling and prone positions. He suggests we devise drills for advancing and retiring in open order retaining the element of control. I expect you to experiment and we will use the sum of your experience to formulate a method that will be common to the regiment. He does add the proviso that the regular drills should still be practised in the event the French choose to meet us in the conventional manner, and I intend to begin there. The nature of our duties in Ireland gave little opportunity to exercise the regiment as a whole. We shall redress this immediately before venturing onto pastures new.'

Peering under his bushy eyebrows at a huddle of Ensigns sprawled on the grass he growled, 'I presume you young gentlemen are totally familiar with the manuals of arms and manoeuvre?'

There were sheepish grins and one or two had the grace to blush.

He glowered at them. 'Be warned! I shall find extra duties for any I catch receiving whispered instructions from a kindly sergeant. Learn your trade, young sirs!'

Later, over a glass of wine, he discussed some of the matters on his mind with Duncan Campbell of Inverawe, his senior major.

'I'm damned if I understand these colonials, Duncan. They cry out for regular troops, yet behave as if we and not the French are the enemy. They refuse to quarter our men on the grounds that it is an infringement of their liberties. Come winter do they expect our men to freeze to death in tents? They have seven thousand provincial troops at Fort Edward and Fort William Henry preparing to move against Fort Carillon. Their officers have informed General Abercromby that if we regulars join them in the campaign, they will resign their commissions and their soldiers will desert en masse.'

'The perennial argument of the Kings' commission superseding a provincial one. Mind, it does seem ludicrous that one of our ensigns is senior to a provincial captain,' Major Campbell commented.

'Indeed! But surely the common aim is the defeat of the French. These controversies can be thrashed out and resolved. Now is not the time to be standing on pride.'

'They have a low opinion of our ability to conduct this war given Braddock's defeat and the recent loss of Oswego. Also, Provincial Regiments working in conjunction with regulars are subject to the same martial law and discipline.' The Major smiled wryly. 'They are volunteers who sign on for a single campaign, or for nine months, whichever is the shorter. A redcoat is to them a 'bloody back.' Martial law and discipline suggests only the whipping post. It offends their sensibilities.'

'Bedamned to their sensibilities,' Grant snapped. 'If they want this war won they had best stop forever whining about their rights, cease their petty squabbling and work with us. As it is I can see no chance of the regiment taking an active part before the campaigning season finishes. We can only ensure our lads are as well prepared as we can make them.'

Chapter 5

'Man! I've herded cattle at the head of the Gareloch where the midges are so bad there were days when all you could see of the cows were their tails waving out of a cloud of the damned creatures,' McPhee moaned, scratching vigorously at his knees. 'But for sheer ferocity the beasties in yon woods have them beat.'

Jamie finished pouring boiling water down the barrel of his musket and swilled it round to clear the caked residue of powder left after a morning spent firing at the mark and practising skirmishing in a thickly wooded area. He had to agree with McPhee. The biting insects of the American forests had been particularly voracious today. He emptied out the discoloured water and set about drying and cleaning the weapon.

'McIvor was telling me that the quartermaster has indented for these campaign gaiters the breeched regiments wear,' John Cameron remarked, staring ruefully at his mud caked hose and brogues. 'We'll look passing strange wearing them and the little kilt. Not a bare knee to be seen.'

'Damn the looks of us,' Iain grunted. 'If they can save my hurdies from being chewed away then the quicker they arrive the happier I'll be.'

Already their experience of the environment they would campaign in had wrought a change in the dress they wore in the field. The belted plaid with it's yards of cloth, all too ready to tangle in branches and undergrowth, had been laid aside in favour of the philabeg, the little kilt, for ease of movement. The red coats had been discarded as a concession to the heat of summer, the men training wearing only shirts and waistcoats.

'Two days rest and we've no duties,' Iain said contentedly. 'What do you think Jamie? A few drams at the sutlers or shall we try one of these grog shops that's opened up on the south of the town?'

'Not today! I have a music lesson,' Jamie said.

It had been three weeks and the 35th had already left for Fort Edward before Jamie had this leisure time to fulfil his promise to the McConnells.

After a few enquiries he located the school on the outskirts of Albany overlooking the river. It was a substantial brick building in the Dutch style with a wooden addition that he assumed was a classroom.

A large lady answered his knock and eyed him suspiciously..

'Would you be Mistress Yonge?' he asked, quickly doffing his bonnet; mindfully aware that relations between townsfolk and the army were steadily worsening with the huge influx of soldiers.

'Ja...and you are?' she said frostily, in a thick Dutch accent, her expression forbidding.

He explained his reason for calling and her broad rosy face brightened.

'Ah! Sarah's friend! Good! Good! I was told you might call. Come!' She ushered him briskly into a spacious parlour at the same time calling for Sarah. There was a clatter of shoes on the stairs and Sarah appeared in the doorway. She looked flustered for a moment and stood smoothing the front of her dress nervously, then gave a shy smile and bobbed a curtsey.

'Mr Campbell...you're here! I have the instruments and music in my room.' She disappeared as quickly as she came.

Mistress Yonge laughed. 'A good girl is Sarah. My only boarder, so we spend much time together and a great help with the younger girls I teach. Please to use this room for your lesson. I shall send for refreshment later.'

Sarah appeared, her arms laden with whistles, a flute and fiddle, and a bundle of manuscript.

'My mother wheedled sheet music from the bandmaster,' she explained, then smiled mischievously. 'Father was not best pleased. He grumbled for days at being beholden to a Donegal man. We're from Kerry,' she added.

'I am sorry I could not come sooner. Your parents are well I trust,' Jamie asked.

She nodded. 'We exchange weekly letters. 'I shall tell them you have arrived to give me my first lesson. They'll be pleased.'

'Then we'd best begin,' Jamie laughed, and looked on by Mistress Yonge beaming benignly from an upright chair, he spread the sheet music out on a table.

The snowball caught Iain Mhor neatly on the back of the head, knocking his bonnet off and sending a shower of frozen particles down his neck. He spun round and glowered at a small group, which included McPhee, all standing innocently studying the sky. He growled and reached down to scrape at the light covering of snow to manufacture his own projectile.

'If you bairns have done playing your games will you kindly fall in,' McIvor said, dryly. 'And put your bonnet on Munro, you great pudden.'

The detachment formed up, Iain mouthing threats at a grinning McPhee, and they swung off down the track toward the river. Young Ensign Ross met them at a jetty where a string of bateaux's, crewed with armed boatmen and loaded with supplies for Fort Edward, were berthed. He was rosy cheeked with the cold air and grinning happily at his first independent command.

'It appears the French have raiding parties out. A woodcutting detail near Fort Edward was attacked a few days ago. Hence the need for extra escorts. So keep a close watch on the banks Six men to a boat, Sgt McIvor, if you will. Myself in the first and you in the rear boat.'

By mid morning there was a little warmth in the late autumn sun, the early sprinkle of snow had melted and the woods on either bank glowed in myriad shades of gold, russet, and reds as the first early morning frosts wrought the change in their leaves.

The fifty-mile journey took two days with an overnight halt at a fortified way station, and passed without incident, much to the disappointment of Ensign Ross. As they drew into the channel separating a large island from the east bank they had their first view of Fort Edward.

Sited where the Hudson became impassable to boats, and guarded on two sides by water, it was a huge structure of earth and wood, with three great redoubts thrusting out to the landward. Barrack blocks and administrative buildings surrounded a central parade. Outwith the main fort, more earthworks were being constructed, enclosing tented lines On the island other defences were being dug, with more barracks and a large wooden building to be used as a hospital, taking shape. The area swarmed with men labouring at the task of extending the fort.

Once dismissed and settled in a cramped barrack room Jamie went off to find Martin McConnel and deliver a letter Sarah had given him. Iain insisted on accompanying him, sensing there might be a good chance of a dram of spirits from what he had heard of Martin.

He was working in the dispensary of the hospital when they found him and he was delighted to see them.

'You shall dine with us tonight,' he declared firmly after the introductions were made. 'No No! I insist,' waving aside Jamie's weak protest. 'Bridget would make my life a misery if she had no chance to question you on how Sarah is. She misses her sorely... as do I. I shall be finished here in minutes.' He noticed Iain peering and sniffing at the medicines he had been working with.

'Chalk and opium, Mr Munro. Chalk and opium for the dysentery and other disorders of the stomach. It helps bind the bowels and in a sorry state we'd be without it. It's these damned Provincials, d'ye see. No camp discipline. Shit where they stand rather than walk to the latrines. Their lines are a disgrace. Filth and ordure everywhere! I will be greatly relieved when we return to Albany in a month's time and leave them to rot in their own sewage.'

He wiped his hands on his apron. 'I blame their officers. The men receive no direction from them. They are as ignorant of the basic rules of camp hygiene as the other ranks. They sneer at us for what they regard as the strictness of our camp regime, yet cannot see that our health is preserved by it.'

He raised a finger in the air and pronounced, rather pompously, 'Disease and sickness can reduce an army more than any battle so we must be ever vigilant in our preventive measures.' Removing his apron and hanging it over a peg he said, briskly, 'Time for a dram and some talk of a pleasanter nature,' and led them off to his quarters.

'Sarah tells me in her letters that the speed of her reading the musical notation is increasing weekly. We are most grateful to you, Mr Campbell,' Sarah's mother said, dishing a helping of a rich stew on their platters. The small room that was the McConnell's quarters was cramped with Jamie and Iain's presence.

'In truth, we spend little time on the theory now. Sarah has learned all I have to offer. We pass much of my visits swapping tunes back and forth, trying out harmonies and the like. A skill at which the pupil excels the teacher.'

'Mistress Yonge is so taken with Sarah that rather than lose her presence in her home and her assistance with the younger girls she teaches she has offered us residence on our return. Poor Mistress Yonge! She is having a battle with the Quartering staff who wishes to lodge some officers on her. She has so far been successful on the grounds of the unsuitability of having young men in such close proximity to her girls. She feels our presence may help stave of more attempts. After this cubby-hole it will be luxury indeed,' Bridget McConnel said happily. 'More stew for you Mr Munro?'

Jamie smiled inwardly. God help any officer unfortunate enough to be lodged with the formidable Mistress Yonge, he thought. She would have them housetrained in no time at all.

'Best not get too attached to luxury, Bridget m'dear.' Martin said. 'Come spring we'll be on the move again. Perhaps with some purpose... for there has been little sign of it this year. An army of seven thousand Provincials sat at Fort William Henry all summer, supposedly to attack the French post at Carillon but with no clear idea of how to go about it. So they sat in their own muck and got sick. A good few died. Then their enlistment's being up they all went home.'

Mrs McConnell rolled her eyes. 'He's been ranting about the poor provincials since we got here.'

'And with good reason. Scum of the earth most of them. Only the poorest wretches in the colonies enlist, for the bounty and the opportunity of being fed. Wastrels and ne'er do wells, the lot of them,' Martin snapped.

' Why, you could almost be describing our own regular soldiers,' Bridget said slyly. 'The present company excepted of course. Is that not how civilians in England view a soldier? Wastrels and ne'er do wells who enlist as a last resort to begging?' she asked innocently.

'That's entirely different!' Martin spluttered, glaring at her suspiciously.

'Why?'

He blew out his breath in exasperation and looked to Jamie and Iain for support. None being offered, he retracted slightly.

'Very well! I admit many choose to serve because they find themselves in straitened circumstances.'

'Or facing a prison sentence?' she smirked.

'Yes! Yes!' he growled impatiently. 'A few perhaps...but they learn to have pride in themselves and their regiment through discipline and a proper respect for authority.'

'And the lash, dear!' she said, brightly

'Dammit woman! Whose side are you on?' Martin fumed.

'Why, no one's Mr McConnell,' she answered placidly. 'I merely point out your comments about provincials are based on an irrational dislike. More stew Mr Munro?'

Martin shook his head in despair. 'Never marry an intelligent woman, gentlemen. They turn your arguments against you and do it with ease. Very well! I confess to some distaste for our colonial brethren, but it is based on observation and contact with them. I have mentioned a few of the reasons. How do you feel yourself, Mr Campbell?'

'We've had little to do with them, but surely they cannot all be as bad as you claim. We hear stories of the ranger's work and these armed bateaux men we came up river with seemed good men. And did not provincial troops defeat the French last year at Lake George?'

'True! The ranging companies do sterling work, as do the boatmen. But they are betwixt and between the Regular Establishment and Provincial troops, subject to the articles of war and led by bold commanders. Captain Rogers is prominent in carrying the fight to the enemy. Lt. Colonel Bradstreet of the Bateauxmen is a regular officer with many years' service and experience. Indeed, these formations are the exceptions that prove my point. Disciplined men under good officers. The Provincial forces have neither.' He shot a triumphant glance at his wife who made a resigned face at him. 'As for the battle at Lake George, the French were badly outnumbered and still it was a near run thing.'

'Do you think these provincials are as bad as he makes them out to be?' Iain asked, as they made their way back to the barracks. 'He's a man of pretty strong opinions, wouldn't you say?'

'He is that,' Jamie laughed. 'Mind! I can see his point. They don't look or behave like soldiers…but neither did we until we we're taught. I suppose we won't find out until we see them fight.'

'We'll hardly be in a position to judge, Jamie, considering we've still to fire a shot in anger,' Iain said disconsolately. 'I'm getting impatient to find out how we'll do ourselves.'

'We're in the 42nd! We'll be fine.' Jamie said firmly.

'That's comforting. Thank you kindly for the reassurance, Mr Campbell,' Iain grinned.

'You are more than welcome, Mr Munro,' Jamie replied solemnly.

New Years Day dawned clear. The company had laid claim to a large frozen pond near the lines for the long awaited curling match between the officers and sergeants and a team from the other ranks. Since the first hard frost every suitable expanse of ice in the area had been utilised by off duty highlanders playing their popular winter sport. Streambeds had been searched for water smoothed boulders and there had been few days when the rumble of their passage over the ice and the shouts of the players could not be heard.

By mid morning the ice had been swept and a half dozen matches were in progress prior to the main event. An enterprising sutler had set up a booth and was doing good trade. Bonfires were blazing to warm the spectators and players and an anxious Iain Mhor was haranguing his team.

'McPhee, I'll thank you to make no more visits to that sutler. I need you sober and not shaming us by falling over in the middle of the match. Now… are we all clear on our tactics? Shall I go over them with you again?'

'Will you stop with your infernal nagging, Iain Mhor,' McPhee groaned. 'You're taking all the pleasure out of the sport. Ach! I'm away for a dram,' and he strolled off, followed by the rest of the team, leaving Iain spluttering with frustration. He went back to polishing the base of his stone, a great thing near forty pounds in weight, muttering all the while.

Mistress Yonge drew up in a horse drawn sleigh, driven by her coloured servant Jonas and carrying the McConnell family, the women well wrapped against the cold. All that could be seen of Sarah's face was the tip of her nose and her brown eyes.

Martin looked at the activity on the ice. 'So this is curling? It looks a fine amusement.'

'The rules are simple. Three concentric rings either end of the rink and whichever stone lies within them scores points,' Jamie explained. 'The skill is clearing away the opponents' stones or blocking them from removing yours. The lowland folk call it the 'Roaring Game' from the sound the stones make as they pass over the ice. It'll be seven men a side for this match. The brooms they all have are for sweeping or scrubbing the ice in front of the stones as they travel. It helps carry them a little further should they need it.'

The three officers and four sergeants arrived pulling a sledge bearing their stones, mysteriously covered over with a piece of canvas. McIvor had a smug smile on his face, which aroused Iain Mhor's suspicions. He reached to lift the canvas but Ensign Ross promptly sat down on the load.

'Ready when you are, lads,' Captain Alex Campbell said complacently.

The ice was cleared of other matches, the ends marked and the company clerk ready to keep score before the canvas was whipped of the sledge.

A groan went up from the crowd and Iain Mhor howled in protest.

'Will you look at that. Handles, by God. They've just gone and used their power and influence to have the armourer fix iron handles to their stones.'

'There is nothing in the rules says we can't,' McIvor gloated. 'Stop your bleating, ye great pudden, and let's be at it.'

Despite the officers and sergeants' advantage with handles on their stones, it was nip and tuck throughout the game. Every scoring stone was hotly argued over and distances measured. After four ends and his team lagging three points behind, Iain demanded the scorer be replaced.

'For there's some folk here would not hesitate to stoop at bribery,' he claimed, glowering darkly at the innocent clerk. A compromise was reached and two men were given the task of hovering menacingly at the clerk's shoulder checking his totals.

By the final end the other ranks team were behind five points and Iain was sweating furiously with anxiety. Alex Campbell's stone sat neatly in the centre circle and it was guarded by two stones outside the scoring area.

Iain wiped his brow and carefully dried his hands. He lined up, both hands grasping his stone, swung once and sent it thundering down the rink. A roar went up as it crashed into one of the blockers, skidded off and struck the other stone, sending them both sliding to one side, his own following.

'Pure brute strength and ignorance,' Alex sneered. 'Block or score, Sergeant McIvor. Just whatever you think yourself.'

McIvor leered at Iain and launched his stone intending it as a block…then saw to his horror it was moving off line.

'Sweep, damn you, gentlemen,' he roared, hoping to at least reach the scoring circles. 'Put your bloody back into it, Mr Ross, begging your pardon, sir.'

His team-mates swept and scrubbed frantically at the ice ahead of the slowly moving stone trying to coax a final few feet from it. It stopped inches from the scoring circle and two feet to the left.

McPhee stepped up with the final stone of the match. He wiped his nose on his coat sleeve and gave the bottom of his stone a perfunctory clean on his kilt.

'McPhee!' Iain said pleadingly.

McPhee gave Iain an evil grin, swung and sent off the truest stone of the match. It connected squarely with Alex Campbell's sending it spinning out of the circles and stopped dead centre for ten points.

The team swept McPhee up onto their shoulders and marched off to the sutlers waving their brooms in triumph.

'It's a family visit, Jamie,' Alex said, strolling up, looking not the least put out with his team's defeat.

'Bad luck, Uncle Alex,' Jamie said, grinning.

'We gave it our best. Iain Mhor was correct in his suspicions. Ensign Ross did try to bribe the clerk, but the man's too honest.' He looked round at the rest of the party. 'Will you introduce me to your friends.'

Jamie did so and excepting a piece of fried chicken from the basket Mistress Yonge had brought, Alex perched on a log and addressed Sarah.

'Miss McConnell, I must thank you for keeping this nephew of mine out of mischief. He's far better off playing music with you than carousing with his disreputable friends.'

Sarah blushed and bobbed a curtsey but her mother protested.

'Why Captain, Mr Munro is the very soul of courtesy. I would hardly regard him as disreputable.'

'Aye! He's a charming man without a doubt,' Alex said. 'A credit to the Regiment, so he is.'

He turned to his nephew. 'Jamie... did I mention that the clerk informed me Iain Mhor had also approached him with an offer of money? And I take it, Mistress McConnell, you have yet to meet McPhee?'

Jamie snorted with laughter. Bridget McConnell looked shocked at all these revelations of dishonesty.

'Which reminds me. I must be off and collect my winnings and buy Iain Mhor's team a dram.' Alex waved his chicken leg in farewell and sauntered away.

'His winnings?' Martin exclaimed. 'He surely never bet against himself?'

'He did that. The whole company knew. The clerk laid the wager for him, but the clerk has a foot in both camps. Mind, though! He missed their fitting handles on the stones. Sportsmanship's fine, but it's the devious tricks that add the spice when other ranks meet the officers and sergeants in a sporting event.'

The winter dragged on in a round of tedious escorts, woodcutting details, and the daily grind of fatigues and duties. The men made the most of their leisure time. Many, intrigued by the sight of Dutch families skating effortlessly on the steel blades bound to their feet tried it for themselves. The ever-popular curling matches continued.

The only excitement came in March when the regiment was hurriedly assembled and marched toward Fort William Henry as news of a French attack on the post arrived, only to be turned back when word came it had been beaten off by the garrison.

Jamie spent much of his off duty time at Mistress Yonge's house with her and the McConnells, often accompanied by Iain, who in his inimitable way, had became a firm favourite with them. McPhee preferred drinking with John Cameron and the others in the company.

As Iain put it, less than kindly. 'It's a blessing... for the man has the social graces of a Barbary ape and would bring black shame on the good name of the 42nd if he mixed with decent folk.'

Iain could be a great snob at times, but Jamie suspected he feared McPhee's presence when he put on his airs and graces for the womenfolk. McPhee had a sharp eye and a great penchant for deflating remarks.

Those times spent at Mistress Yonges' were a welcome break from the bleakness and chill of the overcrowded barracks that had finally been completed just before the first snow. Through her friends it led to requests for he and Sarah to give recitals at various functions and gatherings, the social activity of the better to do inhabitants of Albany increasing as they sought to enliven the dark winter nights.

Having played together so often they now had a wide repertoire, their music varied but with a preference for the Scots and Irish tunes they loved. He found it peculiar that Sarah's shyness and restraint would completely disappear before an audience. She played with confidence and appeared less nervous than he.

They were always given some small fee for their performance. A fee which they would solemnly divide equally as they sat in some warm kitchen eating a supper after their recital.

When the snow and ice finally cleared the Highlanders levelled a stretch of ground and cut and carved their camans, the sticks with which they played their beloved shinty. The 35th, its ranks largely made up of Irishmen, resumed their playing of hurling, an almost similar game stemming from the two races common Celtic tradition.

Martin, a keen player, arranged a match between the 42nd and the 35th. It was agreed that the variations between the Scots and Irish game could be ignored, each team playing their customary way and the teams limited to thirty men a side.

The result was an increasingly violent match that spilled off the pitch and had partisan supporters brawling enthusiastically. The Provost Marshall was informed by concerned townsfolk but declined to intervene and it was left to the officers and sergeants to restore order. The game was abandoned.

'Mistress... that husband of yours is a veritable fiend,' Iain moaned, wincing as Bridget cleaned up a cut above his eyebrow inflicted in a clash for a high ball between Martin and himself. 'A dirtier player I've yet to encounter.'

'I'll warrant he's saying the same about you,' she answered complacently, glancing over to where her husband was having his shin tended by Sarah, his back studiously turned from his erstwhile opponent. 'That hack at his leg was totally uncalled for, Mr Munro. There! You're cleaned up. Now apologise to each other, the pair of you. You'll get no rum until you do.'

In May came the first movements of that year's campaign. To the great delight of the officers and men, the 42nd received orders to march south to New York. The rumour had it they were bound for Nova Scotia and the taking of the French fortress of Louisburg.

Martin was looking glum when Jamie called briefly to make his goodbyes.

'Sure, you're the lucky ones. More garrison duties for us. Fort William Henry this time.'

Bridget looked happy enough. 'Come now. It suits us fine, with no great upheaval. Sarah can stay here and get on with her schooling. My regret is she will no longer have the pleasure of you and she playing music together, Mr Campbell…and of course having to say farewell to good friends. It's been a happy winter.'

'It has that!' Martin cried heartily. 'I cannot think when I've spent a better one. God be with you James Campbell. I trust our paths will cross again. Until then I wish you a safe journey and success in your regiment's endeavours.'

As he left the family and Mistress Yonge waving goodbye, Sarah broke away and raced after him.

'I shall walk with you a way,' she said, her thin face solemn.

They walked along in silence for a while.

'I will write to you, Mr Campbell!'

'Why, thank you, Sarah. And I shall be sure to answer your letters. Now, it grows dark. It's time you turned back.'

She reached out and tugged at his sleeve, her head lowered.

'I will see you again, wont I?'

'Why, Sarah, I hope so. But you know army life as I do. Saying farewell to good friends is part of it, with never a guarantee you'll ever see them again.' Her grip tightened on his sleeve and he heard a hiccuping sob. 'Come, lass! Friends are lost when neither knows where the other is. If we write to each other then that can never happen. We can always find each other. Do you understand?'

She nodded and turned away. Walking back a few paces she stopped and faced him, her arms rigid by her side, fists clenched in the material of her dress, a position familiar to him.

'I hate this war,' she said in a voice barely above a whisper, then turned again and ran off toward the house.

Chapter 6

They heard the news that Fort William Henry had fallen to the French as they waited to disembark from the transport ship that had brought them back from Halifax. With the disappointment of the aborted campaign to take the stronghold of Louisburg still rankling, the news added to the growing realisation that the war was not going as well as planned.

The troops disembarking had received a hostile reception from the civilian population as they landed. Merely unfriendly or indifferent previously, they now openly hissed and booed the redcoat regiments as they marched to their encampments.

Sgt. McIvor had dragged a furious McPhee back into the ranks before he could reach a burly dockworker who had spat on him.

'The man was lucky I was on hand, sir,' the sergeant remarked to Alex Campbell later. 'McPhee was going for his dirk.' He scratched his head in perplexity. 'Why all this hostility?

'For a variety of reasons, Sergeant. They hate the quartering of troops on inns and private homes, yet quibble at the expense of building barracks to house the men. They're not best pleased at the tight controls imposed on merchant ships after Lord Louden discovered that a good few of the patriotic merchants were carrying on a lucrative trade smuggling to the French. It has hit the seaports badly. Recruiting parties are hated as they can lose indentured workers to them.'

Alex Campbell shrugged. 'They want this war won without the expense or any great degree of self-sacrifice, particularly in these areas that are not directly threatened. Finally, Fort William Henry has been taken. Things might change if we were seen to be winning this war. Right now all we can say is we're not completely losing it.'

'All too complicated for me, sir. Soldiering now! That's straightforward!'

'Quite right, Sergeant McIvor,' Alex smiled. 'Inform McPhee that he's confined to the lines until such time as I deem the general population safe from harm before I allow him to wander.'

'Here, Jamie! Is that not the orange facings' of the 35th?'

There was a group sitting outside a sutlers, drinking morosely. They looked up as Jamie approached them.

'Your pardon, but were you with the 35th at William Henry?'

'We were!' a corporal answered in a surly voice. 'What is it to you?'

'I had good friends there with your regiment and I was hoping you could give me some news of them.'

The corporal relaxed slightly and asked in a friendlier tone, 'If I can! What were their names?

'The McConnells! Martin and Bridget. He was a surgeons mate.'

'Ah! The McConnells! Here, sit down and join us.' He took a long swig from his mug and cleared his throat. 'A good man, Martin McConnell… I'm sorry, but he and his wife were killed.'

Jamie and Iain were speechless for a moment. 'Both of them? Both killed?' Jamie said in stunned disbelief.

'I saw it happen. The third day of the siege. They were out tending the wounded. They should have been safe in the casements treating them as they were brought in, but that was not Martin's way. He liked to be on hand when a man was injured. And where Martin went, his wife followed to assist. A mortar shell came over. It exploded a few feet from them.'

Iain cursed in a dull monotone.

'They had a daughter. Sarah!' Jamie asked.

'Ah yes…young Sarah. A fine whistle player. She's still in Albany at that Dutch school. The regiment made a collection for the widows and orphans of the lads that were killed. It came to a goodly sum. She'll have enough to stay on at the school for a while.'

Jamie sat silent, not touching the mug of rum Iain set in front of him.

'Sorry if we seemed a little unfriendly just then,' the corporal said. 'We haven't been feeling exactly sociable lately.'

'Bad was it? Iain asked.

'Worse than bad. We'd have been all right if that thrice damned General Webb had marched to our relief, but he locked himself up in Fort Edward pissing his britches. Colonel Monroe kept sending messages begging him to come. All he got was some advice on making the best terms he could with the French. A six day siege, most of our guns dismounted, the parapets levelled, then a so-called honourable surrender when the French had their breaching batteries in position.'

He leaned to one side and spat disgustedly. 'Trouble was the Indians don't know anything about honourable surrender. They don't understand how civilised folk go about their business. First off they broke into the hospital and killed and scalped the wounded. When we began to march out for Fort Edward then they got really upset.

It wasn't too bad for us redcoats. We had a cordon of French regulars around us. They tore into the poor damned Provincials and their womenfolk who didn't. I can hear the screaming now. They killed a good few but took a lot more away captive before the French intervened. By that time a lot of the Provincials had run off into the woods. It was weeks before all the survivors made it back to Fort Edward.'

He sighed and took another gulp of his rum. 'Our regiment can't fight for eighteen months according to the terms of surrender. So we're to sit scratching our arses and let the rest of the army do the work.'

'Some folk would enjoy that,' Iain joked, weakly.

The corporal looked at him steadily. 'Perhaps! But not me, friend. This war has got somewhat personal.'

The regiment spent little time in New York. Within a few days they were marching north to Albany, their numbers augmented by five hundred recruits who had joined them in Halifax. Marching with them was a battalion of Montgomery's Highlanders, raised in Scotland the previous year. With another regiment, Frasers' Highlanders, who had remained in Halifax, the number of highlanders serving in the Army of the Americas had increased dramatically. Hearing the news that the 42nd had recruited a second battalion, Iain Mhor commented that it would be a rare time to be back in Scotland.

'Just think of all these poor lasses fair desperate for the attention of a man and never a one to be had. All the brisk likely lads gone for a soldier and little left to choose from but old men, cripples and the village idiot.' he said wistfully.

Sarah saw him from her bedroom window, rushed downstairs and threw open the door as he came up the porch stairs.

He stopped and looked at her then put out his arms. 'Oh my poor, poor lass!

Her eyes filled and she ran to him, her thin frame trembling as she wept.

Mistress Yonge appeared at the door and seeing the pair of them she also began crying and led them into the house.

When they had both stopped weeping Mistress Yonge blew her nose loudly.

'Sarah! What are we thinking of! Mr Campbell will be thirsty. Please to go and make some lemonade for him.' Sarah rose obediently and went off to the kitchen.

'I try to keep her busy. It is best for her not to brood.'

'Is there anything I can do to help her?'

'Ja! Play with her the music like before. She has not touched her instruments since she heard. As for the rest, I will care for her. This is her home for as long as she wishes to stay. She is like a daughter to me now. My husband and I, we had no children,' she sniffed, and patted his knee. 'It is good you come back. She needs friends.'

Chapter 7

Sergeant McIvor stuck his head round the door of the long, log built barracks hut that housed the company. It was crammed with two man bunks double tiered, the available space left taken up with arms racks, rough benches, and trestle tables. Blanketed screens either end gave a modicum of privacy to the wives and families of the married men. With the five hundred reinforcements, adding three new companies, and bringing the Regiment's strength up to thirteen hundred men, space was at a premium.

'Munro! Campbell! Captain want's to see you.'

As the pair of them appeared he eyed them suspiciously.

'What have you two been up to that I don't know about?' he growled.

'Nothing at all sergeant,' Iain said in wide-eyed innocence. 'I swear on McPhee's life!'

'Ach! Get on with you,' McIvor snorted.

Alex Campbell was poring over the company returns with his clerk when they entered and doffed their bonnets. He shoved the pile of papers aside with relief when they came in. Picking up a separate sheet he waved it at them.

'I don't know how you got wind of this, although I've a damned good idea,' he said, glowering at the company clerk who kept his head down.

'It's not official until it's published on orders and here's the pair of you putting your names forward the day before. Is there anything you don't let the company know about before I read the damned correspondence myself, Cpl Baird,' he snarled at the clerk who winced and looked repentant.

He turned to them with a sour look. 'You probably know this off by heart, but I'll tell you what's in it anyway,' he said dryly. 'This is a copy of a letter from Lord Howe to all commanding officers. He's enthused with the work of the Rangers and feels we have something to learn from them. So far the dubious privilege of accompanying them has been reserved for the officers He recommends that volunteers of all ranks who are suitable be allowed to go out with Ranger parties. He feels it will give experience to men who will then pass on the knowledge to others. As a first step a company of regular volunteers is to be formed and attached to the Ranger detachment at Fort Edward. As you seem to have stolen a march on your comrades and put your names forward first, your request is granted.'

Iain and Jamie exchanged jubilant glances.

'Munro, you may dismiss and take that damned gossip of a Cpl Baird with you. Close the door behind you.'

'At ease Jamie. It's your uncle speaking now,' Alex said with a smile. 'You know what I'm going to say, do you not?'

'That you had rather I did not volunteer?'

'No! Only that it can be dangerous work. As you know we've already lost one officer.'

Jamie shrugged. 'Which is a way of saying will I reconsider. I'm a good soldier, Uncle Alex. If a spell with the Rangers can make me a better one then it may serve me in good stead some day.'

'As we are now designated the Light Company of the Regiment I can't disagree with that. The more experience I can accumulate within the company the better we will be at carrying out our duties. However, I thought for your father's sake to speak with you on this. To be frank I would have been very surprised and disappointed in you if you had reconsidered. Take care, Jamie!' He turned back to his paperwork with an embarrassed cough.

'You are dismissed Private Campbell.'

Iain was waiting outside with a worried look on his face. 'Well!' he asked.

'We're going to Fort Edward of course. What else?' Jamie grinned.

'Three shillings a day.' Iain said enviously as they filed across the bridge to the island at Fort Edward after a day practising movement and skirmishing in the woods. 'Three whole shillings a day these rangers get. We're in the wrong army, Jamie.'

'Well, I suppose they earn it.'

'You think so,' Iain sniffed. 'Well I don't! We've been here two weeks and all we've done is learn drills that are just plain common sense.'

'They only make common sense after somebody else has thought of them and they're explained to you,' Jamie said patiently. 'Then you say…why that's obvious. Why didn't I think of it.'

Captain Rogers, who commanded the rangers, had put into writing the methods he had formulated for carrying out the tasks he was commissioned to do. The emphases on the use of flanking, advance, and rear parties, however large or small the numbers of men involved.

Methods that encompassed every aspect of movement through hostile territory from the pre dawn stand to arms to the choice of ground in a halt for meals or a night encampment. The use of swift movement and surprise in engaging the enemy and, should they come against a superior force, a system of breaking contact and if need be, scattering to meet again at a pre arranged rendezvous. Above all, the careful use of ground to provide cover, advantage, and the avoidance of dangerous areas that presented a threat of ambush.

The method of engaging the enemy in a firefight was itself nothing new to Jamie and Iain. The use of cover and a system of working in files of two or three men, alternately firing, when either advancing or retiring, was second nature to them after the months spent practising skirmishing. It was now a common tactic for all regulars, particularly those designated as light companies in the regiments.

Jamie decided, on reflection, it was the fact that most rangers were at ease in the rugged environment that made them more effective than the regulars. It was not alien to them as it was to many of the soldiers enlisted from the towns and tamed countryside of Britain. Most were New Hampshire men, with a lifetime of hunting and farming in a wilderness behind them, although not all. In conversation with some he had heard contemptuous and derisory remarks regarding many of the new men recruited. Men from the eastern seaboard towns with no experience of living and fighting in the woods, attracted only by the bounty and high pay of the rangers. Requiring more training than the Regular volunteer company they were rapidly becoming a source of indiscipline, even within the relaxed atmosphere of the ranger lines. Rogers's success and his high standing with Lord Louden and General Abercromby had led to an increase in the number of ranger companies including a company of Mohegans, Christianised Indians from Stockbridge under their own officers. With only a limited pool of suitable men available, the recruiters, desperate to fill the quota, had been somewhat less than careful in their choice.

After a month of training the volunteers began taking part in the patrols and reconnaissance that constituted the ranger's main tasks. Attached to parties of experienced officers and men they swept the northern approaches to the Fort looking for a sign of the raiding parties of French and Indians that presented an ever constant danger to wood cutters and supply convoys coming up from Albany. Three or four day patrols that led to a familiarity with the triangle of country between Wood Creek at the head of Lake Champlain, the head of Lake George and Fort Edward.

Since the fall of Fort William Henry a defensive attitude had prevailed with the ever-nervous General Webb in command and with Rogers in Albany recovering from scurvy there were none of the deep penetration patrols at which he excelled.

Iain grew increasingly frustrated as the weeks went by.

'Where have all these French got to?' he fumed after another fruitless scout around Half Way Brook. 'I thought when we came here we'd find a bit of entertainment. I've had more excitement watching McPhee avoiding a work detail.'

'Missing him are you?' Jamie grinned.

'No!' Iain said, with a snort of derision. He scratched his head and sniffed. 'Well, yes, if you must know. Him, Cameron and the rest. Even that great beast McIvor.'

'We're here to learn, Iain,' Jamie remonstrated gently.

'Well, I'm done learning. I know all the drills. I can shoot as good as any man here and out walk any of them. Now I need some French and Indians to practice on and we can't find a one.'

Jamie had some sympathy with Iain's views, but he felt there was more to be learned. He had watched the Stockbridge Indians, some of whom were normally included in any party of rangers leaving the Fort, checking for signs of enemy tracks. As they all spoke some English he would quiz them on what indications to look for. He envied the officers and sergeants the compasses mounted on the pouring cap of their powder horns, realising that no matter how familiar the terrain might be it was all too easy to lose direction.

He set about questioning some of the experienced rangers how they always seemed to know where north was without the help of a compass. Using the sun and the stars of the Plough at night, he knew already. But how did they keep direction in the gloom of dense woods? They would laugh and wonder at such a question, then have to think hard on how they knew. They would argue among themselves, then fill his head with talk of the little indications. Of spider's webs on the south side, the moss growth usually thickest on the north, tree branches denser to the south. He learned to keep checking behind him for a view of what he had passed by, to pick out landmarks he could identify if he had need to return by the same route. He resolved to acquire a compass as soon as possible.

In early November, Ensign Andrew Ross who was also in the company of volunteers broke the news that they would be returning to the 42nd shortly.

'It was by way of an experiment and unlikely to be repeated,' he told the dozen volunteers from the regiment. 'Volunteers can still go out with the rangers but Headquarters have decided there's no need to keep them in a separate company for training. They can learn in the field. I tend to agree. Providing they're fit and are good soldiers they'll pick it up quick enough. There's a new regiment in the process of being formed. Gage's Light Infantry! The 80th! I hear the intention is to replace the need for rangers.' He shook his head and grinned. 'Well! We shall see. You will be leaving tomorrow. I'm staying on here for a while,' beaming at them happily.

Two weeks after they got back Jamie was summoned to see the company commander.

'The colonel asked me to speak to you first,' Alex said abruptly. 'You've heard of this regiment of light infantry that's forming. Four of the cadets who were in the ranger volunteer company are to be commissioned ensign. There still exists another vacancy. Captain Abercromby of the regiment, who is aide de camp to the General wrote to the colonel suggesting you would be suitable. It appears he received good reports about you. It is unusual but not unknown for privates to make that step. I first have to ask if you are willing.'

Jamie was taken aback for a few seconds.

'Do you want a little time to think on it?'

'No sir!' Jamie said collecting his thoughts. 'I'm grateful for being thought of as worthy of a commission, and I thank Captain Abercromby for advancing my name. But I regret I must decline.'

Alex Campbell looked toward Cpl. Baird and jerked his head in the direction of the door. The corporal rose swiftly and left.

'Can I ask you why, Jamie? Do you doubt your ability to lead?'

'No! I would probably make a good officer. I have an excellent example to follow.' Jamie grinned. 'Do you remember what you told me that day I first arrived in Ireland, Uncle Alex? That a friend is precious to a soldier. I have friends here who mean more to me than advancement. Also, the 42nd is the regiment I chose to serve with. Nothing has changed. I'm content where I am.'

'I should call you a damned fool for turning down a chance like this, but I can't. I applaud your reasons,' Alex sighed. 'I could remind you of the privileged life we officers lead but I suspect I'd be wasting my breath.'

'You would Uncle Alex, and I thank you for not mentioning it,' Jamie laughed 'One thing puzzles me. You told me that if I had joined the regiment as a gentleman volunteer then I could be promoted on merit. Having enlisted I assumed this disbarred me. Can I ask how the Regiment intended to get round the regulations?'

'No you may not! Some things are best kept from the ears of the innocent,' Alex said, then he relented and winked. 'Captain Abercromby despite being an aide de camp is firstly of the 42nd and as such would regard it his duty to advance a deserving member of the regiment. Secondly, he is forever out gallivanting with the rangers and takes a keen interest in their activities and the necessity of a force such as theirs. Thirdly, he is after all, the General's nephew. The rest would have been simply a matter of paperwork. If you have no more questions I shall inform the Colonel of your decision. When I tell him your reasons I doubt if he will be displeased. Dismiss Private Campbell!'

Chapter 8

The smoking chimneys of Fort Edward were a welcome sight and the provision column of horse drawn sleighs increased speed as men and beasts stepped out in the expectation of the warmth and food they offered. A work party of Provincials, desultory clearing snowdrifts from the ditch, leaned on their shovels and watched them pass through the gates. Although it was the first week in March there was little sign of winter easing it's grip. The Hudson remained frozen but afforded an icy roadway between Albany and the fort.

The fug and overcrowding of the low roofed barracks drove Jamie out into the cold crisp air after he had eaten and warmed himself. Iain Mhor was back in Albany nursing a massive head cold, his indiscriminate sneezing and coughing ensuring a wide space around him. McIvor had taken pity on him and stood him down from the escort, commenting that the noise he was making was like to frighten the horses and have every bear in the woods heading for them to see what was amiss.

Passing the outworks of the main fort he crossed the bridge to the island heading for the Ranger's lines he had left three months before, intending to have a mug of something warming at Best's the Ranger's sutler.

A ranger officer was hurrying across the parade and he saw it was Ensign Andrew Ross. Ross pulled up on seeing him and grinned.

'Hail and well met, Private Campbell. What brings you from the flesh pots of Albany and how fares the 42nd?'

'Another escort, sir. What else! It's been that and cutting wood to keep ourselves warm since I got back,' Jamie said glumly.

'I detect a hint of boredom,' Ross chuckled, then looked at Jamie speculatively. 'A big scout going out very soon. Bored enough to volunteer are you? We were to be two hundred strong but we're at least twenty short. Captain Rogers himself will be leading it.'

Jamie did not hesitate. 'Aye, gladly. We'll be hanging about the Fort until a return convoy is put together. I'm sure Lieutenant Graham will give permission should you ask him, sir.'

'I shall speak to him tonight, and if he's amenable report to me at the ranger lines tomorrow and draw rations and snowshoes.' He winked and lowered his voice. 'A chance to see the French fort at Carillon, for that's where we're heading'

Noon of the second day's march saw them halted at the site of Fort William Henry. There was little to see, the ruins covered with a thick blanket of snow. A few charred logs and forlorn stone chimneys like rotting teeth protruded, but only the contours of the ground outlined the ruined ditches and redoubts.

Jamie washed the last mouthful of sausage and bread down with a mouthful of rum from his canteen and slipped his hands into his mittens. He drew his blanket coat closer around his neck and glanced over at his companions. He knew none of them and although they were not unfriendly he was feeling lonely and regretting he had volunteered. He wished Iain Mhor were here.

He was relieved when Ensign Ross returned from an officer's briefing.

Ross quickly briefed the men. 'We're marching to the Narrows shortly, moving up the east side of the Lake. Order of March is Lieutenant Phillip's company who will send scouts ahead on skates. Main body, then us as rearguard. Rendezvous, should we need it, is back here.'

Squatting beside Jamie he rummaged in his haversack for food. Gnawing at a length of sausage he spoke quietly in Gaelic. 'Captain Rogers is convinced the French have wind of this scout. Putnam's Connecticut rangers were out ten days ago. Came back a man short and he may have deserted. Then raiders hit a convoy on the Hudson and captured one of Best the sutlers' men. That we were going out has been common knowledge in the Fort for some time.' He grinned at Jamie. 'Thought I should tell you being as how I asked you along.'

'I wish you hadn't told me, Ensign. Worrying is best left to the officers. How likely is it the French are expecting us?'

Ross shrugged. 'They're watching for us all the time…just as we watch for them. It means Rogers will be extra careful.' He looked at Jamie curiously. 'I believe you turned down the chance of being commissioned Ensign when the regular Ranger Company disbanded.'

'It was a commission in Gages Light Infantry. I didn't want to leave the 42nd. Too many friends. One in particular.'

The Ensign nodded, understanding.

'I'll be glad to get back myself. There have been a lot of incidents lately. Captain Rogers has been away much of the time and when he's not about…. Things go wrong. First was a big reconnaissance to Carillon. Three hundred rangers. It was the first in months and Captain Stark led it. Captain Abercromby went out with us so he was senior Captain. Stark didn't like it and he let the men get unruly.

Would you believe they were shooting at game on the way. Night sentries all asleep and God knows how we got to Carillon without being ambushed. We were near to taking some woodcutters' prisoner when Stark shouted and the whole command started shooting and chasing them. Captain Abercromby got pretty mad then, particularly when he had to cover the withdrawal with only a few of us regular officers. Then we had a mutiny in December. Two men had been whipped for stealing rum and were locked up in the guardroom on the island. A crowd gathered and someone chopped down the whipping post, then they tried to break into the guardroom and release the prisoners. A couple of officers managed to stop them and got them to disperse.'

He took a gulp of his rum and tried to remove a piece of sausage skin from between his teeth.

'How Rogers smoothed that one over I'll never know. Colonel Haviland, the post commander, was for a general court-martial. Then Rogers led a party out himself to Carillon. Took a prisoner, killed their cattle and burnt their woodpile. He was making a point I suppose. Things seem to have settled down again now he's back but I'll be relieved to get home to the 42nd.'

He looked up as a whistle sounded. 'Time to move out!'

After the first days march on the thick ice they began only to move in darkness and two marches later lay up for most of the night in thick woods on the west shore a few miles short of the bottom end of the Lake.

Rogers squinted round the circle of officers gathered in the grey light of dawn.

'This is as far as we go on the Lake. I intend to cut inland and swing round behind the French outpost on Bald Mountain then follow the line of Trout Brook north, keeping the brook on our left. Order of March will be Ensign McDonald leading the vanguard. Captain Buckley's company, then myself with Lieutenant Philips. Ensign Ross, you'll take rearguard again. Ensign McDonald, make sure your men understand to keep well clear of the brook. It's fairly open ground. Your left flank party should keep it in sight though. Rendezvous is here where the sledges are cached.'

The column shook itself out as they left the lakeshore, the advance scouts and flanking parties fanning out from the main body. Their route took them north-west up a valley, the steep wooded bulk of Bald Mountain looming on their right and even with snowshoes the snow made it heavy going. Progress was slow and it was after noon before they swung north, locating the line of Trout Brook and keeping to the wooded high ground above it.

Rogers looked round quickly as the hand signal came back from the advance guard that they had enemy sighted on their left flank. The main body of his column was in dead ground, a low ridge between them and the frozen streambed of Trout Brook. He guessed the French were using the easier going of the icy streambed as a route. He held his musket above his head, waited until the officers and sergeants repeated the signal, then pointed it in the direction of the ridge. He grunted in satisfaction as the column faced left and swept forward in line to the crest.

Jamie settled himself behind a deadfall, shook off his mittens and removed the waterproof cover from his musket lock, then eased his cartridge box to a handier position on his right side. Glancing to his right he saw Andrew Ross kneeling behind a tree peering at the streambed thirty yards away and twenty feet below them. The Ensign looked over, giving him a nod and an eager smile. They were at a slight bend in the line of the brook and could see down the length of the ambush area and beyond. He eased the muzzle of his weapon forward, pulling the hammer back to full cock.

The waiting seemed interminable. He could feel his fingers going numb with the cold and found himself shivering. Suddenly an Indian came into view, his head and shoulders shrouded in a blanket. Then two more appeared. A gap, then a double file of more Indians interspersed with Canadians in grey hooded capotes. He aligned the barrel with the lead Indian. Aim low when you're above the mark, he reminded himself and imperceptibly adjusted his aim to the man's knees. His target was almost directly below him when a single shot rang out from the centre of the ambush, followed instantly by a mass volley. Before the smoke of his discharge obscured his sight he saw the man he had aimed at thrown back in a sprawl of limbs. He fumbled in his cartridge box with frozen fingers and reloaded, feeling the welcome warmth of the musket barrel. The streambed was littered with bodies, some still, others moving feebly. Yelling rangers broke cover and he could see hatchets rising and falling and the flash of scalping knives. Further down the line there were more shouts and screams as Capt. Bulkeley's company flooded down to the streambed to pursue the survivors of that first close range volley. Ensign Ross was on his feet, shouting at the men of his detachment who had slipped down to the frozen surface of the brook.

As Jamie came up he turned to him, his face tight with anger. 'The damned fools! They see a chance of scalp money and they forget everything else.'

There was a crash of musketry in the direction the fugitives from the ambush had taken and the Ensign groaned.

'Oh Jesus! That was only their vanguard we hit. Bulkeley's ran into the main body.' He roared again at the men down on the streambed. 'Get back up here now. Reload and form up. It's not over!'

Rogers had already formed a skirmish line at right angles to the brook as they came up. Beyond it there was heavy firing as the remnants of Bulkeley's company retreated. Rogers waved at Ensign Ross as they approached and shouted. 'Move uphill! Extend the right of the line. They'll try to outflank us.'

As they laboured up through the deep snow Jamie looked left. He caught glimpses of rangers moving back through the trees. Behind them were other figures, so close they were almost intermixed, the war whoops sounding above the crackle of musketry. They had just got into position when the volume of fire increased as the line of rangers opened up on the French and Indians pressing hard in pursuit of the survivors of Bulkeley's company.

A small group of rangers were floundering up toward them. As they watched one spun round and fell the others halting and firing back at the swarm of warriors barely thirty yards behind them.

'That's Ensign MacDonald,' Ross exclaimed. He showed himself and shouted. 'Willie! Willie! Rangers here...Up here, man.'

MacDonald turned and waved...then another of his men pitched forward.

The bolder warriors were close to them now, working their way from tree to tree in swift rushes. Jamie snapped a shot at a fleeting target and as he was reloading saw with horror that Ensign MacDonald had lost a snowshoe. One leg was thigh deep in a snowbank and he was struggling to extricate himself. Two Indians raced forward yelping. The Ensign grasped his musket by the muzzle and twisting his body to face them, clumsily swung at the nearest. Jamie could see the Indian laughing as he easily avoided it...then his hatchet flashed down. The Indian bent over, made a swift cut with his knife, then ripped off the scalp and held it up with a whoop of triumph, the blood dripping from it and staining the snow.

There was a musket shot from next to Jamie, the snow kicking up near the Indian, who ducked back behind cover. Jamie could hear Ross swearing quietly.

Whistles were sounding down the line and they could hear the bull voice of Rogers shouting, 'Pull back uphill! Steady now, boys. Steady!

Jamie would remember little of that slow withdrawal. Fire and retire, the lines shortening as men fell and the flanks pushed inwards as enemy parties probed to get behind them. His musket becoming fouled with burnt powder, making it increasingly difficult to drive home the fresh charge with his ramrod, and the recoil fiercer with each shot. Finally what was left of them were formed in a horseshoe near the summit of Bald Mountain with Rogers frantically patching up holes in the line and all praying for darkness to fall.

'Another half-hour before we break out, boys,' Rogers growled hoarsely, prowling along behind them. 'They'll try one more time. Just hold firm!'

The woods were quiet apart from the odd musket shot then a scream of pure agony echoed through them. Jamie jumped at the sound and looked over to Ensign Ross crouched close by.

Ross grimaced. 'Cutting up some poor bastard,' he whispered.

There was a burst of fire from their right and some one shouted, 'Here they come!'

Dim figures appeared below them. Fleeting glimpses as they flitted from cover to cover, working ever closer. Jamie fired at a muzzle flash then ducked back behind the tree to reload. Bark flew from the trunk as return shots hammered in. He heard Ensign Ross gasp and looked over to see him slumped at the base of a tree. More shots crashed out and he peered round to see an Indian twenty yards away with another just behind him. He fired too quickly and cursed as he saw he had missed. There was a whoop and he knew they were racing forward to take him before he could reload. He knelt, drew his bayonet, locked it on the muzzle, crouched low, and lunged upwards as the first Indian came round the trunk, his hatchet already swinging. The eighteen inch spike took the man under the breastbone and his mouth gaped in surprise. Jamie dropped the muzzle to clear the bayonet and charged yelling at the second Indian who was close behind. The warrior stepped back clumsily on his snowshoes raising his hatchet to throw when a shot blasted from behind Jamie and the Indian's face disappeared in a spray of blood.

Rogers, who had fired the shot, slammed the butt of his musket into the head of the man Jamie had bayoneted, then crouched and reloaded. As Jamie unfixed his bayonet and groped in his cartridge box for another round, Rogers peered at him and seeing his blue bonnet grunted, 'Volunteer from the Highlanders are you? What's your name, son?' When Jamie told him he said, 'Good work!' gesturing at the body beside him.

They scanned the area in front of them, now dark and gloomy but quiet, although musket shots sounded elsewhere.

'Time to go,' Rogers muttered. He pointed. 'Head that way, Campbell, then keep going downhill into that valley we came up. Bear left and you'll hit the Lake. See you at the rendezvous.' He disappeared quickly into the darkness.

Ensign Ross was still alive when Jamie bent over him.

'Don't try and move me,' he whispered. 'I'll be dead soon and right now I'm comfortable.'

'I can carry you.'

'Not in this snow you can't. Take my powder horn. There's a compass on it. Go due south,' Ross gasped. 'In my belt there's a pistol! Check it's primed and give it to me.' He tried to laugh but it ended in a wheeze. 'In case I'm not dying as quick as I think I am.'

Jamie did as Ross asked him and as he pressed the pistol into his hand the Ensign said, 'I'm sorry! Sorry I asked you along. If you make it back to the 42nd, tell them I died well.'

'I'll do that... gladly,' Jamie said, squeezed Ross's shoulder, and moved off through the trees. He had gone no more than a hundred paces when he heard a muffled shot behind him. He paused and sighed, then forced his mind to concentrate on his own survival.

He moved cautiously, stopping constantly to listen for the sound of movement. He saw the glow of a fire away to his left and heard an anguished caterwauling as if of animals and guessed more rangers were being tortured. When the hill fell away steeply and feeling fear now that he was alone and without the blood surge of action to curb it, he abandoned caution, slipping and sliding down the more open ground. A binding broke on one of his snowshoes and he stopped for precious minutes to repair it with fumbling fingers. When he reached the streambed at the bottom of the slope he swung left, within minutes finding himself on the icy surface of the lake. Working along the lakeshore toward the rendezvous he could see in the reflected light of the ice and snow figures moving ahead of him and he stopped, cautiously edging into cover. Then he heard a quiet challenge and a low voice answer. 'Ranger's here!' and almost sobbed with relief.

Rogers was there, meeting his men as they trickled in. He had already sent two men on skates speeding back to Fort Edward requesting support and sleighs for the wounded. The four sledges they had brought with them and cached had been unloaded of the provisions they carried and their place taken by the more badly wounded men.

Jamie took a long swig of rum from his canteen, feeling it's comforting warmth spread from his stomach then gnawed at a piece of hard bread. He heard Rogers asking for volunteers to start dragging the wounded on the sledges back to Fort Edward and stepped forward.

'You still got ice creepers?' Rogers asked and when Jamie said he had, Rogers, recognising his accent, grunted. 'Ah! The Highlander with the bayonet. Campbell wasn't it. All right!.... Join that group.' He walked over to the sledges and spoke to the wounded. 'You're travelling back to Fort Edward in style and comfort, boys. Don't you be going and dying on these nice gentlemen that will be doing the work.'

By dawn the sledges were within four miles of the head of the lake and they were forced to rest on a rocky islet. Jamie was relieved when, after a couple of hours, it was decided to push on. Although near exhaustion, the warmth of their exertions was welcome after lying shivering, their bodies stiffening with the cold.

Noon saw them past Fort William Henry and on the military road leading to Fort Edward, meeting up and passing two companies of rangers with horse drawn sleighs dispatched in assistance of Rogers' party. Just before dusk they staggered through the gates of the fort.

Sergeant McIvor and McPhee found him walking dazedly back from the hospital where the wounded had been handed over and gathered him up.

He woke the following morning, warm with the extra blankets piled on him, and rose reluctantly, his body stiff and aching. McPhee put a steaming bowl of corn mush in his hands and stood grinning.

'I was never more relieved to see a man in my life. Iain Mhor would have killed me if I'd come back without you. Damn it, Jamie! Don't I keep telling you never to volunteer?'

'Didn't I see you with the rest of the lads clamouring to be included in the relief party?' McIvor remarked, coming into the barrack room.

McPhee declined to answer and merely sniffed.

'We lost Ensign Ross then? McIvor asked.

Jamie nodded and related the events of the battle to a quiet audience of his comrades.

'I shall miss that laddie,' McIvor sighed. He coughed in embarrassment and swiped at his nose. 'Lieutenant says we'll be leaving tomorrow morning. You'd best get some more rest, Campbell.'

He was dozing when he heard some shouts outside. John Cameron stuck his head in the door and called. 'Rogers is coming in!'

Jamie got up stiffly and dressed as quick as he was able, feeling the raw weal's the towropes of the sledges had left on his shoulders sting and burn. He reached the main gate as the first of the sleighs carrying wounded passed through. Then came the relief column of rangers, many assisting exhausted men. Last through the gate came Rogers himself, coatless in the cold air and with only a blanket draping his shoulders. He turned at the entrance, staring as if to make sure there was none left behind then followed the remnants of his command through.

Chapter 9

The huge flotilla spread the width of the lake. Nine hundred bateaux packed with the red coats of the regular battalions and the blue or homespun of Provincial regiments made a stately progress up the placid waters of Lake George, bands playing and colours flying. A swarm of swifter moving whaleboats manned by light infantry and rangers formed the vanguard and screened the flanks. In the centre, towed by whaleboats, were two huge rafts carrying the artillery and so constructed as to enable the guns to be used as floating batteries. More than fifteen thousand men were moving north with one purpose. The taking of Fort Carillon!

Jamie stared at the precipitous slopes of a hill on the western shore and remembering that day in March, less than four months before, gave an involuntary shudder. The movement transmitted itself to Iain, pressed close beside him on the thwart.

'Are you all right,' Iain asked, glancing at him.

'Aye! Just thinking of how damned cold it was the last time I was hereabouts.'

He pointed to the hill. 'We made our stand on the other side of it.'

'I'm sorry I missed that stramash,' Iain said, enviously.

'Don't be! Chances are you'd be but a rickle of bones scattered about in the woods up there.'

'Damnation, Jamie! I want a fight. Two years we've been in this country and none but a handful of the lads have even seen a Frenchman It's a black shame! They ship us all the way to Halifax where we sit around for two months, then back to Albany to discover the French have taken Fort William Henry while we were gone. Now there's so many regiments floating down this loch it's likely the French will take one look and be off to Montreal. Or the rangers and light infantry will have all the sport while we're plodding behind. I tell you it's a black shame.'

Sergeant McIvor prodded Iain in the back. 'I'll remind you, Munro, that the Army does not run its affairs to suit your convenience,' he said, dryly. 'However! If you were to write off a wee note to the General listing your grievances I'd make certain he got it. I'm sure he'd be fair mortified at getting the running o' this war so wrong.'

'Aye, aye. Scoff away, Sergeant,' Iain grumbled, sour faced. 'Deny it if you will, though. For all the use they've put us to we'd have been as well sitting back in Ireland.'

The sergeant said nothing, but had to agree with Iain Mhor's point. They had trained hard, learning the new tactics for war in the environment they had found themselves, yet, apart from the officers and men who had gone out with the rangers, had seen no action as a regiment. The move to Nova Scotia with the task of taking the French fortress of Louisburg had been met with enthusiasm and high spirits. When the planned assault was cancelled after reports of a French fleet approaching and they were shipped back to Albany, the frustration and anger was evident throughout the regiment. They wanted to fight and it was continually being denied them. A veteran of Fontenoy, McIvor could remember his own eagerness to taste battle. 'Aye!' he thought. 'They have the need to prove themselves...and that's how it should be.'

'You're a terrible bloodthirsty man, Munro,' he said, teasingly. 'Rest easy! You'll be having your fill of Frenchman soon enough,'

'Away wi' ye, Sergeant,' McPhee scoffed. 'Iain has the right of it. They'll have seen us by now and likely they've run away home to their mammies.'

'Look yonder,' John Cameron called. 'The command boat's signalling.'

A red flag was being waved in the bow of Lord Howe's craft and whaleboats carrying rangers were pulling away from the heavier bateaux toward a wooded bay on the west shore. They watched tensely as the boats ran their bows into the shallows and men scrambled over the sides, disappearing quickly into the forest gloom. There was a spatter of musketry that died away quickly. Bateaux carrying two regiments of Connecticut Provincials peeled off from the main body to join the rangers on their beachhead. The rest of the army continued its slow progress to the main landing area where more boatloads of rangers and light infantry were swarming ashore. There was more musketry.

'Its just a wee spat with the French picquets,' McIvor sniffed. 'We'll be landing shortly... so get off the boat smartly lads and form up with the rest of the company.'

The bateaux grounded and they splashed ashore to the crowded beach.

'I need hardly tell you gentlemen that today has been a bloody shambles,' Lt Colonel Grant said angrily. 'Too many columns moving, guides who got lost, thick woods, regiments blundering into each other and getting mixed. Now half of us are back where we started and the rest of the army is up in the woods somewhere wondering where the hell they are.'

In a quieter voice he went on. 'I regret to inform you that Lord Howe was killed leading the light infantry when his column collided with a body of the enemy. We've lost a very gallant officer.' There was a shocked hush, then a murmur of agreement from the officers around him.

'In the morning we start again. The General is bringing all troops back here to regroup. At first light the rangers will advance to the sawmill. Colonel Bradstreet will be seizing the portage road and rebuilding the bridge the enemy destroyed. All indications are the French have pulled back to the area of the fort. God willing, we should see what they have to offer tomorrow.'

Alex Campbell stood to one side and watched his company cross the hastily repaired bridge over the river Chute. Behind him the falls cascaded down in a series of drops as the river flowed toward Lake Champlain.

He viewed the men tramping past with a sense of satisfaction. Their stride was eager and by the grins on their faces they were in high spirits at the prospect of action. Their dress reflected the changes made to suit the nature of the war in the Americas. Gone were the belted plaids, diced hose and buckled shoes of the parade ground. The dense woods and morasses had quickly shown the impracticality of these garments. Some had feet shod in moccasins and campaign leggings clad their limbs to mid thigh below the philabeg, the little kilt. Their red coats were faded and stained and the cumbersome, uncomfortable pack had been discarded A blanket roll and a haversack held all they needed.

He smiled when he remembered the fierce discussions in the officer's mess regarding the wisdom of retaining the broadsword in the woods. Those officers who had been out with the rangers tended to regard it as an unnecessary encumbrance, citing the hatchet as a handier edged weapon.

The arguments were brought to an abrupt conclusion when the Sergeant Major informed the Adjutant that the men had become privy to the debate and as he put it succinctly, 'Would not be best pleased should their favoured weapon be replaced by a farmyard implement.'

Alex had his own opinion but had kept it to himself, letting the younger officers' squabble on the subject. He recalled that day at Drummossie Moor when the clans had gone into the onslaught in the old style that had served them well in the past. The rapid advance, the quick volley, then the charge with broadswords. It had foundered before the disciplined musketry and the bayonets of steady infantry.

He could see no real use for the weapon in the war they were
engaged in but knew the men took pride in these differences in dress
and the carrying of broadswords. They had a high opinion of themselves and if the loss of the broadsword detracted from the pride in
who they were...then broadswords it was. So each man swung past,
the basket hilt tucked up under the left armpit as high as possible to
avoid the blade hampering their movements.

It had been largely the vision and foresight of Lord Howe who had
wrought the changes throughout the army as a whole. Although the
problems of fighting in this terrain had been recognised long before
he had arrived and much had been done toward adapting tactics to
suit, it was his drive and enthusiasm that honed them. Having gone
out with the rangers he realised the importance of encouraging the
individual soldier to think for himself. 'Each man to a tree and every
tree a fort' was a New England saying. He advocated the trimming of
the men's equipment to a minimum. Gone were the useless hangers,
the pipeclayed crossbelts and the cumbersome packs. A musket,
bayonet, hatchet and cartridge box to fight with, the blanket roll and
haversack to carry the bare essentials were all that were needed.
Tricorn hats were cut down, the long tails of the coat cut off. The
linings of coats were removed in the heat of summer or men wore
merely the waistcoat and shirt. A man could fight better if he fought
in comfort

The army of the Americas was no longer a parade ground army,
but they were far better prepared for the campaigns that lay ahead.

'The best officer we had,' thought Alex. 'Lost in a damned point-
less skirmish.'

He had a fleeting moment of disquiet at the thought.

He saw his nephew passing and when Jamie glanced over gave
him a nod and a smile. He noted the corporal's knot on his shoulder,
looking white and fresh against the faded red of his jacket. 'No talk
of favouritism with that promotion,' he mused. 'The lad earned it after
that outing with the rangers.'

The last file crossed over the bridge and he followed his men
across the open ground to the night bivouac, listening to the inter-
mittent sputter of musketry in the distance as the light troops sparred
with the enemy outposts.

'How long before you can get the artillery in position?' General Abercromby asked. Normally a kindly, bluff man, he looked pensive and
worried this morning. The death of Lord Howe had affected him
deeply. Although a good administrator he had depended heavily on
the advice of his young second in command.

'The smaller pieces should be up by noon,' the artilleryman said. 'The bridge will need reinforcing to get the heavier cannon here by tonight.' He hesitated. 'Sir, if I could get my guns down to the south of the river I can take their field works in enfilade. It would need a road cut, but three days could see them in position'

'That's too long! Reports are there's three or four thousand more French on their way and every hour that damned fieldwork is getting stronger.' He turned to a junior engineer officer who had carried out a reconnaissance of the French lines the day before. 'You've had a good look at their works. Do you think they can be stormed successfully?'

'Right now, sir. Yes! It's a long perimeter and there are a few areas that are incomplete, but as you noted they are continually strengthening their position. I couldn't answer if an assault is delayed.'

Abercromby chewed at his lower lip and stared at the map spread on a tree stump. Colonel Thomas Gage, now his second in command since the death of Lord Howe spoke up. 'If we attack on a broad front we can deliver weighty assaults at several points. With our advantage in numbers he would be pressed to bring enough force to counter them all. I would advise we do it soonest.'

Colonel Bradstreet, the aggressive commander of the Bateauxmen growled his agreement.

Abercromby sighed and reluctantly came to a decision.

'Very well! We do it now.' He turned to his staff and the senior officers.

'The light infantry, rangers and bateauxmen to drive in the enemies outposts, then clear the front moving to the left flank. Provincial regiments will move forward in line to the edge of the abattis and put down fire. They're to leave gaps for the regular regiments who shall attack in column of companies. Brigaded Grenadier companies will take the centre. The 42nd and 55th regiments to remain in reserve.' He hauled out a pocket watch from his waistcoat and glanced at it. 'Seven of the clock! Begin the attack in one hour. Go to it gentlemen.'

The 42nd watched in sullen silence from their position on the crest of a low hill as the light troops moved across their front having successfully driven in the French outposts. They had received the news that they were in reserve, at first with disbelief, then anger. Officers and men alike smarted with hurt pride.

A haze of powder smoke drifted among the felled trees of the abattis that stretched the length of the French position to a depth of two or three hundred yards out from the logs of their palisade. The French had used the cut tops of the trees they had used in building their palisade to thicken the abattis. It looked a formidable barrier.

Provincial troops passed them to take position at the edge of the tangled mass. Then they could hear the drums beating the advance. Bands were competing in playing regimental marches, the shrill sound of the fifes carrying in the still air… and the columns came into view, in solid blocks of red. For minutes there was no sound but the drums and the music then the leading companies reached the beginnings of the abattis and the steady advance slowed as the tangle of fallen trees broke up the formations. The enemy palisade vanished in a cloud of smoke as the defenders opened up with a mass volley and the formations shredded still further. Even at long musket range men were dropping in the companies that had still not reached the abattis.

The attackers opened fire and with not a breath of wind, the powder smoke settled like a pall and the scene was lost. Men began to appear, staggering, limping and crawling back over the open ground, and bandsmen rushed forward to assist them. Faintly through the noise of the weaponry they could hear the shouts of men and the mutter of the drums still beating the advance.

Alex Campbell glanced round at his company and frowned when he noticed they had imperceptibly edged forward ten paces. He looked along the line of companies and saw the regiment as a whole had lost its alignment as the men were unconsciously drawn toward the fighting. Sergeants were moving to the front and holding their halberds horizontally in an effort to stop the movement. He signalled to Sgt McIvor and he and the other company sergeants did the same.

'Steady now, lads,' he shouted. 'Our turn will come.' But he sensed the men were not listening. The drift forward continued.

Lt Colonel Grant stared anxiously in the direction of the sawmill where the General and his staff were positioned. 'Give us the word, damn ye! Give us the word,' he muttered.

His adjutant came up red faced and breathless.

'Sir! We're barely holding the men back. Most of the officers are making little effort to restrain them. If we don't go soon….' He left the rest unsaid.

'I know, Archie! I know.' He turned abruptly toward where Major Proby stood, next to the colours of the 55th. They were Lord Howe's regiment, composed mainly of Lowland Scots and trained by Howe in the role of light infantry.

Taking off his bonnet he waved it above his head. When he had Proby's attention he drew his sword and pointed it toward the enemy lines. He smiled when he saw him repeat his actions.

'We'll not go in piecemeal,' he growled. 'You can let them loose, Archie!'

There was a roar as the drums thundered out the advance and the Regiment surged forward, the sound of the war pipes driving them on, as it had driven on their forefathers.

A spread of grapeshot smashed into the branches of a felled tree on their right. Two men close by went down kicking and McPhee let out a yelp as a splinter gouged into his cheek.

Iain paused from his hacking at the thick tangle that blocked their way and glanced back in concern, then reached over and plucked the offending splinter out. McPhee cursed him roundly, pawing at the blood flowing down his face.

Jamie and others dragged the cut limbs to one side and they pushed through into a relatively clear space. All along the line broadswords were swinging as others did the same. The ground behind was littered with bodies and the wounded were crawling back as best they could.

The fire grew heavier and the three of them took shelter behind a tree stump and caught their breath. They were a mere fifty yards from the French works and they were grateful for the thick powder smoke that gave them at least cover from more accurate fire. It was an illusory safety as the musket balls kicked up the leaf mould around them and grape shredded the broken limbs and entwined branches of the felled trees. They had been forcing their way forward for almost two hours and they were nearing exhaustion.

John Cameron crashed through into the little clearing, tripped over a branch, landed at their feet, and looked up, swearing under his breath.

'Good day to you, John.' Iain said, grinning. 'And how does this compare with Drummossie Moor?'

'Drummossie? How in hell would I know,' John snarled, 'for I never was nearer than four miles of the place. I fell asleep on the march from Inverness and slept through it all.

Then I spent three days dodging bloody English dragoons. Now! If you would kindly make a bit of room for me?'

Alex Campbell was crouched some twenty yards forward of them and peering at the base of the French palisade. He was near the edge of a shallow ditch dug by the French for the earthworks. It was bare of obstacles. He cursed as a billow of smoke obscured his view for a few seconds, then grunted in satisfaction at what he saw as it dispersed. He beckoned to Sgt McIvor.

'Any other officers around?'

McIvor shook his head. 'They both went down early on, sir.'

'There's a tree cut down near the palisade but its close and some of the limbs are resting on it. Gather as many of the lads as you can and put down fire. Keep their heads down while we get nearer, then if we make a lodgement bring the rest up over that parapet.' When the Sergeant moved off Alex looked round at the men scattered about him 'No more than twenty,' he thought. 'Can't tell them what I intend. Too damned noisy. But they'll follow me when I go forward...and they're smart lads. They'll see what's needed when we get close.'

He sat down behind the stump he had peered over, stretched out his legs and yawned hugely. He saw a couple of the men exchange looks and grin.

'Nothing to do but wait for McIvor,' he mused. His mind began drifting. 'I had it wrong about the broadswords. Never would have reached here without them...and we'll need them when we get over that damned palisade.' He inspected the blade of his sword, frowned when he saw the sticky wood resin adhering to it and scrubbed at it with a handful of loam. He leaned back against the stump, and yawned again.

'Make sure your pieces are charged,' McIvor bawled, upright and ignoring the musket balls flicking past. 'Fire when I tell you and not before. We're nearly there lads'

He turned and forced his way through the entangling branches followed by the remainder of the company. There was a growl from them when they could at last see the palisade and fleeting glimpses of the heads of the defenders. They quickly formed a ragged line and the first volley crashed out, raising splinters from the parapet.

Alex Campbell surged to his feet at the sound and without looking behind him raced for the felled tree. A broad limb extended up from the trunk at a gentle angle, its branches above the height of the logs of the palisade.

'Careless of them,' he thought, then cursed as he tripped over some debris and went sprawling. Before he could recover himself four men were past him and already on the limb. A bullet caught the last man and flicked him off, but the first three were up and vaulting into the French works, broadswords already swinging. He could hear shouting and the clang of metal on metal as he swarmed up the broad limb...then he was at the parapet and he paused to gather himself. He took in at a glance the tangled bodies of his men on the firestep and the fierce faces of the defenders... then a bayoneted musket darted up taking him under the ribs. He tried to cut down with his sword but there was no strength in his arm and he toppled back, crashing into the tree limb before hitting the ground in a sprawl of limbs

Jamie gave an inarticulate shout when he saw his uncle fall back and frantically scrabbled the few yards to where he lay, shrugging off McIvor's restraining hand. Kneeling, he cradled his uncle's head. Alex Campbell's eyes flickered open and he stared at Jamie unseeing. There was a gout of blood from his mouth, his body spasmed and then went limp.

More French heads and shoulders bobbed up over the parapet and a volley swept away some other Highlanders attempts to climb the limb. Jamie felt a hammer blow on his left side that hurled him forward over his uncle's body. A return burst of fire from McIvor's group sent two of the Frenchmen reeling back and had the rest ducking behind cover.

John Cameron spun back, his musket falling. Still on his feet he looked down in surprise at his right arm, the wrist and hand attached only by some sinews and the blood spurting.

McPhee standing next to him took one look, whipped out his dirk, held the arm firmly, and slashed down, the hand dropping into the leaf mould. He cut the sling off his musket, whipped it as a tourniquet above the stump, twisting the dirk to tighten it until the blood stopped jetting out.

'Why, thank you kindly, McPhee,' John said faintly.

'Damn the thanks,' McPhee grunted. 'Just make sure you return my good dirk. Now, away back with ye.'

'Keep up that fire,' McIvor roared and watched anxiously as Iain, who had bounded forward on seeing his friend struck down, throw Jamie over his shoulder and rejoin them. Two other men carried the body of Captain Alex Campbell back behind the remnants of his company.

He glimpsed others from the Regiment crossing the ditch on the right and cursed as he saw many crumple up before they reached the palisade. Small groups were chopping at the logs to make foot and handholds. Some even standing on other's shoulders to mount the ten foot breastwork. An officer he recognised as Lieutenant John Campbell of Number 4 company, using his men's backs, clambered up and sitting astride the parapet, coolly reached down and hauled others up. He saw the broadswords swinging as a group of defenders charged them, then the bayonets and musket butts rising and falling until the last red coat disappeared.

Somebody called out. 'Listen Sergeant! They're beating the retire again.'

'Aye!' he thought. 'That's the third time of telling so they must mean it.' He swiped at the sweat and tears on his face in irritation.

'Half of ye keep up the fire...the rest gather what wounded you can. We'll not be leavin' them. Go back slow and steady, lads. They'll never boast they routed us.'

'Put me down, Iain,' Jamie gasped. 'I can walk.'

They had reached the edge of the abattis and there was an unnatural stillness, the firing having died as the assaulting troops retired.

Iain stooped and lowered him to the ground carefully, holding him upright, his powder stained face twisted in concern. 'Where are ye hit? Let me look at you.'

Jamie indicated his left side, wincing at the searing pain below his armpit. Iain peered, then ripped at the already torn tunic and shirt, feeling the flesh gently.

'A wee hole where it went in and I can feel the ball where it never came out. There's a great gouge on your broadsword hilt where it hit first. Man! You fairly frightened me when I saw you go down. Here! Lean on me and I'll get you to the surgeons.'

'My Uncle Alex…'

'We have him Jamie lad. McIvor and McPhee are carrying him in.'

'Bury him proper Iain, you hear!'

'We'll do that. I promise!'

'Bring up the guns, sir. I beg you!' the artillery commander pleaded. 'I can make these works untenable.'

Abercromby shook his head. He looked grey faced and haggard. 'No time! No time! We face the same problem we did this morning. With Montcalm reinforced it would be a long siege. Were he to send a force up Champlain and strike toward Fort Edward there is little in his way. I cannot risk it. The Army must retire to the head of Lake George.'

There were murmurs of protest from his senior commanders and he looked up at them sharply.

'You disagree, gentlemen,' he said harshly. 'I would remind you that you urged me strongly to press the attack today. In particular yourself, Colonel Gage, and you Colonel Bradstreet. As Commander in Chief, I of course bear the responsibility and shall shoulder the blame for the decision that has cost us many brave men. However… you will understand if I chose not to seek your advice regarding this withdrawal. I do not intend to compound the errors made here by leaving our rear areas open to attack. The Army will retire and there's an end to it.'

Lt. Colonel Grant stared at the neat lines of blanket rolls and knapsacks his Regiment had discarded prior to advancing over the ridge. There were gaps where men had retrieved their own after the action, but those that still lay there bore mute witness to a soldier killed or badly wounded.

'All my fine laddies,' he thought and the tears ran down his cheeks. He remembered in Ireland when the command of the regiment had become vacant. He was senior major, but he had not the money to purchase it. The men had voluntarily contributed the money from their own purses, although in the end it had not been needed as he was granted the promotion without purchase. He heard a movement behind him and hurriedly brushed his wet cheeks.

'Yes Archie! What is it?'

'We're ready to march, sir. The wounded are already on their way to the boats. We've buried what dead we could recover. Major Campbell's badly hurt and his son's dead. A lot of other officers killed and wounded. I can't reckon our full casualties until we check the muster rolls.' The adjutant saw what the colonel was staring at and winced.

'Damned near half the Regiment, Archie. I counted 'til I couldn't bear to count any more. And I'm to fault. I let them go without orders.'

'No, Colonel! We couldn't hold them. Nobody could have. We beat the retire three times before they came back. They wanted this fight. We all did.' He touched the colonel on the arm. 'Sir! We must get back. There's but a few hours of daylight left.'

The Colonel took one last look at the French works in the distance. He could see the flags of the French regular regiments flying above the palisades and there came a distant sound of cheering as the defenders watched their foes march away.

He growled. 'Aye, cheer away. You earned it, damn you. But there will be a next time,' then he turned and walked slowly back to where his shattered regiment waited for him.

Chapter 10

Sarah had gathered with others to read the bulletins that had been posted throughout the town giving an account of the battle at Carillon The regiments still sat at the head of Lake George but wagons and bateaux carrying the wounded quickly began arriving at the Military hospital.

She spent anxious hours at its gates, along with the wives and womenfolk of the regiments, frantic with worry for their men. She scanned the tired faces of Highlanders that passed through them, but found she was unable to ask about Jamie for fear of hearing the news she dreaded. It seemed to her that every other man was from the 42nd.

Then a party of walking wounded arrived in a bateaux and she cried out with relief when she saw his familiar figure, clothing torn and bloodstained, his face still smudged with powder smoke.

She ran up to him and he had looked at her in surprise.

'Why, Sarah! This is no place for you. Away home lass!'

'I will when I find out how you are,' she'd said stubbornly.

'Ach! I'm fine. It's only us lightly wounded they've sent on here to Albany.'

'You don't look lightly wounded,' she said. 'Is Iain Mhor all right?

'Aye, and McPhee also. I'll look better when I'm washed and cleaned up and I'll be round to see you as soon as the surgeon says I'm fit to be let out. Now off with you.'

As he passed through the gate of the hospital he looked round and she was still there, her eyes fixed on him, hands tight clasped in her dress.

The light company of the 42nd filed past the burnt out wagons, the oxen dead in their traces and bloated with the heat of late July. Scattered among the shambles the corpses of the drivers and the escort were also swelling and blackening. The stench was overpowering and the men quickened their pace to be clear of it.

They had been called in the early hours of that morning to march out in support of rangers and Connecticut provincials already despatched to the area. One thousand men, comprising the light companies of the regular regiments encamped at the head of Lake George.

The word of what had occurred spread as they marched. A large convoy ambushed. A New Hampshire colonel at Fort Edward who had refused to supply men to strengthen the escort. A Massachusetts regiment posted at Half Way Brook, marching out after word of the ambush reached them, catching up with the rear of the enemy intoxicated with the liquor they had plundered, then refusing to attack.

Iain glanced over anxiously at Sergeant McIvor who marched along, his face showing no expression but his eyes flickering toward each body they passed. His wife, Jenny, had been travelling in the convoy to join him.

Camping a half mile from the site, parties were sent back to bury the dead. They buried over a hundred bodies. Iain, McPhee and others in the company spoke to those who carried out the nauseous task and discovered that they had found no females among the corpses.

'Sergeant,' Iain said hesitantly, joining him at the campfire, where McIvor sat staring blankly into the flames. 'We've been asking around and it appears they made off with around eighty captives. There were some dozen or more wives with the convoy and the burial parties didn't find one female. Your Jenny's alive, Sergeant. Captive, but alive.'

McIvor looked up, his face haggard and seeming more elderly than Iain could remember.

'I'm obliged to you and the rest, Munro,' he said slowly. 'Perhaps she is alive. But for how long? You know my Jenny. She's likely to take to cuffing them about the ear if they upset her. Caught you a few licks as I remember. And she's getting on in years...like me. I hope she's alive but that's all I can do. Just hope!'

Rangers came in the next day with the news that the raiders had got too far ahead to catch up with but that there was sign of more incursions. As the bulk of the light companies retraced their steps to Lake George, eighty regulars marched to join the rangers and provincials for a sweep of the area, including half of the light company of the 42nd. For a frustrating week they searched, and laid ambushes until, within a half day march of Fort Edward and provisions low, they headed back to the fort..

'Damn these Provincials,' Iain fumed, as another shot sounded ahead of them. 'They're on their way home so they think it's all right to take pot shots at game.'

'Ever since you went out with the Rangers, you've become a greater bore than ever, Iain Mhor. Always chattering on about your experience,' McPhee sneered, winking broadly at the men marching nearby. 'Man, you'll be looking for promotion on the strength of it.'

'Aye! Scoff away, for the ignorant man that you are, McPhee. One thing I learnt was you stay alert until the gates of the fort close behind you.'

They marched on for another half an hour and the head of the column walked straight into an ambush.

Lieutenant Grant shouted, 'Tree up!' as the crash of muskets sounded to their front and the half company spread either side of the track in a skirmish line.

As Iain took cover behind a tree he looked over at a cursing McPhee who'd found a patch of stinging nettles and wiggled his eyebrows at him. 'A great bore am I, McPhee?' he asked smugly.

Panic-stricken Connecticut provincials came streaming back down the track ignoring the angry shouts of the officers in the thin skirmish line. Captain Dalyell of the 80th, in command of the regulars lashed out with the flat of his sword at men fleeing past them. A company of Boston provincials moved up and extended the left flank, then Rogers arrived and his rangers pushed out to the right.

Rogers stood bellowing at the Connecticut men, cursing them for cowardly poltroons, and slowed their retreat. Most shamefacedly turned about and thickened up the firing line in time to face the French and Indians surging forward.

Iain held fire until he had a clear shot, waiting for a French militia-man to break cover from behind a large tree not ten yards away. As the man slipped into view making for another tree, Iain shot him, letting out an Indian whoop as he saw him thrown back to slump at the base of the tree he'd just left. He reloaded smoothly and peered round his cover listening to the volume of fire increase as the enemy closed with the skirmish line. Bullets were clipping at branches and leaves and wisps of powder smoke threaded their tendrils through the woods.

McPhee scuttled across to join him.

'Feeling lonely, McPhee?' Iain grinned.

McPhee scratched under his kilt at the nettle stings and ignored him.

A provincial only a few feet away rose from behind a fallen log and fired, then stayed upright peering into the smoke of his discharge. A volley of return shots hammered into him and he fell forward over the log. There was a scuffling of leaves and a chorus of triumphant yelps.

McPhee stepped round his side of the tree and shot the lead Indian racing forward to claim the provincial's scalp, then fell back hurriedly to reload as Iain took his place in time to fire at another Indian, hitting him in the arm. The warrior spun and disappeared into some under-growth.

Lieutenant Grant appeared close behind them, slipping from tree to tree.

'All right here, are we,' he asked, breathlessly.

'Ach! Just fine sir. Just fine! McPhee has a terrible itch under his kilt, but then, hasn't he always,' Iain answered cheerfully, applying his ramrod vigorously to the fresh charge in his musket. 'And how are things elsewhere, lieutenant?'

'The centre's holding nicely, but we think they're pushing round the right flank, so keep an eye in that direction.'

The sound of musketry increased from that flank and the three listened to the discordant howls of the Indians and the shouts of the French as they pressed forward against the rangers.

It went on for some time then gradually the woods quietened. Rangers began appearing carrying their dead and wounded back to the centre, and whistles were blowing for units to reassemble.

Iain looked down on the dead provincial sprawled over the log and turned him over.

'Why, he's but a bairn,' Iain said sadly. 'Do you take his legs McPhee, and I'll take the poor laddie's shoulders.'

They carried him back to join the long line of bodies laid by the side of the track.

Sarah reached under her pillow and took out the small bundle of letters neatly tied with ribbon. She moved her chair close to the window for better light and extracted the latest one. Over six weeks old, she had reread it a dozen times. She carefully unfolded it and read it again.

At Camp on Long Island this 16th day of February 1759

My dear Friend Sarah,

It may be that by the time you receive this the Regiment will be on its journey back to Albany for we have been told we shall return there in the spring, but of course the Army moves in slow and mysterious ways.

This sojourn on Long Island, although welcome after the events of last year, has become somewhat irksome to my comrades and myself despite our rations being abundant with fresh vegetables and meats and the climate mild to compare with what we had grown accustomed to in the north. To put it frankly, we are bored and wish to be about our business. We are now fully rested and many of our wounded are returned to their duty, but alas, so many familiar faces are missing from our ranks. Our losses have meant a rash of promotions and I am delighted to inform you that I have been made Sergeant. I trust you will be suitably impressed at this news. Iain Mhor has been made corporal and with the power going straight to his head, has become insufferably efficient. Poor McPhee, whom you have met on one or two occasions, complains loudly that he is continually being victimised by the aforementioned Cpl Munro. We can only hope that when the novelty wears off Iain will return to being his normal self.

When we do return you will be astounded at the splendour of our dress having at last received an issue of new plaids and coats with facings of blue now that we are designated a Royal Regiment. A far cry from our sorry appearance when we left Albany in September last. I have been busily engaged in sewing up philabegs from remnants of our old plaids for Iain Mhor and myself. His needlework is not of the best. He is peering over my shoulder at this moment attempting to read what I have penned and begs to be remembered to you and Mistress Yonge.

May I thank you for your kind enquiry as to the state of my injury and am pleased to inform you that it has left me with no discomfort apart from a slight ache when the weather turns wet and cold.

I have succeeded in purchasing some folios of music that I will deliver to you personally, not wishing to risk their damage by sending them to you. I confess they contain some rather turgid airs but they will suffice as an aid to your musical reading.

Please to give my regards to Mistress Yonge and I hope to enjoy her hospitality once more when I come to visit you on our return.

You're Friend.
James Campbell, Sgt. 42nd Royal Regiment of Foot.

Laying the letter on her lap she stared out the window. There were patches of slushy snow in the hollows and ice in the ruts of the track. 'Go away winter,' she said aloud.

She wiped the mist of her breath off the windowpane and peered at the tree branch that tapped on her window when the wind blew. There were flecks of green where the new buds forced through the bark and she smiled. Spring would come slowly as it always did and no words of impatience from her would hurry it along. But spring set armies to marching and although she would see Jamie again she dreaded what the year might bring.

Chapter 11

Mistress Yonge laid a comforting arm around Sarah's shoulders as the last company disappeared over the crest of the hill on the road that led to Lake George. The faint sound of the pipes could still be heard in the hot still air.

'I saw him so few times and when he did call it was different. He was different,' Sarah said, her voice breaking.

'How so, Sarah?

'I don't know. Serious! Distant! His thoughts elsewhere.'

'You can hardly blame him, girl,' Mistress Yonge said firmly. 'They marched off last year going to the same place and you remember how they came back. Perhaps Jamie has grown into this war and now knows there's little honour or glory in it. Besides, as a sergeant he has more responsibilities.'

'Iain Mhor remains unchanged by it all.'

'And will remain unchanged until the day he dies,' Mistress Yonge chuckled. 'Your Jamie has a serious side to him. Iain Mhor goes through life with barely a thought on what may happen tomorrow. He's a great child in the body of a large man and if I were thirty years younger I'd...' She stopped abruptly and coughed in confusion.

'Why, Mistress Yonge, I do declare your blushing.' Sarah said, her mood lightening.

'It's the heat!' the Dutch woman snapped. 'Come along Sarah! Time we went home.'

Jeffrey Amherst, who had taken over command from Abercromby, was a deliberate man who made no precipitate moves. The Army at the foot of Lake George waited in the sweltering heat, periodically lashed by torrential thunderstorms and grumbled at his caution. Finally in late July with the knowledge that the attack on Quebec by Wolfe's Army was well under way and would have drawn off French forces from the Champlain Valley he launched his attack on Fort Carillon.

The landings were unopposed. Rangers and light infantry swiftly pushed up to the Chute river and finding the bridge had not been destroyed, crossed over, taking up a position near the sawmill. A weak sally from the fort was easily fended off and the rest of the army began arriving.

By noon the next day the fort was invested and the heavy guns moving up. The first traverses had been opened and were inching their diagonal way toward the fort's defences.

There was to be no headlong assault. Amherst intended to conduct his siege operations by the book.

'Here Jamie. This is where we buried him,.' Iain Mhor called, clearing dry withered grass off the low mound of earth.

Searching around Jamie found a slab of fieldstone and carried it over to his uncle's grave. With his bayonet he began gouging out lettering in the soft limestone.

Ian sat watching the activity below him with interest.

The French guns were bellowing shot at the sapheads of the traverses, the ground around them churned up with the ball strikes. There was little the French they could do to stop the relentless slanting approach. No targets presented themselves. Merely the shovel blades tossing the new dug earth onto the parapet.

'A slow business,' Iain commented.

Jamie brushed chips of stone from the lettering then looked up and surveyed the scene.

'Aye! But there's an inevitability about it. When the traverses are close enough they'll set up the breaching batteries and then the French are finished. Nothing left but to surrender. Unless you'd prefer to go about it the way we did last year?'

Iain grimaced. 'No! Slow is fine. Just as long as they don't have us down helping scrape out that ditch. I took the shilling to get away from that sort of labour. Digging for peat and such.'

'I'm done here. Give me a hand to set it up.'

They scraped a hole at the end of the grave and stood the stone upright in it, packing the earth around the bottom. Before they left to go back to the regiment they stood quietly for a time.

Two nights later a huge explosion startled the army.

'God save us! Will you just look at that,' McPhee exclaimed.

They watched as the sky was lit with lurid flames from the fort. There were more explosions as fuses set off guns overcharged to destruction.

McPhee sniggered. 'Seems the French have decided not to wait around and surrender.'

Next morning parties entered the fort and discovered the destruction was far from total. Almost immediately work was begun restoring the defences.

It would no longer be called Carillon. It would be known by the name that the Indians had given the land where it was sited. Ticonderoga!

A week later the bulk of the army marched the few miles north to another fort the French had destroyed in their retreat to the Richelieu River and the defences on Isle au Noix.

Chapter 12

'Have you heard the rumour?' Iain asked in a hoarse whisper.

'Which particular rumour would that be? The one that has the French Army's paychest under the rubble we're clearing, on account they forgot to load it before blowing the place up.... Why are you whispering?'

Iain grinned. 'Not the paychest. It was myself started that one just yesterday. I told McPhee, and him being a rare one for the gossip, before I knew it there was a whole crowd of Provincials shifting stone and timber like their lives depended on it.... And I'm whispering because this rumour is secret.'

Jamie looked at him blankly, then shook his head in bemusement. 'I'm not going to ask you how a rumour can be secret, so out with it.'

'Seems the Rangers are getting ready for some ploy or other. Can't find out where their going but I had a wander down to their lines and they're working on their whaleboats.' When Jamie made no comment he grimaced in annoyance. 'Don't ye see. They'll be looking for volunteers from those who've ranging service. Like us. It'll get us away from this damned hard labour for a spell.'

'We don't labour. The Provincials do most of the work, and even if we did some of us just supervise.' Jamie remarked, smugly.

'Sorry, Sergeant, I forgot,' Iain said disgustedly, then pleadingly. 'Ach, Jamie, think on it. A wee jaunt on the loch and a chance of some excitement, maybe. And you know fine their rations are better than ours.'

'You were less keen on the boating last month when we happened on these French gunboats and they were like to blow us out of the water.'

'That was last month,' Iain sniffed. 'I thought we'd be in Montreal with them French mam'selles by now... yet here we are building another damned fort.' He stalked off in a sulk.

Curiosity and the feeling that perhaps for once the camp rumours could be right had Jamie wandering up to the Rangers' lines at the edge of the lake. Their whaleboats were pulled up on the shingle of the beach in a neat line but the men had finished work for the day and most were lounging by their tents. A few had lines out fishing. He stood watching for a while, scanning faces for someone he knew.

'Well! Well!' a deep bass voice rumbled. 'Campbell isn't it? I see you've made Sergeant.'

Jamie swung round to find Rogers eyeing him from the grassy bank above the beach. He was surprised and not a little gratified that Rogers had remembered him.

'Congratulations on your own promotion to Major, sir.'

'Why, thank you Sergeant. I wont ask what brings you to the ranger's lines It didn't take long for the whole damn army to know there's something afoot. Worse than a load of old women at a sewing bee.'

He shook his head disgustedly, then stared at Jamie with his unblinking protuberant eyes. 'You in a mind to come along, Sergeant?'

'Come along to where, sir?' Jamie asked, innocently.

Rogers chuckled and tapped his fleshy nose with his forefinger. 'Now then! You know the rules of the game. I let you know when we 're well away from all the loose chatter in the camp. Your Lieutenant Grant will be taking the names of volunteers from the Highlanders. Be glad to have you along.' He turned and walked away briskly, stopping to make some remark to a group of rangers that had them guffawing with laughter

'Suagothol is where we're headed,' Iain said, with certainty. 'The whole Army knows it.' He finished tying up his blanket roll to his satisfaction. 'Where's Suagothol, Jamie?'

'Ask Rogers…. But wherever it is you can be sure it's not called Suagothol,' Jamie scoffed, testing the edge of the hatchet he had been sharpening.

The last three days had been spent in the Ranger's lines. The volunteers, from Regular regiments and Provincials, all of whom had done ranging service, mingling comfortably with those enlisted as rangers, renewing acquaintances with men they knew. They were a microcosm of Amhurst's army. Hardened veterans of the years of campaigning, with a confidence born of recent success and the knowledge they could match the enemy in the environment they fought in.

They were moving out that night, the men already in groups up the bank from the whaleboats they would man. The campfires were masked with brushwood on the side facing the lake so they could launch and move off in the darkness. Until then there was little to do apart from checking and rechecking their arms and equipment.

'Happens it was Rogers himself who came up with that name,

Suagothol,' drawled a lanky ranger. 'Overheard him say to one of the officers that if we give them a name to chatter about they ain't likely to do any thinking and maybe come up with the place they ain't supposed to know about in the first instance,' he chuckled. 'Ain't he the one though.'

He turned to Jamie. 'I remember you from the Battle on Snowshoes. You helped haul me back down Lake George on a sled. Didn't introduce myself at the time on account of how I was lying on my face all the way 'coz of the bullet in me arse and feeling a tad unsociable. Name's Ezra…Ezra Shawcross.'

He spat in the fire. 'Damn me if I didn't lose a little toe from frostbite as well. Just fell off a couple days after we got back.' He sighed and stretched. 'Still! We're the lucky ones. Lot of good rangers lost their hair that day.'

'I'm glad we're finally introduced Ezra.' Jamie said. 'As I remember it you were doing so much cursing we didn't linger when we handed you over to the surgeons.'

They were a mixed group. A corporal from another company of the 42nd called Charlie Hutchinson, and Terry Murphy, a cheerful Irishman from the 27^{th,} along with seven rangers, made up their whaleboat crew.

'Here we go boys,' Ezra said, as a stream of officers emerged from Major Rogers' tent hurrying off to their units. The bulky form of Rogers appeared. He stood peering around and sniffing the air, for all the world like a hound scenting.

Lieutenant Grant, their boat commander, strode up. 'Get her launched, lads…and no talking from now on. A couple of French gunboats were reported off the mouth of the Otter two days back but they could be anywhere now.'

There was a rumble of gravel under the keels as the whaleboats were run into the dark waters of the lake and the splashing of oars as the boats formed up in a line stem to stern. A long minute of silence then a whisper passed from boat to boat. 'Rendezvous is Buttonmould Bay.'

The oars dipped in the water, the rowers leaned back, and the long line of dark shapes headed north.

A dull thud jerked Jamie from his doze. All around, men sat up and stared anxiously down toward the lakeshore where a cloud of grey smoke rose above the tree line.

'The French found us d'ye think? Iain asked, checking the priming of his musket.

Jamie shook his head. 'It sounded like a powder explosion. Stand to just in case. We'll find out soon enough.'

The wind dissipated the smoke quickly. They heard a few shouts from the area below them, then all went quiet again.

This was the fifth day they had lain at Buttonmould Bay, the boats drawn clear of the bank and carefully hidden with brush while a party of rangers and Stockbridge Indians had scouted overland toward the Otter River to locate the French gunboats. They had come back yesterday evening with the news that they were still moored off the river mouth.

Lieutenant Grant came up, looking grim faced and worried. 'It's a damned shambles down there. A powder bag exploded. God knows how. Nobody killed but a lot of men injured with burns.'

A ranger came hurrying up. 'Major Rogers compliments, Lieutenant. All officers to join him for a conference, sir.'

'What happened Captain, and how many hurt? Rogers asked, quietly.

Captain Williamos, a Regular officer, the leggings burnt through on his right leg, the flesh blistered and flecked with unburned powder grains, grimaced and shrugged his shoulders.

'We were reallocating boat stores, I can only think one of the Stockbridge Indians got careless. It happened opposite their boat and there are thirteen of them injured.... Plus four regulars, three rangers, two provincials.... And myself.' he said dejectedly.

'That's a bad burn Captain. You'll take two boats tonight and get yourself and these injured men back to Crown Point.'

'Two men hurt in that accidental discharge and six Rangers carrying them back. Then Captain Butterfield and these seven sick men you sent back yesterday. Now this. That's almost a fifth of our force gone and we've only just set out,' Ogden, a hard-bitten Ranger captain commented. 'Why, that's more than we'd lose in a fight.'

Rogers shrugged. 'Can't be helped! Fortunes of war, gentlemen. Although it's time we had a smidgen of better luck.' He grinned and studied the sky. 'It may be coming tomorrow the way my old wounds are aching. Cold and rain tends to bring it on. I think there's dirty weather on its way, so warn the men to be ready to move tomorrow night. Give them as much rest as possible. We've ten miles of narrows to get through plus a dogleg over to the western shore. I intend to give these French ships as wide a berth as possible, and if the weather comes on as foul as I hope... it'll be a long hard night. Post extra pickets for now in case that smoke was spotted and someone decides to investigate.'

'Major! The men are curious as to where we're headed. Are you intending to let them know?' Ogden asked.

Rogers shook his head. 'Time enough when we get passed these damned French ships.

'How are you enjoying our wee jaunt on the loch so far, Iain? Was that not how you described it?' Jamie asked solemnly.

A gust of wind shook the branches of the tree they were crouched beside and showered them with drops of water. Iain blew a drip from his nose disgustedly.

'Don't crow, Jamie Campbell. You're as daft as I am to be here,' he grunted, bitterly.

They peered northwards over a leaden grey lake flecked with whitecaps and swept by rainsqualls.

'Twelve hours of rowing and bailing on a night as black as the Earl of Hell's waistcoat and we draw first spell on picket,' Iain moaned. 'Why do you listen to me when I get these mad notions. I'll happily build forts from Crown Point to Montreal when we get back. Catch me volunteering for anything again and you have my permission to shoot me.'

'Hush, you great bairn. Here! This'll cheer ye.' Jamie reached in his haversack and produced a lump of soft bread and a flask. The mouthful of rum soaked bread spread comforting warmth in their chests.

The previous night had been one of unremitting toil, discomfort and tension. They had crept up the western side of the lake, lashed by rain and a chill wind, the whaleboats linked with lines, stem to stern, to avoid separation in the pitch darkness. There was a heart stopping period when the rain had ceased and they lay quiet, watching the glimmer of ship's lanterns no more than half a mile off, then the relief as another belt of rain swept in. About twenty-five miles they had travelled so Lieutenant Grant had told them.

Now the narrows were passed and the wider part of the lake lay opened up before them.

It was almost dusk when they at last found out where they were headed. They had assembled where the boats were hidden, ready for that night's move. Rogers signalled for the detachments to close in around him.

He grinned at them. 'Here's where you find out where Suagothel really is.'

'By order of General Amherst', he began formally, reading from his orders and speaking quietly but clearly. 'You are to proceed to Missisquoi Bay from whence you will march and attack the enemy's settlements on the south side of the River St Lawrence in such a manner as you shall judge most effectual. Remember the barbarities committed by the enemy's Indian scoundrels on every occasion where they had an opportunity of showing their infamous cruelties on the King's subjects, which they have done without mercy. Take your revenge but do not forget that although those villains have dastardly and promiscuously killed women and children of all ages, it is my orders that no women or children are killed or hurt.' He paused, then went on. 'So! Now you know. We're on our way to wipe out St Francis for good and all. The St Francis Indians have been raiding our settlements for years. Long before this war started. Some of you have lost kin to them. Most of you have lost friends. Time to even up the score... Now! Man your boats.'

Chapter 13

'A foot more of water and a damned sight fewer trees and we could have rowed all the way,' Charlie Hutchinson remarked to Iain as they cut spruce boughs to make a sleeping platform for the night.

It was the end of the second day's march through a spruce bog that seemed interminable. The whaleboats and provisions for the return had been cached in the swampy wilderness at the head of Missisquoi Bay. That same day the column had splashed off into a nightmare landscape of spruce thickets, fallen waterlogged trees, and cold muddy water that hid the broken branches and roots that tore at the legs and feet. Even if fires had been allowed everything was sodden and the nights were cold miserable affairs, wrapped in a thin damp blanket on rough bowers perched above the water.

Jamie, with Ezra, Murphy and another ranger were on picket some hundred yards in the rear, watching the column's back track when they heard a splashing and a call of 'Rangers! Rangers coming in.' and two Stockbridge Indians came into view.

'That's Lieutenant Jacob. They were left to watch the boats,' Ezra said.

Jamie stood up, and called back. 'Rangers here! Come ahead.'

The two men were swaying with fatigue and the Indian Lieutenant gasped breathlessly as he waded past. 'The French found the boats!'

'Yesterday afternoon around four hundred French and Indians discovered our boats. About half of them started off after us. Thanks to Lieutenant Jacob here, we've got a full day's march on them.' Rogers looked round the assembled officers, their faces barely visible in the dusk. 'As I see it we have only one option. That is to carry out our task and return by another route'

'We could wait and ambush them, major,' Captain Ogden suggested.

'It would be too chancy a business in this terrain. Flat and feature-less. Nowhere to site an ambush we could guarantee they'd walk into…. And they'll be wary. We'd take casualties and be no better off. We'll be short of food and a hundred miles from Crown Point. We take St Francis and we'll find food there.' He paused and cleared his throat. 'Lieutenant McMullen… you'll take six rangers and make your best speed back to Crown Point. I suggest you strike out east for some way to get you clear of those following us. No written orders...for obvious reasons...so commit this to memory. I intend to retire up the St Francis River to Lake Memphremagog, then down the Passumpsic Valley to strike the Connecticut at its junction with the Wells River. Tell General Amherst to send provisions up the Connecticut from No 4 to the Wells...That is the way we'll return...if at all. You have that?'

'I do sir...and I won't fail you.'

Rogers chuckled. 'I sincerely hope not, Lieutenant.' He yawned and stretched. 'Let's get some sleep. The past two days we've been sort of strolling. From now until we hit St Francis we needs open our legs. I intend to gain a bit more of a lead.'

On the morning of the ninth day after leaving the boats they at last hit dry firm ground and by noon they were hidden up on the western bank of the St Francis River.

Murphy eased off a moccasin and sourly inspected his pallid, water wrinkled foot. 'We've rare bogs in Ireland, boys...but I never saw the likes of that one.'

'Myself, I regard it a blessing the French found the boats,' Iain grunted, gnawing at his last piece of sausage. 'Saved us traipsing back through that again.' He looked up as Lieutenant Grant approached.

'You dried out then, Cpl. Munro?' the lieutenant asked solicitously, a faint smile on his face.

Iain Mhor eyed him suspiciously. 'Just about sir.'

The Lieutenant leered. 'Ach...That's a pity. Sergeant Campbell... yourself, Munro and Shawcross hand over your weapons and packs to the others and head down to the river The Major wants the tallest men to form a chain across to get the rest over without half the detachment washing downstream.'

'What are you grinning at ye wee Irish dwarf,' Iain snarled at Murphy as he set off. 'I've still a dram of rum left in my canteen and it had best be there on the other side of this damned river.'

Jamie breathed a sigh of relief when the whispered order to fix bayonets and advance came. It had been a long night. The careful approach toward the village, then the wait while Rogers and a small party had crept forward to observe and come back with the news that there appeared to be some big celebration with dancing and drinking. Charges were drawn and the muskets reloaded with buckshot and ball but left unprimed for fear of an accidental discharge. The officers had briefed their detachments on the plan of attack and then there was another cautious move to within a thousand yards, the glow of the fires showing above the low ridge behind which they crouched and the sound of drums and drunken whoops heard clearly. Then all was quiet as the revels finished. Only a cold wait in the predawn chill remaining.

The long line of men swept down toward the village through fields of harvested squash and maize, the only sound the heavy breathing and the swish of leggings through the stubble. They could make out the dwellings now. A hodge-podge of substantial log built cabins and bark wickiups. They halted fifty yards from the first huts and primed their weapons. No sound came from the sleeping village. The line started running now and as the first wickiup doors were kicked open, rangers bursting in wielding bayoneted muskets and hatchets, a solitary cock greeted the dawn.

Lieutenant Grant's detachment of thirty men had been allotted the task of cutting off any escape by the river and they ignored the dwellings they passed as the first screams rose and muskets banged. They reached the riverbank and settled in a line awaiting the expected fugitives.

'Independent fire, lads. Take them as they come,' Lieutenant Grant shouted. A cabin door near them burst open and an Indian staggered out looking around wildly. Two muskets fired and the man was thrown back inside. Jamie saw another slipping between two huts, waited for him to appear again and shot him as he came into view.

'You led him nicely there,' Ezra called, approvingly.

All along the line, men were firing as figures emerged from the cabins, confused and befuddled with sleep and the drink they had consumed the previous night.

Flames were taking hold of some of the bark houses and they could hear the screams of women and children above the rising crescendo of musket fire.

'Ware behind!' someone shouted and Jamie swung round to see two Indians in the water swimming desperately and a canoe with a man crouched low, paddling. There was a volley of shots and the swimmers rolled over and disappeared. The Indian in the canoe stood, his face shot away, then as he fell, tipped the craft. Another three bodies rolled into the water from it and were swept downstream.

'God save us Jamie,' Iain said, sorrowfully. 'That was a woman and bairns.'

More huts were blazing now. The musketry had died away apart from the odd shot but the screaming continued. They waited but no more targets presented themselves and Lieutenant Grant called, 'Sweep through and tidy up. Rendezvous in the centre of the village. Sergeant Campbell! To me! There's a hut over there I think is a corn store. We'll check it and if it is make damn sure no fool puts a torch to it. We're going to need it.'

'What's the butchers bill,' Rogers asked his orderly sergeant.

'One Stockbridge Indian killed, a half dozen minor scratches, but Captain Ogden was shot through the body.'

Rogers frowned. 'Badly hit?'

'He says not, major. Reckons he can still walk.'

'He'll damned well have to.' Rogers grunted.

He wrinkled his nose at the smell of roasting flesh from the blazing cabins and wickiups then walked over to the group of twenty or thirty women and children huddled together around a Jesuit priest. Another smaller group of white women captives stood some distance away.

'They were expecting a raid, Major. Not here...further west at Wigwam Martinique. They say there's two or three hundred French and Indians waiting there. A lot of the menfolk from St Francis are with them,' Lieutenant Jacob said. 'They were celebrating a wedding last night.' he added. He had been interrogating the prisoners.

'Expecting us were they? We must have been sighted on the lake. That accounts why they found the boats so quickly.' He walked over to the prisoners, selected two young boys and two girls and pushed them over to the white women.

'Tell the rest they can go.' He walked over to a fire where a number of large kettles were bubbling away.

'Have the men all been provisioned?' he asked the group of officers. 'I trust you told them to fill their packs? We've a fair way to go before we find anymore.'

'There's been some looting. The church ornaments have gone. The priest says they were silver. He's not best pleased,' Lieutenant Dunbar, a regular from Gages Light Infantry said, disapprovingly.

Rogers shrugged. 'Can't be helped. Soldier's loot and we don't have time to be searching them. The men that took them are fools if they gave up room in their packs for silver instead of food. A week from now they'll be sorry they did.' He sniffed the aromas from the kettles. 'Get the men fed. We move off in a half-hours time. By sunset I want to be well passed where we crossed the river and if there's any moon we keep moving. There's French at Wigwam Martinique, a half days march from here. Burn the rest of the huts and make sure what's left of the corn is destroyed. Leave the French nothing. If they're hungry they can dine on roast relatives,' he said, brutally.

Lieutenant Grant's detachment spooned into their mouths the first hot food they had eaten since leaving Crown Point.

'Hurry up and pack it in, lads,' the lieutenant called. 'It's the last hot meal you'll have for a good while.'

'There he goes, spoiling the taste of it with his hurry up,' Iain mumbled, his mouth full. 'A man can't take the time to enjoy anything without somebody rushing him in this army.'

Jamie was studying the white captive women squatting a short distance away. They wore shapeless Indian smocks, their faces grimy and smoke blackened, indistinguishable from the Indian women who had been released. Most seemed frightened, the violence of the morning cancelling any overt feelings of relief or gratitude toward their rescuers. One woman, however, was staring around boldly.

'Jenny?' he called, hesitantly. 'Jenny McIvor?'

The woman looked in his direction and rose slowly, her eyes scanning the group of men.

'Jamie Campbell,' she said in the Gaelic, her voice quivering. 'And Iain Mhor himself.'

She rushed over and hugged them. 'A hundred thousand welcomes to you. Quick now, tell me! How is that old goat McIvor?'

'He's well Jenny. He's missed you badly,' Jamie reassured her.

'Thank the Lord! I thought the old fool would have pined away for the want of me. What are ye gawking at, Munro?'

'Aye! It's yourself right enough, Jenny. I wouldn't have recognised you dressed as you are. Man, did they work you hard.'

'No harder than I worked scrubbing the company's dirty linen.' She started in astonishment as Lieutenant Grant came over. 'God save us, but has the whole of the 42nd come all this way for an old biddy like me?'

'It makes the journey worthwhile, Mistress McIvor. A pleasure to see you safe and well,' the lieutenant grinned. 'We'll soon have you back in the loving arms of the good Sergeant McIvor.'

'Glad as I am to see you, I wish it could have been done without all this.' She waved her hand at the burning cabins and the litter of dead bodies all around. 'They weren't bad people once you got used to their ways.'

She looked over and saw her fellow white captives moving off.

'I'd best away and the quicker you're gone as well, the better. There's going to be some pretty angry people coming after you when they see what you've done,'

Picking up a large basket packed with corn she swung it on her back and slipped the strap on to her forehead and caught up quickly with her companions. They saw her put her arm round one of the young Indian girls in a comforting gesture then disappear into the smoke from a burning hut.

'What you got there Ezra?' Murphy spluttered through a mouthful of parched corn, eyeing something large wrapped in greasy linen that Ezra had hauled from his haversack. 'This, my boy, will keep me hale and hearty, with a spring in my step, when you are grilling your cartridge box.' He unwrapped the object and sat back admiring it.

Iain Mhor stared at the grey greasy ball as big as his head and sniffed at it cautiously.

'Damn me! It's beef tallow... and old beef tallow, by the smell of it. You plan to eat that?'

'Not yet. I ain't hungry enough,' Ezra said, carefully rewrapping it.

It was well into the fifth day of the march from St Francis. They were still following the river along a well-beaten track and Rogers had forced the pace. He had been up and down the column chivvying them on with curses or words of encouragement. Now they were at the fork of the river that would lead them to Lake Memphremagog. They had come seventy miles.

The column was on the move again and the men forced their tired limbs into the rhythm of the march. Charlie eased up beside Jamie.

'You think the French and Indians are still after us, Jamie? They might have given up by now.'

'I wouldn't count on it Charlie. We've just wiped out a whole village and killed a lot of their kin. The Abenaki will be after a reckoning. Wouldn't you be?'

'I suppose I would.' He coughed and looked uncomfortable. 'Jamie! I looked round that village and I didn't count much above thirty dead men... but there were a lot of women and children and God knows how many were burnt up. It doesn't sit easy with me. I keep hearing the screams.'

'So do I, Charlie. So do I.'

'Ezra! I mentioned it to him. He just laughed, called me a soft-hearted bugger and said something about lice breeding more lice.'

'I know what he means,' Jamie sighed. 'What scares you most, Charlie? What do you dread the most?'

Charlie scratched at his beard. 'Being taken alive, I suppose.'

'Right! It scares all of us. We've seen the results of what they do. We fear it and we start to hate those that cause us that fear. Ezra's lived with it all his life... so he's got a lot more hate in him than you or I. The Indians think nothing of it. It's their way. It shakes you and I to see women and children killed. They look on it different because it's all part of war to them. Ezra thinks as they do. You and I! We haven't learned to hate enough, Charlie.'

'Not entirely sure I would want to, Jamie.' Charlie said, a wry grin splitting his beard

'Go away you soft-hearted bugger,' Jamie said, with a laugh.

Memphremagog looked as forbidding as its name sounded. Slate grey under a blanket of dark clouds, it stretched south to the horizon, gloomy woods lining its shores.

Lieutenant Grant had returned from a council of the officers, quietly furious. Without explanation he divided his small detachment into three roughly equal groups then led his two sergeants a short way off.

'It's been decided to split into smaller parties,' he said sourly. 'A lot of the men have run out of food and there's more chance of coming on game than travelling in a large body. I can't say I agree. The Major was reluctant as well. I think we stand more chance keeping on as we are for a while yet. Safety in numbers if the French catch up with us. But we took a vote on it and that was the decision of the majority.' He shivered as a shower of sleet swept in and scowled at the sky. 'That's just what we need,' he grunted.

He produced two rough sketch maps. 'The best I can do. You both have compasses?' When they nodded, he paused, digging moodily at the leaf mould with a stick.

'Your route is up to you. Once we split up you decide what's best to get your party home safely. The rendezvous is the junction of the Wells and the Connecticut. Any questions?'

Sergeant Evans, a stolid, taciturn ranger shook his head, as did Jamie.

The Lieutenant stood up abruptly and shook hands with them both. 'Good luck to you.' He watched them go off to their groups, kicked angrily at the leaf mould, and went off to join his own party.

Jamie felt a moment of doubt, almost panic, as he approached the figures huddled in the lee of a thicket, their faces turned toward him in curiosity. It was the responsibility. The fear of making the wrong decision that caused it. As quickly as it arose he put it from his mind.

He squatted beside them. 'You've probably guessed what's happening.. We're splitting up in the hope we can come across more game this way.' He looked round his little party. Iain, Charlie, Murphy, Ezra and two other rangers, Bourne and Lorrimer. 'Ezra, you've been hunting all your life. What's the chance of shooting some meat.'

Ezra shook his head. 'In this weather...poor, lest we step on it by chance. We're the only critters stupid enough to be movin' around in this.'

'We could fish the lake.' Bourne suggested.

'Back home in Scotland I lived on the banks of a loch. Weather like this the fish go deep and won't bite. I doubt they're any different here.'

'It's worth a try. I'm pretty hungry and a mess of trout wouldn't go amiss.' Bourne said stubbornly.

'The trouble with fishing is you tend to sit in one place. You don't get any nearer where you want to go, and if you catch nothing, you're a day hungrier and fifteen miles short of where you could have been.'

Ezra nodded in agreement.

'Here's how I see it,' Jamie went on. 'We've about finished the food we have, but right now we're in more danger from the French catching up on us, especially if we waste time looking for game, than dying of hunger. Most of the parties will keep to the east of the lake. That's the shortest route to the rendezvous. I intend to go west of the lake. I say we push on hard while we're still strong until we're beyond the southern end. The French must be running short of food as well. Another two days march and we can ease off and then think about hunting up some meat.'

'If we go west about it'll add miles to the rendezvous,' Bourne complained.

'True! If we were heading for the rendezvous. I intend to strike south-west. Head straight for Crown Point.'

There was silence for a long moment, then Ezra let his breath out in a whoosh.

'That's a deal of walking, Jamie.'

'I know! But think on this. We can't be sure if the message got through about the rendezvous. We don't know if there'll be food there. All these men moving south wont make the hunting any easier, even if they are split up. Whatever we do, it's a gamble… but I think we'll fare better this way.' He looked around the haggard, bearded faces. Bourne was shaking his head.

'No offence, Sergeant,' Bourne said quietly. 'But I don't like the idea of striking off on our own…and you're a regular. I think I'd feel better with a ranger leading me.'

'No offence taken, Bourne. We're at the point where every man has to look to himself and decide how best he can survive. Go see Sergeant Evans and ask to join him.'

Bourne stood up and looked around at the rest of the group. 'You comin', Lorrimer?' he said, hesitantly.

Lorrimer shook his head. 'The Sergeant makes sense. I'll stay with him!'

They watched Bourne walk off slowly to Evans. The Sergeant cocked his head to listen, then shrugged his shoulders and beckoned him to sit down.

'He ran out of food yesterday morning. His stomach is tellin' his brain what to do most likely,' Lorrimer remarked.

'If he thinks ol' Evans is going to let him squat by the lake fishin', he's badly mistook,' Ezra snorted.

'There's an hour or so of daylight left. We can get on a couple of miles,' Jamie said. He rummaged in his haversack and produced a bottle. 'I was keeping this for when it was really needed. Picked it up in St Francis. I think now is as good a time.'

'Brandy, by God! Iain exclaimed. 'Damn you, Jamie. You never said a word.'

'You'd have been nagging me all the way from St Francis if I had.'

'Here's health to us all,' Ezra toasted, raising the bottle. He smacked his lips and let the mouthful trickle down his throat. 'If the worst comes we can always eat Iain. Enough meat there to get us all to Albany.'

'Don't even joke about it,' Iain said, sourly. 'Pass that bottle!'

Chapter 14

They heard the faint report of a musket ahead of them and they looked at each other, dull eyes lighting up with hope. Bent over to ease the stomach cramps of hunger, they lurched unsteadily as they walked. The last three days had seen them eat no more than a few handfuls of wizened beechnuts. They came out of the trees into a wide meadow rising up to a ridge. Then another shot sounded and on the crest of the ridge they could see a figure capering and waving.

'Two shots,' Jamie said. 'That has to be something big.'

'Charlie's dancing, God love him.' Murphy said. 'And there's Ezra, joined him in the jig. It's meat tonight me boys.'

They staggered up the hill and found Charlie and Ezra sitting, grinning and panting from their celebration. Ezra said nothing, merely pointed to a carcass a few yards off.

'An elk!' Iain breathed reverently. 'A damned great elk.'

'Not the best shot of me life.' Ezra drawled, modestly. 'A lung shot and I was fair mortified when he took off. He didn't go far though.'

He drew his knife and set about butchering the beast. 'There's a good stand of trees further down. Be a grand place for dinner.'

'Well, Jamie! Looks like we'll make it after all,' Ezra murmured. He was roasting a strip of meat over the embers of the fire. The others were wrapped in their blankets, snoring.

'It's thanks to you and that shot you made, Ezra.'

'Maybe! But I'd have never made that shot had I not been in better trim than the rest of you. I guess we all thought you crazed when I offered to share that lump of tallow and you said I was to keep it for myself on account of one of us needed the strength for hunting. Little Murphy was like to burst into tears 'He chuckled and inspected the meat. 'Mind though. It was damned embarrassing sneaking off to eat it and the rest of you with nothing, but there's a heap of strength in beef tallow.' He cut a chunk off the meat and passed it to Jamie.

They had run out of food after the first day's march from the north end of Memphremagog. On the third day Ezra had downed a partridge and two squirrels which had afforded them barely a couple of mouthfuls each, merely increasing their need. The next three days the weather had again turned foul but they had pushed on knowing their survival depended on marching to the limit of their strength. Ezra and one other would start off before the rest to decrease the risk of startling game with their approach. Each day ended in disappointment and an increasing despair, until this morning had changed it to buoyant hope.

'We'll rest up for a couple of days. Get some of our strength back. We've more meat than we can carry now. So it's just eat all we want and roast enough to fill our haversacks. It can't be more than another four or five days to the Point.' Jamie said. 'I'll be happier when we sight the Lake. We'll slip more to the west when we set off again.'

Three days later, on the top of a hill, high above the tree line, they looked to the south and saw the unmistakable bulk of the Green Mountains and north of west the sheet of water they had travelled in the whaleboats, five weeks before.

They lost Lorrimer crossing the Otter.

The river was swollen and fast flowing and there was no choice but to fashion a rude raft for their equipment and muskets and cling to it in the freezing water, kicking with their feet to propel them to the far bank. They were within yards of it when a fallen tree swept down on them, its branches spread in a fan ahead of the main trunk.

There was a strangled shout and they saw Lorrimer caught by a branch and swept off with the tree. His white face had a look of despair, then the tree rolled and he disappeared from sight.

It was a subdued camp that night. To lose a comrade so near to safety and the end of their hardships was bitter indeed.

Then Murphy broke his ankle within a mile of the lakeshore and three miles from Crown Point.

'Damn it!' he cursed. 'I can smell the soddin' rum from here.'

'You're a damned nuisance, Murphy. No mistake.' Iain said, unsympathetically. 'Here! I doubt if I'll need this now.' He passed his and Murphy's packs to the other three. 'I'll carry him down to the shore. Send a boat back for us. Make sure there's rum aboard. Climb on my back, you Irish midget.'

'You're a darlin' man, Iain, so ye are.'

'Shut up, Murphy!'

The pair disappeared through the tress and the others could hear them amicably squabbling long after they were out of sight.

'Glad you made it, Sergeant,' Captain Ogden said. 'You took the long way round. You weren't the only ones. We picked up sixteen at the mouth of the Otter yesterday. A mix of rangers and the white hostages. I got here four days ago. You probably fared better than those of us that headed for the Wells. Not an ounce of food when we got there. Seems they thought they'd waited long enough and took it all back to No 4.

Jamie had already heard how Rogers and Ogden had rafted down the Connecticut to No 4 and organised provisions for the rendezvous. Ogden had then come overland to Crown Point to deliver a report while the Major had gone back up to the Wells with the food for his men. He remembered Ogden keeping up with the column as they retired from St Francis, ignoring the pain of the shot through the body, and he marvelled at the hardihood of the man.

'There were still a few parties to come in when I left the rendezvous. I know we lost Lieutenant Dunbar and most of his men and they caught up with Ensign Avery and took all but him and another. Your Lieutenant Grant made it you'll be glad to hear,' Ogden went on. 'You have any trouble of that sort?'

'I lost a man drowned crossing the Otter, but no trouble from the French, sir.'

'So its back to the 42nd for you then,' Ogden grinned. 'I believe your regiment is heading to Albany for the winter. Pretty soon I believe.'

Jamie's tiredness lifted at the words, and the thought of seeing Sarah again brought a smile to his lips. 'I hadn't heard.'

'You did well, Sergeant Campbell. I'll make sure the Major drops a note to your Colonel saying so.'

'Thank you sir.' He hesitated before leaving the tent. 'Captain Ogden. All that effort, All these men lost…. Do you think it was worthwhile?'

Ogden gave a wry smile. 'Come to think of it…no I don't. But that's hindsight, Sergeant. We did what we were asked. No! What we were ordered to do. Best leave others to judge whether it was worthwhile. The rest of the army seems to think so.'

Ezra, Iain and Charlie were waiting outside the tent after delivering a drunk, singing Murphy to the hospital.

'Goodbye, Ezra. I won't say it's been a pleasure, but you know what I mean. You take care.'

'Plan to, Jamie. See you all come next year's campaign no doubt. What with Quebec having been taken we might get this business over and done with.' They all shook hands and he walked off jauntily toward the Ranger lines.

Jamie looked at the other two and smiled. Their hair was unclubbed and lank, faces hairy and grimy, leggings torn and ragged…and they all stank to high heaven.

'God knows what the Sergeant Major will say if he catches sight of us but let's get back where we belong. We've a lot to do. I'm told we're moving back to Albany soon.'

'There it is again. Always hurry. A man has no chance to catch his breath,' Iain groaned. 'Charlie and I planned to get good and drunk tonight. What say we all go down to the Ranger lines, make ourselves halfway respectable and get drunk with Ezra,' he wheedled. His voice took on an unctuous tone. 'Nobody knows we're back and I'd say we deserved it.'

Jamie barely hesitated. 'Corporal Munro...I'll be damned if for once you're right.' And led them off to the Ranger's lines.

Chapter 15

Cecile moved in her sleep and her warm breast pressed against his arm. Reluctantly he decided it was time to creep back to his own bed. He eased himself away from her carefully but the movement disturbed her and she murmured in protest. Groping for his plaid on the floor where he had discarded it, he bundled it up and moved toward the window. He trod carefully remembering to avoid a particular area where the floorboards creaked noisily and was easing open the window when he heard her whisper his name.

'Stay a little longer,' she breathed.

He smiled and moved back to the bed, his hand finding the mop of black curls on the pillow and moving down to her cheek. He bent and kissed the tip of her nose.

'It's close to dawn,' he whispered in the hesitant French he had acquired over the winter. 'You're Papa will be up soon. I'll see you at breakfast.'

He grinned as she blew out her breath in disgust and slipped quickly out of the window.

He had barely settled himself on his straw palliasse in the room he shared with the others quartered on the farm when he heard the heavy breathing and low cursing as Iain Mhor squeezed himself through the window.

'How was the Widow Dupont?' Jamie whispered, grinning.

'Grateful! As always,' Ian answered hoarsely. 'It's the damned walk back across the fields that undoes all the previous entertainment.'

The widow lived in a farm a quarter mile away.

'Visit Cecile did you?' Iain asked, throwing himself down on his palliasse with a grunt.

'I did! I just got back minutes before you.'

'Far be it from me to grudge you pair of fornicators your pleasure,' McPhee interrupted caustically. 'But is it necessary to waken the rest of us with your night visiting and your thrice damned chattering about it.'

'I detect a hint of frustration from Private McPhee, Jamie. It's a full two weeks until payday. What do you say we lend him some money and he can nip into Montreal and buy himself a whore.'

'There's one thing you can be certain of, my smug Corporal Munro. I'd do my tupping and there'd be no damned discussion about it afterwards, keeping men from their sleep.' McPhee snorted contemptuously.

Jamie chuckled and as the room quietened drifted off into a contented sleep.

The past year had been a momentous one.

When the campaign season opened it was obvious the French were all but defeated. Still dangerous but with three armies set to converge on the remnants of their forces defending Montreal and deserted by their Indian allies there was little they could do but wait for the arrival of these armies.

The Quebec garrison under General Murray pushed up from there, whilst Amherst brought the main army, including both battalions of the 42nd, down the St Lawrence from Oswego by boats. A hazardous journey, where more men were drowned in boat accidents on the rapids than through any action by the French. A smaller force under Colonel Haviland thrust up from Crown Point through St Johns and Chambly.

On the morning of the 7th of September 1760, in a feat of logistics and planning the three armies arrived almost simultaneously in the environs of Montreal and invested the city. The next day Governor Vaudreuil capitulated to General Amherst and the war for Canada was over.

Both battalions of the 42nd remained in Montreal as part of the garrison and went into winter quarters.

The farmhouse Jamie and five companions were quartered in was a substantial building owned by a cheerful, garrulous Canadian called Cadotte, a man in his late forties. Although initially reticent and resentful of their presence he quickly thawed when he was paid the quartering charges which he had rarely received under the French regime. It took only a few days for he and his family to adapt to the presence of their enforced guests. For Jamie and the rest their quarters in a cramped room was luxury after the months of campaigning. They still drew rations and would hand them over to Cadotte's wife, a competent cook, to prepare and share with the family.

Duties were light. A company muster each morning with a cursory inspection and an hour or two of drill, then back to the warm spacious kitchen of the farmhouse. With time to fill they began to help with the chores and any other farm work, although with winter setting in there was little of that.

To McPhee's great embarrassment, Cadotte's youngest girl, a

moppet barely four years old, decided he was her favourite and would clamber on his knee at every opportunity. She would chatter away happily to him in French, peering up at his face and tugging his nose if she thought she was losing his attention. Most evenings she would fall asleep on his shoulder while he sat glowering at Iain Mhor who took delight in crooning Gaelic lullabies to them both with McPhee speechless for fear he'd wake her.

There were also two teenage sons and an older daughter, Cecile.

A small, attractive, dark haired girl in her twenties, she had a continual sulky expression on her face and was distinctly unfriendly. If she caught any of the men casting an admiring glance her way she had a habit of staring back boldly, then her lips would curl in a sneer and she would toss her head in a gesture of contempt.

As Jamie's French improved her father told him she had been married only one month when her husband had been killed on militia service, barely four months before they arrived.

Acquiring a fiddle on a visit into Montreal, Jamie livened up the evenings in the kitchen with his music. The family would respond by singing French Canadian songs, Cadotte bawling the choruses and beating the time on the kitchen table. Cecile would sit silent, her face expressionless. Even when her family was howling with laughter at some badly mispronounced French word as Iain Mhor attempted to communicate, her look remained stony.

The frozen farm ponds were utilised as the Highlanders again took up curling, drawing crowds of locals who quickly took to the game and tried it themselves and as Christmas drew near there was a constant round of social activity with families visiting each other.

On the morning of Christmas Eve, Cadotte and his family dressed in their best clothes and accompanied by three of the Highlanders who were Catholic, trooped off to attend the Christmas Mass.

McPhee and Iain had disappeared on some jaunt of their own and Jamie was sitting alone in the kitchen with his fiddle idly practising a French Canadian tune he had heard when the door opened and to his surprise Cecile entered wearing her usual sullen look.

She ignored him and began preparing vegetables for the soup, clattering the kitchen utensils deliberately noisily. Jamie sighed and put down his fiddle.

'You are not attending Mass?' he asked.

'I prepare the meal for everyone. I shall go to the evening service.' she answered in a surly voice.

Her obvious hostility annoyed him and in a moment of irritation he said sharply, 'Cecile! I am sorry about your husband. I know it must be difficult for you having us here, but your family has accepted us. I wish that you would also. The war is over. If you stay angry at us for your loss you hurt only yourself.'

Her back stiffened and he prepared himself for the flash of temper he had witnessed before, but then her head bowed and she went still, the kitchen knife clattering on the table. Her shoulders heaved and she began to cry with deep rasping sobs. He crossed the room quickly and laid his hand on hers.

'I'm sorry, Cecile. I had no right to say what I did.'

'Three nights!' she whispered fiercely. 'That was all that I had with him before he went off. I am a widow who never really knew what it was to be married.' She swung to face him. 'Look at me. Is it fair this should happen to me. I see the way you men watch me. What it is you are thinking. I have stayed angry because if I did not I fear what I would allow myself to do.'

She reached up and touched his face then pressed close against him. 'I am tired of being angry, Sergeant Jamie. I want what I only tasted on these three nights.'

Standing on tiptoe she crushed her lips on his, her face flushed and hot, then she took his hand and led him, bewildered at events, up to her bedroom.

Spring came at last and with it an end to winter idleness. Military activity increased as regiments drilled and honed skills grown rusty over the cold months. There was an air of expectancy among the men. The conquest of Canada may have been successfully concluded but the war with France continued and the men sensed their peaceful sojourn was soon to end.

With the Gulf of the St. Lawrence free of ice, ships began arriving again carrying provisions and badly needed equipment and uniforms for the army. They also carried mail.

Jamie tore open his father's letter eagerly. It had been over a year since he had had news of home. As he read it he went still and the letter fell from his nerveless grasp.

Iain glanced over and seeing the look on his friend's face asked questioningly, 'Jamie! What is it?'

'It's my mother. She died nine months ago.'

'Och, laddie. I'm sorry for your loss.' Iain went over to him and gave his shoulder a comforting squeeze.

The others in the house learned of it and men came up with a murmured word of condolence. Cadotte's wife hugged him, wiping tears from her eyes and Cecile quietly came up to him when they were alone, and sat with her arm round his shoulder in sympathy.

It was a quiet household for a day or so but gradually the numb sense of loss eased and Jamie recovered his spirits as the days passed. His duties helped keep him from brooding excessively and pushed away the feeling of guilt that perhaps his decision to go for a soldier may have hastened his mother's passing in some way.

The marching orders finally came in April. They were to proceed south to a camp on Staten Island, there to await transport ships for an expedition to the West Indies.

Men they spoke to in the 2nd / 42nd were less enthusiastic, having already fought there in a campaign, capturing the French island of Guadeloupe before joining the 1st Battalion prior to the taking of Ticonderoga. They had lost many from disease.

Cadotte and his family gathered to say a final farewell to the men they had shared the winter with. There was genuine regret on their part to see them go. He and his wife had tears in their eyes as they went round each man and embraced them. His youngest daughter clung to McPhee's kilt and bawled until he swept her up, kissed her cheek and handed her carefully into the arms of her mother. Only Cecile was dry eyed. She and Jamie had said their goodbyes earlier. They both knew that whatever had drawn them together it had not been love in it's proper sense and that when he marched that would be the end of it. Yet, when the drums began beating the muster and the men set off she ran up and gave him their first public embrace, her dark eyes bright with tears.

Her father and mother looked at each other knowingly, smiling and nodding at what they had suspected for some time. Only grateful that their daughter had finally ceased grieving for the husband she had lost.

Chapter 16

The Light Company was spread across the barren hillside, its only vegetation low growing thorny shrubs. They were on the forward slope a hundred yards below the crest and before them, across the valley, they could see the hill that stood between them and Fort Royal.

The brigaded Light and Grenadier companies of the Army had taken the hill they were on two days before in a breathless, sweaty scramble. Aided by guns, mounted on a ridge flanking the hill and manned by sailors of the fleet, the action had been more exhausting than dangerous and casualties had been light.

Now the army was getting into position for an assault on the higher of the two hills. Morne Garnier was a more daunting proposition. A hill with entrenched batteries and prepared defensive positions, its approaches broken up by ravines.

The early morning sun was warm but not yet oppressively so and Jamie ignored the dryness of his mouth and resisted taking a sip from his canteen. The water in it would need to see him through a long hot day.

Captain Murray accompanied by Sergeant McIvor strolled along the skirmish line of men exchanging words with a few. There was an occasional burst of laughter. He stopped beside Jamie.

'A fine day for it Sergeant Campbell. We're just waiting for Lord Rollo's brigade to wend its weary way up the hill then we should be off,' he said lightly.

There was a puff of smoke from the hill opposite, then seconds later a cannonball ploughed into the ground a good hundred yards below them. The boom of the discharge echoed seconds later.

'Bless my soul!' Captain Murray exclaimed. 'Whatever are they up to? That's no way to behave. Unmasking a battery for no good reason.' He reached in his pocket and extracted a notebook and made a note of the battery's position on a sketch he had drawn the day before.

More cannon opened fire, the shot smashing into the hillside sending up showers of stone splinters and dust. All the rounds dropped short.

'They'll reach when the guns warm up. We'll withdraw the company back fifty yards Sergeant McIvor, if you please. No need for any unpleasantness at this stage.'

McIvor was about to shout the orders to retire when Captain Murray held up his hand.

'Cancel that, Sergeant. Now what are they up to?' He put a telescope to his eye and studied the base of the hill opposite. 'Well, damn me! I do believe they're attempting a sally.'

Jamie could see ant like figures swarming from the broken ground in the valley, beginning to coalesce into columns.

'Ensign!' Murray shouted to an officer twenty yards away. 'My compliments to the Colonel. Inform him the French are coming out. Quick as you like.' He watched the Ensign run up the hill and disappear over the crest, then resumed his stroll behind his company.

The formations below them were advancing and beginning to lose their compactness as the steep hill and broken ground took its toll. By the time they had got within three hundred yards they were a shapeless mass of groups and individuals.

'We'll fire and retire on my whistle, lads.' Captain Murray called, and as the ragged front of the enemy crept to within one hundred paces and a spatter of musketry came from it he blew a single blast.

They fought the way they had learned in America, the widespread files keeping up a continuous fire as each man leapfrogged back a few yards to reload after firing. They had barely begun to withdraw when whistles blew again and there was a shout. 'Clear the front. Move to the right flank.'

Jamie looked over his shoulder and saw the regiment sweep over the crest in line and advance down toward them. He shouted to his men and they scrambled along the hillside to the flank.

They had no time to form up before the line of companies halted and muskets came up to the present. Jamie saw the cloud of men below them pause, some turning their backs on what was to come. There was a single ripple of fire from the line and he could see the heavy balls throwing men down before the smoke of the discharge obscured his view.

Another explosion of musketry as the 2nd Battalion, Montgomery's Highlanders and the brigaded grenadier companies came up and discharged their weapons and when the smoke cleared all could see the French in headlong retreat.

A roar went up from the 42nd and with a shout of 'Broadswords' the whole line leapt forward.

Iain and Jamie paused panting at the foot of the hill after the scrambling rush down the hillside. A shallow gully cut across their front, a dried up watercourse at its bottom. Across it they could see the enemy scrambling up paths on the far side. The 42nd had advanced so swiftly the swinging broadswords had cut down a few of those enemy troops slower in retiring. Highlanders were already slithering and sliding down in pursuit. Captain Murray waved his broadsword. 'Keep on! They won't stand,' he shouted, his voice cracking with excitement and led them down and across the watercourse, littered with muskets and equipment discarded in panic stricken flight.

Groups of Highlanders and Grenadiers were streaming up paths toward the French redoubts and batteries from which very little fire was directed at them.

Jamie saw the foremost group mounting the earth works of the nearest redoubt and stream over its parapet, the metal of bayonets and swords flashing in a frieze of light before Captain Murray led them slantwise across the hillside toward the embrasures of a gun battery.

A single unaimed cannon belched, its ball passing high above their heads, then they were pushing through between the guns and the fascines of the embrasures. The defenders were scurrying over the earthwork at the back, a few halting to fire a scatter of shots.

Jamie saw Captain Murray stagger, then sit down abruptly and ran over to him.

'Damn me, but that's inconvenient.' he heard him mutter angrily, peering at the wound on his thigh.

He waved Jamie off. 'Keep pushing on, Sergeant. Tell Lieutenant Grant he's in command.' He set about binding the wound with a kerchief.

Leaving the battery they found themselves among the huts and houses used by the defenders for shelter. They halted in the shade of the buildings and thirstily drank tepid water from their canteens. Numbers of prisoners were being herded back down the hill and parties of redcoats were clearing the trenches and broken ground their long bayoneted muskets probing before them.

Iain grinned at McPhee who was vainly attempting to inspect the back of his thigh where he had picked up thorns from a bush he had fallen into.

'McPhee, you fairly attract pieces of wood when we're in action,' he jibed. 'Come over and I'll tend to you again.'

'Go to hell, Munro!' McPhee growled. 'I prefer you where I can see you. There's no telling what mischief you'd get up to behind me. Jamie will do it.'

McIvor came up, breathing heavily, the dust on his face caked with sweat.

'I'm getting too old for all this running around,' he grumbled.

'We're to clear these huts and buildings. Any prisoners you find take them back to that gully we crossed. They're holding them there.'

He walked over to the nearest one and casually pushed open the door. A musket exploded inside and he was thrown back.

McPhee reacted first, leaping up and slipping through the doorway. As Jamie reached it he saw McPhee knock aside a bayonet thrust with his arm and step in close, his dirk driving into the side of a mulatto militiaman. As the man slid to the floor a woman screamed and in the dim light he saw her crouched in a corner with a child in her arms.

McIvor lay on his back, his shirt scorched with powder burns and soaked with blood from the massive chest wound. Iain was crouched beside him, his face twisted with grief.

Jamie bent over the Sergeant who murmured. 'That was careless of me,' his breathing shallow and laboured. His eyes flickered and he looked up at Iain now openly sobbing. The corner of his mouth twitched in a smile and he said affectionately, 'Munro...ye great pudden!

His eyes closed and his breathing grew shallower, then ceased.

Jamie felt his eyes prickle with tears and he turned away.

McPhee stood by the doorway looking white and shaken.

'The woman and bairn inside. The man I killed was her husband. I think he thought he was protecting them. Damn it, Jamie! Why didn't he just surrender like the rest of them. We'd never have harmed them.'

Jamie reached out and squeezed McPhee's shoulder but could find no words to say to him.

With most of the militia dispersed to the hills and the citadel and town invested on all sides it would be only a matter of days before Port Royal fell. The besieging army sweated and laboured at the traverses, cursing the French for delaying the surrender, knowing that once the breaching batteries were in position the defenders would have to bow to the inevitable.

The water they drank was foul and the rations rancid. Men began to sicken and die of the things that plagued an army in the West Indies. Dysentery, fevers, and heat exhaustion took a far greater toll than enemy fire and when the French finally surrendered it was a relieved 42nd Regiment that embarked both battalions on the now familiar transport ships to sail from Martinique, north for Cuba and the taking of Havana from the Spanish.

Chapter 17

As they crossed the strip of soft white sand the water dripped from kilts made heavy from their immersion as they'd waded ashore from the line of boats that were now backing water to make room for the next wave. The rumble of shot passing overhead was continuous, crashing into the wooded slopes ahead of them as the heavy cannon of the warships sought to neutralise any resistance to the landing.

Before the first of them reached the trees fringing the beach the gunfire stopped abruptly leaving a silence broken only by the screeching of flocks of parakeets disturbed by the noise.

The light companies skirmished up through the vegetation as more troops poured ashore, quickly forming into their battalions.

Captain Stirling, their new company commander, halted them on the crest until the light companies of the 2^(nd) battalion and Montgomery's Highlanders came up abreast of them.

There was open ground ahead and Jamie could see a troop of horsemen off in the distance. He could hear no sound of musketry from anywhere around and with a sense of relief realised the landing had been made unopposed.

'Cavalry!' Iain said, moving forward to kneel beside him. 'Now there's a change. We've never faced cavalry before.'

The line swept down, the men closing to a tighter formation as they reached the open ground and the advance boldly continued toward the cavalry, the tips of whose lances flickered in the sunlight. A loud jeer went up as the troop of horsemen wheeled to the rear and trotted off.

They advanced for some way until a halt was called short of a river with a fort and earthworks guarding the crossing. They watched gleefully while a seventy-four gun man of war worked it's way in close and opened fire, reducing the fort to rubble and dismounting the guns within an hour. A party of marines from the ship swarmed ashore and secured the fort and the advance continued. As night fell they halted and lay on their arms through a night of torrential rain. They were within two miles of the objective that was the key to the capture of Havana. The formidable Morro Castle.

Crouched in the shade of the thick woods that grew just beyond cannon shot of the Morro they watched as engineers went about their business of marking the ground in preparation for the siege.

'That's almost solid rock, that is,' McPhee sniffed. 'Lets see them solve how to dig traverses in that.'

There was bare ground with little earth or vegetation all the way to the ditch, with the walls beginning twenty feet above a steep sided scarp cut from the bedrock. Cannon peered out of embrasures and from salients designed to sweep with fire the ditch and scarp.

'I can hazard a guess how they'll solve it,' Iain groaned. 'It'll be us and the likes of us with picks.'

It was a week before they were called to take their turn in the labour of digging the traverses. The rains had eased off and they worked under a pitiless sun that sapped the strength from them quickly. Men dropped from heat exhaustion and were carried back to the shade of the woods to recover or die. Water grew scarce as the rains ceased altogether and they became dependent on what little could be spared from the ships, themselves on short rations. Yet the traverses crept closer, until eighteen days from when the siege was first opened the breaching batteries were in position.

The day before they were to open fire the Spanish landed a force to take and destroy the batteries.

The light company was in the woods mounting guard for the workers in the trenches when the attack came in from the seaward. As the first warning shots sounded they stood to arms and moved to the edge of the woods where the pickets were mounted.

The attack was futile and the fire from the guard companies and the men in the trenches cut the attacking force to pieces long before they got near the batteries and they fell back, leaving half their number dead or wounded.

The next day the batteries commenced firing while three ships of the line bombarded the Morro from the seaward, but despite the heavy fire little impression was made on its defences and more heavy guns were brought up.. It was decided that saps be pushed forward to mine the walls.

The assault companies formed up, their ranks desperately thinned by the sickness that had swept through the army. Fevers and fluxes had left most of the regiments at half strength or less. Thousands of men lay on the beaches or in the nauseous cramped troop decks of the transports, shivering, sweating, or vomiting. The sheer numbers of sick men overwhelmed the medical staff and orderlies who had escaped the fever themselves.

Jamie's company was down to thirty men.

He felt light-headed as they squatted in the hot sun waiting for the mines to be exploded. Splashing some precious water from his canteen on to his bonnet he mopped his face with the foul smelling liquid and felt momentarily better.

The batteries thundered away raising splinters from the wall. Mortars threw shells into its interior driving the defenders into the casements. Then the mines exploded and men held their breath, waiting for the clouds of dust and debris to subside.

There was a roar from the assault companies as they saw the breach, the wall having slid in a mass of broken stone masonry into the ditch, creating a ramp that would take them into the citadel. The columns of attackers surged forward eagerly, anxious to have done with this obstacle that had held them back for so long and cost them so much sweat and hardship.

There was little resistance as they clambered up and through the breach, the defenders demoralised and retreating. The assault was over in less than twenty minutes. Four hundred Spaniards lay dead or wounded at a cost to the assault companies of a mere handful of men wounded.

Iain looked round for Jamie and spotted him sitting upright in the shadow of a wall. He ran over and his friend looked up at him, his eyes glazed. He opened his mouth to speak, then choked and vomited a thin liquid.

'Oh Christ, Jamie!' Iain groaned. 'Not the fever! Not you!'

He crouched beside his friend cradling his head and shouted, 'McPhee! McPhee! To me, man!'

Chapter 18

The barge pulled in to the familiar landing, less busy than he remembered it, with the war over and the regiments gone. A few provincials from the garrison were lounging around, some fishing. His was the only red coat in sight. He shouldered his pack and made to step ashore, when he was overcome with a wave of faintness. He reached out blindly and grasped the gunwale for support.

'You all right, sergeant?' one of the boatman asked. 'You don't look too perky.'

'I've had a fever. Still feeling it. It'll pass.' He sat down on a bench, his legs trembling with weakness.

'Here! Have a swig o' this,' the boatman said, handing him a bottle of rum. 'Won't harm none. Pick it up in the West Indies did ye?' When Jamie nodded, he clucked sympathetically. 'Heard it was bad there. You serve up this ways?'

'From before Ticonderoga, then all the way to Montreal.' The rum had cleared his head somewhat and he handed the bottle back to the boatman.

'A right old hand. Probably our paths crossed a few times. I was one o' Bradstreet's bateaux men.' He sighed and grinned, 'Life's sorta boring now, tho' she's a mite safer.   He stared at Jamie in concern. '42nd are up in Schenectady. You ain't fixing to walk there are ye? You don't look exactly full o' beans.'

Jamie smiled ruefully. 'You're right there. I'll be staying in Albany for a few days. I've someone to see. I'm due my discharge when I get back to the Regiment.'

'Going home or fixin' to stay round these parts?'

'Maybe further north. I hear there's some land grants going around Champlain.'

'There is that. A heap o' land. There's a fair parcel o' folks movin' north since the war finished. You'd best get in quick or the best farmland'll be gone.'

Jamie shook his head. 'I'm no farmer. I'm looking to setting up a sawmill. Build boats. I think there'll be a call for them up on the lake.'

'Happens you're right. That ol' lake is gonna get busy.'

He helped Jamie ashore and passed up his pack. 'Good luck to ye,

Sergeant. If you're staying around a while, we'll split a bottle some-day. Name's Amos Catchpole.'

'James Campbell...and thank you for the rum.'

The boatman watched him walking away, noticed a slight waver in his stride, and frowned. He glowered at the Provincials staring curi-ously and bawled irritably.

'Ain't ye got better to do than clutter the place up and gawk at real soldiers, ye blue coated poopheads. Get the hell off my jetty!'

Sarah sat under a large maple, reading aloud to the two girls with her. One of them tugged at her dress. 'Miss Sarah... there's a soldier coming this way and I think he may be drunk.'

She looked to where the girl was pointing and saw the red coat and plaid of a Highlander. The man was definitely unsteady as he walked. He was coming directly toward them and she was about to get up and usher her charges away when she hesitated and studied him as he approached. She could not see his features, but something in the way the man held himself, the long rangy stride, wavering as it was, made the breath catch in her throat. She clasped her hands tight to still their trembling.

He was very near before he noticed them. He hesitated, then clum-sily doffed his bonnet and made to pass them by

'Jamie Campbell! You stop right there,' she called, softly

He paused and turned to see the woman hurrying toward him. The big bonnet shaded her face, but her voice had sparked a memory.

'Sarah? Sarah is that you?'

She lifted her head to look at him and he could see her face, still and composed but the brown eyes misty with tears.

'Why.... You've grown. You're a...a....'

'A woman? It's been almost two years. Did you expect to find me just as I was?'

'Never thought on it,' he mumbled. Her face blurred and a wave of dizziness made him sway.

She gripped his shoulders and steadied him 'Ah, Jamie! What have they done to you? You're but skin and bone.' She reached up and touched his cheek and felt the heat of it. 'You're burning up. Here now! Sit down!'

She turned to the young girls who were watching open-mouthed. 'Stop your gawking, the pair of you. Heide... run down to the river and fetch water. Use your bonnet and don't fall in. Ilsa run back to school and find Jonas. Tell him Miss Sarah wants the trap down here straight away. Then tell MistressYonge that Jamie's back and he's sick. Quickly now!' She clapped her hands sharply and the girls scampered off.

'You act just like our old dominie back home,' Jamie said, grinning weakly. He leaned gratefully against the tree trunk.

She knelt beside him removing his accoutrements and loosening his jacket and shirt, then said severely. 'Four letters in two years and nothing this past twelve month.'

'I wrote from Martinique, but French privateers were busy we heard. Likely they took the ship the mail was on.'

Heide arrived back with her bonnet sodden and shapeless and using her kerchief Sarah mopped his brow and chest with the cold water.

'I was at the jetty when the 42nd arrived back.' She bit her lip to hold back the tears but could not hide the quaver in her voice. 'I looked for you…. And looked for you…. And you weren't there and I thought you dead, then Iain Mhor saw me and told me what had happened.' The words came out in a rush.

'I told him to find you and let you know. I thought you might worry.'

'Worry!' she flared. 'I've done nothing but worry these two years past.'

'Sarah, there were times I was a little worried myself,' he murmured faintly, with a hint of reproach in his voice. His eyes closed and he let the waves of dizziness carry him off into a fevered sleep.

He woke between cool sheets. The room was bright and airy and a light breeze wafted the curtains at the window. He tried to sit up but there was no strength in his arms. A hand raised his head from the pillows and a glass was held to his mouth.

'Apple juice,' a voice said and Mistress Yonges broad, rosy cheeked face swam into view. He drank gratefully.

'I sent Sarah to bed,' she went on in her thick Dutch accent. 'She sat with you all night. Here! Drink this. The doctor left it. An infusion of Jesuit bark he called it. Good for fever he says. I have sent Jonas off to Schenectady with a message to your regiment. I did not want to see you accused of desertion. '

He drank the bitter medicine and made a face. 'I was given this at the hospital in New York,' he croaked. 'Tasted just as bad there.'

She gave him another sip of apple juice.

Sitting back in her chair she smiled at him fondly. 'Is good to have you back, James Campbell. No more problems with Sarah now.'

He looked at her in surprise. 'Problems! Sarah has been a problem?'

'No! No! Sarah is a good girl. The problem is you damned men. For a year now I keep tripping over young men. Boys from the town. Officers from the army. Miss Sarah…will you do me the honour of accompanying me to the soiree. Miss Sarah… please to partner me to a ball. Miss Sarah…come walk with me by the river,' she said, mimicking them. 'They loiter about cluttering up my porch. Stupid boys with the mouth hanging open,' she snorted. 'I tell her. Go! Enjoy yourself. Flirt a little. Make each jealous of the others…But no! This she will not do.'

'Why would she not?'

Mistress Yonges' china blue eyes widened and she sat back in the chair. 'You ask why? You don't know?' She shook her head in disgust, muttering in Dutch. 'Because of you…you stupid Scottish man.'

'How can that be. It's been almost two years since we last saw each other. I could have been dead for all she knew.'

'Ja! But until she knows for sure, she will not look at any other man. That Sarah! From when I first met her. Jamie this…Jamie that. Sick of hearing your name I was.' Her smile belied the words and she leaned forward and patted his cheek. 'She's loved you for years, James Campbell. Did you really not know?'

'Mistress Yonge. Affection …yes! We're good friends. She was but thirteen when I first met her. She was barely full-grown when I last saw her.'

'She was sixteen. Lot's of girls are married by that age. I was. You should marry her! Soon! Before she changes her mind and decides on some young officer with the fancy manners.' With that she got up. 'I go wake Sarah. Tell her you are still alive. Stupid… but still alive!'

Sarah came in minutes later, her brown hair tousled from sleep.

'How are you feeling now,' she asked, sitting by the bedside, concern in her voice.

'I'll live. The surgeon in New York warned me the fever might recur,' he said, reaching over and clasping her hand. 'Thank you for nursing me. Mistress Yonge said you sat up all night.'

'Oh, I did nothing,' she said softly. 'You frightened me a little. You talked in your fever. Was it bad, Jamie?'

'I don't remember much of it after I got sick. The voyage back to New York was pretty bad as I recall. The time in hospital was boring, waiting to get better and with little to do but think.'

He studied her face. It was fuller and softer than he remembered. The mass of freckles she used to produce with the merest touch of summer sun now reduced to a golden sprinkle across her nose. Her eyes were the same warm brown but less large with the fullness of her face. It finally came to him she was no longer the thin gangly girl who shared their common love of music but had somehow changed into this confident lovely woman.

'What did you think about, Jamie.' Her voice broke into his musings.

'Oh, what I might do other than be a soldier. I made plans. Changed my mind. Made other plans.'

'Did you come to any decision?'

'I thought to stay here in America after my discharge. Find land, and use my hands to make things again. I'll have to speak to Iain Mhor first of course.'

'Of course,' she said, tightly. 'Any other plans?'

'No! Not at present,' he laughed. 'A lot more thinking to do still.'

She rose, her face slightly flushed. 'I have a class soon and you need more rest. I'll leave you to your thinking,' she said quickly, and left the room leaving him with an uneasy feeling he had said something that had upset her.

The heavy tread on the stairs and the girlish giggles of Mistress Yonge woke him from a light sleep, knowing who it would be before the door opened and the room filled with the bulk of Iain Mhor.

Mistress Yonge smiled from the doorway. 'I bring some tea up for you shortly.'

'A drop of something in it wouldn't go amiss. That was a cold walk from Schenectady, Mistress,' Iain said with an ingratiating grin.

She sniffed disgustedly. 'Soldiers! Always the rum. I may have some in the medicine chest.' She winked a blue eye and went off.

'Mr Grant told me you'd arrived and gave me two days furlough. He sends his regards. You look better than when I last saw you.' Iain swiped at his cheeks with a massive hand and mumbled. 'I thought you were going to die on me.'

Jamie reached out and grasped his friend's hand. 'I couldn't do that. Who would keep you out of trouble.'

Iain gave a watery grin. 'Seems to me you're the one that always needs looking after.'

'The regiment? How is it?'

Iain's eyes filled with tears again. 'McPhee died just before we took ship to come back. We were drinking together one night. The next day he was dead and buried before sunset. Martinique and Havana near finished us, Jamie. We can barely muster four hundred men...and that's with the second battalion joining us. There are few of us left from five years ago.'

'Old McIvor...well, you were there when we took Martinique.. You saw him die. He at least was killed like a soldier. Not sickening with something you couldn't see to fight.' He produced a grimy kerchief and blew his nose loudly. 'Martinique and Havana ruined the whole damned Army of the Americas. Most of the regiments are like us. Half strength or worse. It's a mercy the peace has been signed.'

They were silent for a while thinking back on all the men they had marched and fought beside. Buried in graves from Canada to the West Indies. Discharged through wounds or sickness to an uncertain future and a niggardly pension.

'What of us, Jamie? We're due our discharge soon. Have you thought on it?

'Aye! I have. I've had little else to do but think on it for the past three months…Do you miss home, Iain?'

'Whiles! But Scotland's just a memory. The regiment's been our home for so long '

'How would you feel about staying here? I'm told there's land grants for discharged soldiers. Two hundred acres for sergeants and corporals. Think on it Iain…four hundred acres between us. I want to build a sawmill! Work with wood again. Build boats, make furniture! There'll be a call for these things when folk start moving in. They already have by all accounts.'

'I'd be little use, Jamie. I'm no carpenter!'

'Perhaps not…but I've yet to meet a man who can make friends easier than you. You've a natural gift for making yourself welcome wherever you go. Why, I'd wager folk would buy things from you just for the pleasure of your company. D'ye see now? I make them and you sell them.'

'In effect, a peddler!'

'Call it what you want. I would prefer the term, purveyor of quality wooden items.'

Iain Mhor beamed. 'A purveyor of quality wooden items is it? By God, Jamie…I'm your man.'

'It'll be hard work to begin with. I'll write off to my father. Explain what I intend and ask for a loan to get ourselves started. I'd like him and my brother to join us. They are craftsmen, Iain. There'll be a need for craftsmen with these new lands opening up.' The words tumbled out in his enthusiasm. 'We can make a good life here on our own land. Something we can never have back home.'

'Aye! It's time I started looking for a wife and settling down. Some nice lass to be company for Sarah when you and she wed.'

'Have you been talking to Mistress Yonge?' Jamie said irritably. 'She was on about Sarah and I. It seems that everyone has decided its some perfect love match without asking either of us.'

Iain looked at him in surprise. 'Well! Isn't it?'

'Damn it Iain! She and I have been good friends. In all the years we've known each other, nothing has ever been said by either of us that would change a friendship into something else. Most of the time I've known her she's been a mere slip of a young girl.'

'Well, she's not a slip of a girl now, and hasn't been for long enough.'

Iain poked a large finger into Jamie's chest.

'Listen! You're either blind, stupid, or your wits have been addled with the fever. When we'd come visiting here, didn't I used to see her, watching you with those big brown eyes, and you too busy scrape, scraping away on your damned fiddle to notice. She was no skinny wee slip of a girl the last time you saw her before we marched off to Oswego, the year we took Canada. And did I not see the look of her when the 42nd got back and she was searching for you and you weren't there,' Iain rumbled. 'And what of yourself? Was it just friend-ship and a chance to play music that had you trotting up here every time you had a spare moment?'

'We are fond of each other. I'll admit that...but not in the way you all seem to think,' Jamie snapped, his face reddening.

'Perhaps not at first, but it's far from being fondness on her part now...and damn it man, it's time you took the blinkers from your eyes and stop thinking of her as some bairn you befriended years ago.'

There was a knock at the door and Mistress Yonge nudged it open with her broad hip and came in bearing a tray.

She looked at the pair of them and smiled complacently.

'An extra tot of rum for you, Mr Munro, for being so perceptive. Isn't it strange. The closer something is under someone's nose, the more difficult it is for him or her to find it.'

'Aye, Mistress,' Iain said, glowering at Jamie. 'There's times you need take them by the scruff of the neck and wave it in front of them.'

There was a little warmth in the winter sunshine as he sat in the shel-ter of the covered veranda that stretched the length of the building. He could hear the shrill voices of the girls chanting their arithmetic times tables to the rhythmic cadence of Sarah's wooden pointer in the classroom. He smiled, remembering the old dominie at Killin using the same method of constant repetition to drum it into he and his classmates.

His lack of strength was frustrating. He was impatient to be about his plans for the future, resolved in the long hours of inactivity.

Then there was Sarah! This change in how he viewed her. Seeing her for how she was now, and not as he remembered her. No longer the young gawky girl with their shared love of music but a woman grown, confident and mature All that Mistress Yonge and Iain Mhor had said. Their surprise that he had never seen what had been obvi-ous to them.

For the last five years she had been a constant in his life. A softer world he could escape to for brief periods. The long absence had dulled her importance to him, yet, on the journey up from New York the knowledge that he would be seeing her again had reawakened memories of her. He drifted off into a light sleep.

The sound of a horse's hooves woke him from his doze. A young lieutenant of the Royal Americans, dressed in immaculate regimentals, dismounted and strode up to the steps.

'See to my horse, will you,' he snapped, then looked at Jamie curiously. 'I was unaware Mistress Yonge had employed a discharged soldier. How long have you been here?'

'A few days. However, I'm neither employed nor am I yet discharged. Sgt Campbell, sir, and I'm a guest here.'

'Guest or not, it is usual for an enlisted man to stand when an officer approaches. If you're not yet discharged you will do me the courtesy, Sergeant.'

'Stop being all military, Lieutenant Willis. The Sergeant is recovering from an illness contracted in Havana and is in no condition to be leaping around on your say so.' Sarah had come out of the classroom frowning and tight-lipped. The snap in her voice flustered the young man.

'Ah! Ill d'ye say. Of course…remain seated by all means, Sergeant. Good day Miss McConnell.'

'Good day, Lieutenant,' Sarah replied coolly. 'You have a reason for this visit?'

'Why yes.' He glanced at Jamie. 'Perhaps we could speak privately,' he said, inclining his head toward the door.

'I have a class,' Sarah said, shortly. 'I'm afraid I have no time for entertaining.'

The lieutenant flushed, growing ever more uncomfortable. Clearing his throat he stammered, 'The Mayor of Albany is holding a Grand Ball a week from now. I would be most honoured if you would accompany me to it.'

'Thank you kindly for your invitation Lieutenant, but I regret I must decline.'

'I beg you Miss McConnel! Please reconsider. It will be a most auspicious occasion. The cream of Albany gentry will be attending.'

'I have no doubt it will be a very grand affair. However I shall be otherwise engaged.'

The lieutenant was not about to give up and continued to plead with her to change her mind. Jamie could see Sarah was becoming increasingly embarrassed by his persistence.

The words were out before he knew it. 'With respect, Lieutenant. Could I ask you not to keep pressing your attentions on the lady I intend to marry.'

The officer gaped in surprise and Sarah went still, her hands clenched in the folds of her dress.

'You and she? To be married? Miss McConnell is this correct?' Lieutenant Ellis stuttered.

Sarah walked slowly over to Jamie and laid her hand on his shoulder.

'It would appear so,' she said quietly, her eyes bright, high spots of colour on her cheeks.

The young man succeeded in looking both puzzled and crestfallen, searching for words that would allow him to withdraw with a modicum of dignity.

'In that case I do heartily apologise to you both,' he said ponderously. 'I wish you joy of it. You are a most fortunate man, Sergeant.'

They watched him set off disconsolately to retrieve his horse, which had wandered away.

'You have a strange way of proposing marriage, Jamie Campbell,' Sarah murmured, her hand coming up to rest on his cheek.

'I've been unwell,' he answered, grinning. 'I can be excused from going through the usual formalities.' He reached up and clasped her hand. 'I've also been blind. Abrupt as it was…you do accept it?'

She bent and kissed his cheek. 'With all my heart,' she said.

She listened to the increasing noise from the unsupervised girls in the classroom. 'The class can wait. Shall we go in and break the news to Mistress Yonge?'

He smiled. 'I'll wager she will be delighted, but not be in the least surprised!'

Chapter 19

Lieutenant Grant, perspiring freely from the vigorous reel he had partnered her in, returned Sarah to Jamie. Iain Mhor, who had left MistressYonge collapsed in a chair, flushed and feebly fanning at herself after dancing with him, immediately snatched her up. As he led her on to the floor, Sarah gave Jamie a despairing look. He grinned and waved to her. The predominance of men at the wedding meant the women present were in great demand for dances, although it did not prevent highlanders pairing together to make up the sets.

Some Dutch friends of Mistress Yonge and Sarah sat in shocked silence, keeping tight hold of their giggling daughters, as kilts flared, exposing unseemly glimpses of naked, hairy thighs.

'Well Sergeant! Out of one enlistment and straight into another. From military to marital bondage in the space of a week.' the Lieutenant chuckled, settling beside Jamie. 'She's a fine woman and I wish you joy. How goes your plans for the future?'

'I await a letter from my father and hopefully word of a banker's draft. Meantime Iain Mhor and I can get on with making application for the land grant and looking for a likely site. The site is crucial if I am to build a sawmill. A stream with a good flow and close to the Lake for boat building.'

'Whale boats and bateaux's. We spent enough time in them, did we not?'

'We did that! But these will be put to a more peaceful purpose. Have you plans for your own future, sir?

'Ah! You've heard that I'm to go on half pay then. It was to be expected, for the regiment is well over establishment for officers with the influx of those from the 2nd Battalion. We have barely six under strength companies.' He shrugged and smiled wryly. 'I had hoped to make Captain before this war ended. Like you I shall stay in the America's and attempt to make my fortune. Take my land grant and farm I suppose. Or rather hire others to farm it for me,' he grinned.

He saw Sarah returning from the floor and rose with a bow. 'Take my seat Mistress Campbell, for if ever a young lady looked to need one, you do.'

'Thank you Lieutenant. Iain Mhor's dancing is more physical than graceful. We Irish tend to do our dances on the one spot more or less. You Scots cover far more ground.'

She sat down gratefully as the Lieutenant bowed again and wandered off to refill his glass.

'You have done very little dancing,' she said, accusingly.

'No! I'm saving my strength,' Jamie grinned, smugly.

She coloured up. 'Are you indeed,' she murmured. 'Speaking of which…when can we slip away without attracting undue attention?'

He was about to answer but was interrupted by Iain loudly calling for silence, He came across to them carrying Jamie's fiddle and Sarah's flute.

'You'll not be leaving without giving us a tune.' He winked broadly. 'I'm assuming you will be leaving us soon?' he said in a hoarse audible whisper

'So much for slipping away without attracting attention,' Jamie muttered in disgust and Sarah giggled as he led her to the centre of the barn.

'What shall we play?' she asked,

'D'ye mind that tune you taught me when I first started coming to Mistress Yonge? It was a favourite of yours.'

'Give Me Your Hand?'

'Aye! That's the one. I think it appropriate.'

She nodded and smiled.

They played the lilting tune through three times. First the straight melody on both instruments, then, as their fingers remembered, the flute and fiddle each taking its turn in weaving a harmony round the other's melody.

Jamie broke the seal on the letter and removed the outer layer of water stained paper and began to read.

The Parish of Kenmore,
This 12th day of June 1763.

My dearest son,

I received your missive the other day with the news of your marriage. I am delighted for you, as is Callum. Having mentioned your bride in past letters, I rejoice that another musician has been added to the family. I look forward to meeting her and seeing you again, for Callum and I have arrived at the decision to join you as you suggested.

I confess it was with some trepidation on my part. Callum, of course, was enthused with the idea immediately and set about convincing me.

The prospect of seeing you again weighed heavily of course and with the loss of your dear mother, our old home is an empty place, the memories of happier years now painful to me. Perhaps it is time, old and set in my ways as I am, to venture out and view different horizons. With the news of your wedding all my nagging doubts have straightway disappeared.

Since the peace was signed, numbers of our countrymen have decided to take advantage of the new lands opened up by the conquest of Canada. Broadsheets have appeared offering passage to the America's and I hear of whole communities leaving together to start afresh. So, we will not be alone in coming to our decision to abandon our native soil.

You should by now have received a draft allowing you to draw on monies I have deposited with an agent in Edinburgh. He assures me the sum will be available to you through an associate in Albany. It should give you the wherewithal to press forward with your plans.

Callum and I will be disposing of the property and making arrangements for our passage next spring, hoping to arrive in Albany by mid summer. Our woodworking tools will travel with us. I could not bear to sell them and they will be needed in this new venture. I have written also to your friend Mistress Yonge thanking her for offering to make her home available to us on our arrival in Albany. We look forward to our reunion and count the days.

You're Affectionate Father,
James Campbell.

'Well?' Sarah asked eagerly.

'It seems that next year we'll have a quartet playing.' he said, grinning.

She looked puzzled for a second then she realised what he was implying.

'They're coming!' she cried delightedly. 'Oh, Jamie! I'm so glad for you. Here! Let me read that letter.'

He went out to tell Iain and Mistress Yonge the good news.

'Now the hard work starts, Iain,' he said later. 'We'll be leaving tomorrow. There's a few supplies we still need so we'd best purchase them today.'

They had been busy for the first half of the year and at times it had been frustrating dealing with the authorities issuing land grants. Before the snow had cleared the pair of them had set off north to view a strip of military patent on the eastern shore of Lake Champlain. Midway between Ticonderoga and Crown Point they had found what Jamie had visualised. A stream with a good flow, tumbling down into a sheltered cove, the land covered in tall stands of timber.

'It's not the best of areas for farming,' Jamie had commented. 'Hilly and a lot of rocks, but will you look at the trees. That's the crop we need.'

Standing on the high ground above the cove looking north they could see the narrows between Crown Point and Chimney Point.

'We're within a couple of miles of the Military road between the Point and No4. Folk will be using that road Iain, to get up here and settle.' he said jubilantly. 'This is the place Iain!'

They had hurried back to Albany to finalise the details and a few days later Iain had added another two hundred acres to their entitlement.

'I met Willie MacKay today,' he had announced casually. 'Remember him! Corporal in the grenadier company. He's discharged and wants to get back to Scotland. Say's the army is not supplying passage back. Anyway, we had a few drams and he agreed to apply for a land grant, which he'll sell to us for fifty dollars. I took him down to the surveyors' office and he applied for the plot adjacent to ours. All that's left to do is tying up the title all legal like. Do we have fifty dollars lying around?

'We will when I draw it from the agent,' Jamie had exclaimed admiringly.' You're a born businessman, Iain Mhor Munro. You were wasted as a corporal.'

'I know!' Iain said modestly. 'Didn't I keep telling them that.'

They finished making their purchases and crossed the street to an inn for some ale to quench their thirst. Jamie had picked up a newspaper to read the latest news of the Indian uprising away to the west. Pontiac's rebellion, the broadsheets and newspapers were calling it, from the name of the Indian chief who had raised the tribes. Most of the posts in the west and along the Great Lakes had been overrun.

'Any mention of the lads.' Iain asked.

The 42nd had been marched south into Pennsylvania when the uprising began.

Jamie shook his head. 'Just that Detroit and Fort Pitt are still under siege and efforts are being made to relieve them. Then there's an article accusing the French of stirring the tribes up. It's hard to tell who to believe. I spoke to an Indian trader a few days's ago and he told me it was all because of Amherst cutting back on the trade goods and gifts.'

'It makes you feel guilty. I mean, us discharged and then all this trouble,' Iain said wistfully.

'They'll manage well enough without you and I. We're civilians now and we've done our share,' Jamie retorted, although as he said it he felt a twinge of regret. The 42nd were marching again and he was no longer part of it.

A shadow fell across their table and they looked up to see the familiar face of James Grant smiling down at them.

'Do you mind if I join you, gentlemen?'

They noticed he was in kilted plaid and redcoat and seeing their questioning look he smiled.

'As you can see, I'm back in harness. Off half pay and restored rejoicing to the colours. God bless this gentleman Pontiac.'

'Rejoining the Regiment, Lieutenant?' Iain asked, a touch of envy in his voice.

'I am! Off down to Pennsylvania shortly. It appears there has been a few vacancies made from among my brother officers, hence the call to arms,' he said lightly.

His voice changed and took on a serious note. 'You'll not have heard yet but some of the regiment were involved in a big fight recently. I read a full report at Garrison Headquarters here. It had only recently arrived'

Jamie and Iain edged forward in their seats and listened avidly to his account.

'They were marching to relieve Fort Pitt. Most of the 42nd, with detachments from Montgomery's Highlanders and the 60th, around five hundred strong altogether. Lt Colonel Bouquet was commanding and they had a big supply train of packhorses. About twenty-five miles short of the Fort, near a stream called Bushy Run, the advance guard was attacked. Bouquet pushed our Light Company forward and the lads saw them off. Then the Indians attacked again and got on some higher ground. It went on like that for the rest of the day. Usual tactics! Fire, then pull back when our troops went forward to clear them out. The trouble was that more were arriving. Come evening, Bouquet pulled back to the top of a hill and built a redoubt with flour bags from the supplies to shelter the wounded. When morning came the Indians were in a horseshoe round them. Bouquet feigned a retreat back to the flour bags by his two forward companies and the Indians followed them up but he had slipped two other companies round the back of the hills on his right and left. They came over then and he'd caught the Indians in the flanks and front neat as you like. That must have hurt them badly for they abandoned the siege The column got into Fort Pitt two days later.'

'What was the butchers bill. Lieutenant,' Jamie asked.

'Ah! Pretty high I'm afraid. For the regiment, twenty-nine killed and thirty-six wounded. Many from our old company I'm sad to say. About sixty killed altogether in the column.'

Iain grunted as if he had been struck. 'That's a lot of men downed. It must have been a hot fight. Have you any of the names, Lieutenant?'

Grant shook his head. 'I'm sorry to bring you news like this.' He beckoned a serving girl over and when she had brought over the drinks he raised his glass.

'A toast, gentlemen! To fallen friends!'

They echoed his toast and drained their glasses.

Chapter 20

It was her favourite part of the day Sarah decided, settling into the rocking chair in the shade of the porch. The menfolk had been fed, out and away from under her feet. The children busy at their morning chores. Young James was industriously hoeing in the vegetable garden and his sister Bridget ostensibly assisting but distracted by the study of some beetle she had found, while Ilsa's five-year-old son Iain, straw haired like his mother and father, searched the hencoops for eggs. She could hear her father in law whistling some Gaelic air in the little workshop Jamie had built for him. Ilsa would be over shortly for their ritual morning tea and old James would emerge from his workshop to join them, then take the children off for their lessons.

She sighed contentedly and raised her face to the warm sunshine of late spring.

Their little community had grown over the years, from that first twelve-month of unremitting toil. Damming the stream, building the sluices and the sawmill, all the while living in a cramped sod roofed cabin of logs. There had been little leisure that first year, Jamie and Iain returning each day, exhausted and barely able to stay awake long enough to eat the meal she had prepared.

There had been the bright moments, ones of exhilaration, when, for instance, the great saw blade had arrived and been fitted. And then that day when Iain had opened the sluice, the water mill turning, slowly at first, then gathering speed and Jamie fed a log on to the blade and cut that first plank.

When they went off to Albany to collect James Campbell and Callum. Sarah was heavy with their first child. All three sailed south in the whaleboat to the growing settlement of Skenesborough, then by land to a decaying Fort Edward, and a barge down river to Albany.

Jamie's father and brother were waiting for them at Mistress Yonge's and the reunion was a joyful affair. She had taken to the pair of them at the first meeting. Jamie's father with his soft spoken, gentle manner and Callum, a quiet, rather solemn man who took after his father much more than Jamie himself. Fine musicians both, with Callum preferring the pipes, the evenings were lively affairs and the house was filled with the sound.

They stayed only a few days, Jamie being eager to show his father and brother their new home, but as he came to the narrows at Ticonderoga he turned the whaleboat's prow up the Chute River and berthed her beneath the overgrown mounds of the old French Lines.

The abattis had long been cleared and the ground planted. They walked easily across fields that had seen so much death and suffering up to the low grassy ridge.

Iain and Jamie searched in the long grass until they found the rough slab of fieldstone that had toppled on top of the grave and upon which Jamie had carved in crude lettering.

Capt. Alexander Campbell,
42nd Regt. 8th July 1758.

'We can make a better headstone, Father,' Jamie said.

'No! This one is just fine,' the old man answered, his eye misting up. He turned away and walked off a short distance as Callum played a lament on his pipes, the sound carrying eerily and causing men working the fields to raise their heads. Jamie and Iain set about re-erecting the stone.

Sarah joined James and stood beside him quietly.

'It feels very strange,' he murmured

'We were all strangers to this land at one time, Father James. It will grow on you as it did us.'

He smiled and waved his hand at the vista. 'The land is not what I find strange. Why, I could be looking over a Scottish loch. No, it is the circumstances that brought me here. To be standing on this ground where my son fought and my brother died along with so many of my countrymen. I find it difficult to believe. I've lived through turbulent times, Sarah, but have personally never known anything but peace. War and violence never came my way... nor have I ever raised my hand in anger to a living soul. Yet here I am an ocean away from where I was born partly because of what happened at this place.'

She reached out and took his hand. 'Years ago a young Highlander stepped out of the woods near Albany and chased off some men who were harassing my family. It was your son. Happenstance, fate, call it what you will. It brought us all together here, .We have no control over chance...but sometimes the bad things that happen can lead to happiness.'

He nodded and squeezed her hand. 'I forget you've had your share of bad things happening to you. Have you seen your mother and father's grave, Sarah?'

She shook her head. 'Jamie and Iain searched the last time they were at Fort William Henry. There were some old French grave markers but as for the rest that died there…'

'I don't profess to understand what gives men the courage to face death in battle,' James said quietly.

'Pride, discipline, a fear of being less brave than the man you stand beside. All that…and the certain knowledge that whatever happens to someone else it will never happen to you,' Sarah said firmly.

He looked at her in surprise and she smiled.

'Jamie told me that and only because I asked him the same question. Mind! He did say that the last reason tends to lose a bit of its certainty once you've been wounded,' she laughed. 'He doesn't talk of the war much. He says it's over and best forgotten, but it doesn't stop him when he and Iain get to reminiscing. It's strange but they never speak of the bad things. They talk and laugh about the men they knew and the funnier things that happened.'

'We'd best get on if we're to get home before nightfall,' Jamie called, and they set off back across the peaceful fields.

Others came to join them as the business prospered. A raw-boned ex soldier from Montgomery's Highlanders called John MacKenzie arrived. His skill as a blacksmith was required, fashioning ironwork for the whaleboats, and making or repairing farming implements. A lean taciturn man, who limped slightly from a wound taken at Bushy Run, he had been recruited by Iain in Albany, and he settled in quickly, adding to the services that Jamie could provide to those who farmed the area.

Itinerant workers would come for a season or two, tree felling, clearing ground for fields and meadows or improving the track they had cut to link up with the military road that ran from Crown Point to No 4 on the Connecticut River. A young Irishman, called Liam O'Donnel came and stayed, sharing the spacious cabin they had built to house John MacKenzie. A hard worker, he had landed in Boston as an immigrant only a year before.

A skinny thirteen-year-old orphan, who immediately aroused Sarah's motherly instincts, closely followed him. Billy Ferguson, scatterbrained and forever cheerful, joined the two in John MacKenzie's cabin, learning quickly that, old soldier as he was, John tolerated no sloth or untidiness in his living quarters.

Iain would be gone for days or weeks at a time, drumming up trade, collecting material that was needed or delivering items they had sold. It was he who suggested they build a larger vessel with a greater carrying capacity than the whaleboats and when it was built opened up a brisk trade carrying cargo and mail from Skenesborough or on occasion north to St Johns in Canada

To the great delight of Sarah and the immense surprise of Jamie, Iain came back one day from a trip to Albany with a lively blond haired Dutch girl called Ilsa, who clung to his arm and gazed up at him adoringly.

'We got married a few days ago,' he explained sheepishly. 'Sort of in a hurry…if you know what I mean.'

He grinned down at the girl on his arm, who Sarah guessed was around three months pregnant. 'We'd planned it different, but events sort of got ahead of themselves. Isn't that so, Ilsa?'

Ilsa laughed and smiled happily around at her new family.

'That has to be the only secret you've kept in your life,' Jamie commented later, as Sarah and Ilsa chattered away in the kitchen..

'I meant to tell you. Thought I'd surprise you.'

'Well, you certainly succeeded there,' Jamie said dryly.

Iain, through his travels, had been the main source of all the news from further afield. The friction between the colonies and the British Government that had developed mainly in the towns of the eastern seaboard had had little impact on their lives, engrossed as they were in making a success of their venture.

'From what I can gather Boston appears to be run by rioting mobs,' Iain explained after a trip to Skenesborough. 'I met a man who'd just come up from Boston and he told me he would hate to be a customs man, a sheriff officer, or a magistrate in that town. If the rioters take the notion they'll come along and ransack their house then pull it to pieces.'

'That's terrible. Why would they do such things?' Sarah asked.

'Seems their angry with just about everything right now. The Sugar Act for one, now it's this new Stamp Tax.'

'The Sugar Act lowered the tax on sugar, for God's sake. Why would they be angry with that?' Jamie scoffed.

'Because most of the molasses that came in before was smuggled and no one bothered much about collecting tax. Now the government is tightening up on collection and smuggling and the merchants and rum distillers don't like it,' Iain said pityingly. 'You really want to get out and about more, Jamie.'

'That doesn't explain why ordinary people would be rioting. They don't deal in molasses or rum distilling. Like us, they just drink it.'

Iain sighed. 'According to this man I talked to, the merchants and distillers are the very people who are stirring folks up. There's newspaper and broadsheets being printed, full of talk about how the rights and liberties of colonists are being trampled on with these taxes and telling people to defy them. There's groups called the Sons of Liberty all over. They make sure folk are informed and can all act in concert.

Some of them can get pretty heavy handed as well, tarring and feathering folk who disagree with them too loudly. Now this new Stamp Tax is coming in. A tax on newspapers, legal documents, contracts, playing cards and whatnot. That's got them even more riled.'

'I fail to see why. It's not like a tax on flour or eggs or milk. Things that they need everyday,' Jamie snorted.

'Look!' Iain said impatiently. 'I'm only telling you what I was told. I don't understand but half of it myself. If you choose not to believe me you can go to hell. Or better still go find yourself a newspaper.

Chapter 21

Giving a last stroke of the whetstone to an adze he was sharpening, Jamie tested its edge and laid it aside. He liked to re sharpen all his tools at the end of a day's work, ready for use the next morning, a habit his father had insisted on. The rest of the men had gone off to clean up for the evening meal and he was alone in the workshop.

He straightened his back and stretched, viewed with satisfaction the sleek lines of a whaleboat requiring only the ironwork to be fitted before she was launched and was heading for the door when a figure appeared in it.

'How are you Jamie? It's been some time.'

He peered in the gathering gloom of evening at the man's face.

'Charlie? Charlie Hutchinson. God! It's been years, 'Jamie cried delightedly, clasping his friend's hands. 'What brings you here, man? No! Come up to the house and eat with us and tell me then. Iain Mhor's there.'

Leaving the workshop he noticed the fully laden canoe tied to the jetty.

Charlie was quiet during the meal, despite the cheerful talk of Iain Mhor. Jamie thought him subdued, as if the spirit had been beaten from him.

He waited until Sarah and Ilsa had cleared away the platters and a jug of ale was going around before he asked.

'Something's happened, Charlie. Would you like to tell us what brings you here?'

Charlie's voice was hesitant as he began to tell them, then grew stronger as a deep anger surfaced.

'You know I had a farm down New Perth way. I applied for a military grant when I was discharged from the 42nd back in 67. Just before the regiment sailed for home. Worked for over two years in Albany to get together money to buy tools and such. I was a happy man when I finally set to working that land, Jamie.' He stared down into his mug of ale and there was a tremor in his voice.

'I've never had anything much before. Soldiering was all I knew. Then there I was with two hundred acres of my own. Well, you know the feeling yourself. Its a good feeling is it not, Jamie? I worked like the devil. Had a cabin built and twenty acres cleared in the first year and things just got better. I had good neighbours and we helped each other out. Got myself a yoke of oxen, a milk cow, and planted up a vegetable garden. Aye! I was pretty happy.'

He fell silent, his hands so tightly clenched his knuckles showed white through the weathered tan.

'What then, Charlie?' Jamie prodded gently.

'You'll have heard of Ethan Allen and his kinfolk and the Green Mountain Boys that's formed to stop New York authorities turning folk off land they'd purchased on a New Hampshire grant. Its an unholy mess down there with New York making land grants on ground that's already settled by folk who bought it from New Hampshire speculators. Allen, he's one of them speculators.'

'I thought the King personally had instructed New York that those who had New Hampshire title were to be left alone even if he had found in favour of New York having the sole right to make grants,' Iain interjected.

'He did, but he's three thousand miles away and the New York Assembly decided there was just too much money to be made, so they ignored it. The provinces hate one another more than they hated the French. They're forever squabbling with each other,' Charlie said heatedly, his face growing flushed. 'New York! New Hampshire! They're each as greedy and jealous as the other. Throw in the speculators like Allen who buy land from New Hampshire to sell on and some big New York landowner who claims the same land and its no wonder there's a lot of bad feeling.'

'You were saying about Ethan Allen, Charlie. Did he have something to do with you being here?' Jamie asked curiously.

Charlie gave a harsh bark of humourless laughter. 'You could say that. About two weeks ago, Allen, that cousin of his, Remember Baker, and seven other men I don't know, paid me a visit one night. They dragged me outside and knocked me about a bit, then they tied me up and put a halter round my neck.' His voice broke slightly. 'Jamie! I'm no coward but I was pretty scared then.'

'They set fire to my farm. Cabin, barn, everything. Trampled my vegetable plot and run off my animals and chickens. While it was burning, Ethan Allen... why he ups and makes a speech. I don't know for whose benefit, because I sure as hell wasn't listening. I was just thinking of all that hard labour burning up and what they might do to me next. I remember him saying something about they had resolved to offer a burnt sacrifice to the gods of the world and this being a beacon to light the way from tyranny. It made no sense then and it makes no sense now.'

'He burnt you out? Iain said incredulously. 'Is the man raving mad?'

'No! I thought about it afterwards when they told me to take myself off and never show myself on the land again or they would hang me. He did it to scare off any other folk who might take up land on a New York grant especially those that might settle on land that he was trying to sell off. No, he's not mad. Just another ruthless, uncaring, greedy bastard,' Charlie grated bitterly.

Those around the table sat quiet, shocked at the story they'd heard.

'Why you, Charlie? Had you any dealings with him before this?' Jamie asked.

Charlie shook his head. 'I'd never met him and that's a question I kept asking myself. Why me? All I can think is that I was on land in dispute. Land that he or some of his kin laid claim to. He can't harm the people who allocate the land so he chooses to terrorise the folk who farm it.'

Jamie felt a seed of anger inside him growing. Anger at the ruthless intolerance, the growing lawlessness, and the constant carping about rights and liberty all about him.

He had heard of Ethan Allen and his campaign to resist the New York authority's attempts to apply writs to remove tenant farmers that had purchased land through New Hampshire. A campaign that involved raising a militia that chased off sheriff officers and surveying parties. His Green Mountain Boys! From what he had gathered there was some justice in their resistance. He had sympathised with Allen's claim that no title of disputed land could outweigh the cultivation and possession of it, particularly when, as was the case, New York had been specifically told not to pursue a policy of removing New Hampshire tenants by the King himself.

Yet here was a man who seemingly claimed that right only for New Hampshire tenants. Who had denied another man that same right in a particularly brutal fashion, purely on the grounds that he held it on a New York title.

The sheer hypocrisy of it was breathtaking.

'What do you intend to do now Charlie?' he heard Iain ask.

'I'm heading for Canada. I have a brother there. Start all over again I suppose.' His face flushed up and he snarled vehemently. 'Damn them all to hell. I've had enough of this country. It's getting to be full of hate. You take care, Jamie. Most of the trouble is east of the Hudson right now but it'll work its way north. You'll see!'

'Charlie! Winter's coming on. That canoe's a bit fragile for what you intend. Winter here with us.' Jamie offered.

'I'm obliged for your offer Jamie, but I want to push on.'

'I can't have that Charlie. Look! Iain and I will sail you up to St Johns in the ketch if you insist on going.'

'Of course we will,' Iain boomed. 'And I guarantee it'll be a more comfortable trip than the last time we three travelled up the Lake together. You remember that one, Charlie!'

'I do that Iain,' Charlie said, his face sagging with tiredness, and his eyes filling with tears.

'Your good friends and I'm sorry to be a burden.'

'You're no burden, man. The day we can't help old comrades in arms will be a sad one. Now, there's a bed for you upstairs. James, show Charlie where it is.'

He watched his son lead Charlie away then exchanged a grim look with Iain.

'Charlie's right you know,' Iain said. 'The trouble is going to move up this way. You know these seven thousand acres that Colonel Reid acquired north of the Otter, then brought over tenants from Scotland to farm. There are some families on it with Hampshire grants. I've heard he's intending to issue writs to have them ejected. I wouldn't be surprised if that doesn't bring a few of these Green Mountain Boys up here.'

'I didn't know Reid in the Regiment. What's he like?'

'I just knew him from hearsay. He was only with us a few weeks before I was discharged. Came as a major after the second battalion joined us. He was wounded in Martinique serving with them. By all accounts he's a bit of a cold fish.'

'Well! He's bringing trouble down on all our heads. All of us who hold land from New York.

Chapter 22

A mild westerly wind was blowing, the last vestiges of melting snow dripping from the tree branches, soaking riders and horses.

The lake had still been frozen over when they had left to travel down to Skenesborough to check on the ketch, ice bound there since December by a sudden hard freeze. Now they were riding east to strike the Military road and collect some moneys owed them from a farmer in Pittsford.

'There's a good inn in Rutland village I stayed at once,' Iain said, easing the wet cloth of his breeches away from his thighs. 'What say we lodge there? It'll be a soggy night for camping in the woods.'

'We might as well,' Jamie agreed. 'There's but two hours of daylight left and we'll not reach Pittsford before dark. Some hot food and a dram or two would be welcome.

For all its size, the inn was a cosy place. At either end of the long taproom were massive fieldstone fireplaces with cheerful fires blazing, the intervening space filled with tables and benches. The air was redolent with tobacco smoke, the pungent odour of rum, and the appetising smell of stew simmering in pots hanging from irons in the inglenooks of the fireplaces. A small group of men had gathered near the fire at the far end and they merely glanced up as Jamie and Iain entered. Nearer the taproom counter, a dark haired man sat alone, his head bent over some documents carelessly scattered amongst the dirty plates of a recent meal. The innkeeper was wrestling a five-gallon keg of rum onto a trestle behind the counter. When he had it in place, he turned to Jamie with a friendly grin.

'Good evening to you, sirs. And a damp one sure enough. What would be your pleasure?'

'Hot buttered rum would go down well I think,' Jamie smiled.

They waited while the man bustled about, dumping a knob of butter and brown sugar into large mugs, and half filling them with rum, then over to the fireplace to top them up with hot water and plunge a red hot fire iron into the mixture. He brought them over, steaming and heady with the fumes. Jamie warmed his hands on the mug then took a gulp feeling the warmth spread through his chest.

The innkeeper disappeared into a backroom at some task, and Iain walked over to the fire and contentedly warmed his backside, the steam rising from his clothing.

Jamie sipped slowly at his drink and studied the lone man, well dressed in good broadcloth, still engrossed in his paper work and now scribbling busily with a pen. The man raised his head and studied the ceiling for a few moments as if looking for inspiration and Jamie noted the overlarge pugnacious chin, protruding underlip and dark deep-set eyes. He remembered Charlie's description of the man who had burned him out.

When the innkeeper returned Jamie caught his eye. 'The gentleman at the table there. I think I know him. Do you happen to have his name?' he asked quietly.

The innkeeper looked nervous and glanced around him shiftily before answering.

'Why, that's Ethan Allen,' he whispered. 'He's staying here. Has some business in these parts.' Then he hurriedly found some other chore to busy himself with.

Jamie joined Iain at the fire. 'Where's your pistol?'

'In my saddlebags, where else,' Iain said in surprise. 'Why are you asking?'

'Don't stare! The dark man alone at the table. He's Ethan Allen.'

'Is he now. Are you intending to kill him for what he did to Charlie...Or do you want me to do it?'

'Don't be daft! No!. I just want a word with him and he may not like what I have to say. I think that's some of his cronies at the other fire. Saddle the horses and bring them out of the stable then get your pistols and slip back in the other door.. It's by way of a precaution. I'll give you a few minutes.'

Iain finished his rum and sniffed longingly. 'That stew smells appetising. Can't we have a plateful before you start whatever you have in mind to start.'

'No, Iain we can't. We'll do it now.'

'There you go again, always hurry and rush,' Iain grumbled and headed out of the door

He waited until he saw Iain come in the other door, and exchange a few words with the men round the fire. He shook his head despairingly as his friend helped himself from the pot of stew and ambled over to a corner table where he sat unobtrusively spooning the food into his mouth.

Draining his mug, he walked over to where the dark man was still busily writing.

'Mr Ethan Allen?' he asked quietly.

The man looked up, leaned back in his chair and stared at him, his deep set eyes suspicious and watchful.

'You have the advantage of me, sir. Should I know you? Have you some business with me?' his voice was rasping and loud.

'My name is James Campbell. As to my business with you…it regards a friend of mine.'

The door behind them banged open letting in a gust of cold air. A lean figure barged in and back heeled it shut, rested a pack and a musket against the wall, then headed for the counter, bringing with him a strong smell of wood smoke and damp leather.

'Rum…and a bowl of that there stew, Aaron. Soon as you like,' he called to the innkeeper.

He looked round the room and his eyes widened.

'Great God almighty. Sergeant Jamie Campbell himself,' he bawled, bustling over to the table and taking Jamie's hand in two grimy fists. 'What are ye doin' here. Must be four or five years since I last called in on ye. I keep meaning to swing by and visit.'

'It's good to meet with you again Ezra. Still running the woods I see.'

'You know this gentleman, Ezra?' Ethan Allen broke in.

'Know him! I should say so. Rowed all the way up Champlain with him. Splashed eighty miles through a spruce bog to St Francis with him, then near starved marching back to Crown Point with him, Makes for more than a passing acquaintance I'd say.'

'Well now. Yet another one of Rogers heroes.' There was the merest hint of a sneer in Allen's voice. 'Now, if you will excuse us Ezra I believe Mr Campbell has business to discuss with me.. I'll take your report later.'

'I've been doing some survey work for Ethan here, up on the Onion River, and I wintered over there. I'll get some rum down me and eat, then we'll do some catchin' up.'

'No! Stay Ezra. I know this will be of interest to you. My business with Mr Allen has to do with an old friend of ours. You remember Charlie Hutchinson, don't you?' Jamie watched Ethan Allen's head jerk up at the name.

'Charlie! God, yes. Saw him over in Albany a couple of year's back. Working in a stable and saving every last penny to set up on a piece o land. Took me all my time to drag him out for a few rums. You seen him lately? How's he doin?'

'Charlie got his bit of land, Ezra. Down about New Perth way. He doesn't have it now though. He called in on me around four months ago. I helped get him get up to Canada to start again. Seems he got burned out.'

'Burnt out? Damn! An accident like?'

'I should have said burned out… and driven off his land. Mr Allen here can tell you all about it. From what Charlie told me, Mr Allen here declared that Charlie's burning farm was a beacon to light the way to freedom from tyranny.'

He turned to Ethan Allen. 'Like Charlie Hutchinson, I hold my land on a York grant. There's bad feeling enough around our way, with all this disagreement over who has the rights of it. So far it's only talk. I don't agree with anyone losing his land whether he holds it from New York or New Hampshire. Your argument with New York had some merit although your methods were questionable.'

He took a step closer to Allen and locked his gaze on the man's dark eyes.

'When you burned Charlie out you stepped beyond the bounds of fair argument, and from what I have heard you intend to continue using fear and intimidation on New York tenants.'

His voice dropped to a throaty growl. 'I give you fair warning. Set foot on our land and we'll shoot you down.. That goes for any of your Green Mountain Boys as well. If anything untoward happens… livestock killed, a barn fired… anything at all. I will hold you responsible and come and kill you myself.'

Allen's face had darkened with anger as Jamie spoke.

'You dare to threaten me, sir. We have a way of dealing with people like you in these parts. The last man who threatened me we hoisted in a chair up to an inn sign. A few hours hanging there cooled him down.' He gave a quick glance to the far end of the room and men were moving up having heard his raised voice. 'Perhaps you would benefit from a few hours swinging there yourself.'

He stiffened as Jamie's pistol dug into his breastbone.

'I heard of that. I believe you took the pistols from the man who had forgotten to cock them. Of course, the man was in his seventies. You'll note mine is cocked and I'm not in my dotage.' Jamie smiled without humour. 'If your friends have a mind to intervene they should perhaps look round first.'

'Good evening to you, Ezra,' Iain Mhor boomed from the other end of the room, a horse pistol levelled. 'I'd advise you to stand well to the side. I may have overcharged it a trifle. Bird shot half way up the barrel,' he grinned.

Jamie edged back toward the door and opened it. 'I'm sorry we met again like this Ezra. Call by any time you've a mind to.' His face hardened and he addressed Ethan Allen again. 'You take heed! Cause any trouble to me or mine and I shall certainly kill you.' With that, he disappeared into the darkness, as did Iain.

Men moved up and one said. 'You want we should go after them, Ethan?'

Allen, his face pale now with suppressed fury snapped. 'No! No, they'll keep for another day.' He glared over to where Ezra leaned against the bar counter regarding him thoughtfully. 'Seems you have a few Yorker friends, Ezra, Any more I should know about?'

Ezra continued to stare and he snapped 'Something on your mind, Ezra?'

'Surely is, Ethan. Did you really spout that horse manure when you burnt Charlie's' farm down?' Ezra drawled then took a long drink of rum.

'I'm sorry he happened to be a friend of yours. There was nothing personal about it. Someone had to be made an example of to teach these goddamned Yorkers a lesson.'

'Nothing personal ye say. I recall you telling me a while back that you had some plots down that ways to sell. I'm thinking maybe that plot Charlie farmed was one o' them.'

Ezra drained his mug and cracked it down on the counter, then took a step closer to Allen.

'Lemme tell you a little story, Ethan. When we hit St Francis and were movin' through the town to clear it, I stopped to recharge my piece. I was a bit careless on account of the shootin' being over, and an Abenaki I thought dead was playin' possum. Jumped me from behind, took me down an' was about to split my skull with a hatchet when a ranger put a bayonet to him and forked him off me like a sheaf of corn. No prizes for guessing who that ranger was. So Charlie was a little more than a friend. He saved my skin, did Charlie.'

Ezra's face grew mottled with anger. 'I look around you pissants here and I don't recall any of you at St Francis or anywhere else,' he spat. 'Charlie and folk like him helped open up this damned country. Where the hell was you bastards?'

'I did my share in the war,' Allen said stiffly.

'Your share!' Ezra snorted in disgust. 'I know about your share. A couple months sitting on your arse at Fort Edward in a lousy militia regiment then you ran off back to Connecticut. You never saw a Frenchmen or an unfriendly Indian.' He took another pace forward and grinned fiercely as he saw some of the men edge nervously back.

'I've never took to you much, Ethan. Always thought you were a pompous, arrogant, son of a bitch. Always thought you were brimful o' wind and big words that sound nice. I'd bet you didn't ride to Charlie's farm on your own. You're good at getting folks worked up and doing the business for you. Jamie Campbell's right. Like him I don't hold with folks bein' run off their farm if they've put the money down in good faith. Like Charlie. He warn't the brightest button on a weskit.

He wouldn't have known a damned thing about who had the rights of it. Just that he had a bit of land at last…and you burnt him out. You used big words to justify what you were doin' but it warn't about whether New York had the right to grant land in New Hampshire. It was all about Ethan Allen making money.'

He turned abruptly and retrieving his pack and musket headed for the door.

'You're forgetting something Ezra,' Allen rasped. 'I hired you to do some work for me. I want the results I paid you for.'

Ezra paused at the door. 'You can go to hell, Ethan. You want to know about that land you can walk your arse up there. As you paid me though I'll give you a little good advice. You'd best take Jamie Campbell serious. If he says he'll kill you should you mess with him, then that's what he'll do.'

'He can come and face up to me anytime. I'd be more than willing to meet him with any weapon he may choose,' Allen said, truculently.

Ezra guffawed contemptuously. 'You think Jamie would play that game. He'd do it the way he's larned. Last you'd know would be a bullet through your head from a hunnert yard off or a knife in your throat as you strolls down to the privy. Jamie don't fight like a gentleman.'

'That would be murder and he would hang for it.'

'My, my! That from a man who ignores the law whenever it suits him. Ain't burning a man out of his farm agin' the law. Why, it might even be a hangin' offence for all I know.' Ezra snorted. 'Anyways, the way your goin' it could be hard to pin your killin' on any one man. The way you're goin' there'll be a whole heap of folks with a mind to snuffin' you out.' With that, he slipped out the door.

He made up with them by dawn. Catching a whiff of wood smoke he left the track and following the scent downwind spotted the two of them by a small fire waiting for the tea to brew. They looked up unconcernedly as he approached.

'Gettin' a mite careless in your old age, Jamie,' he said dryly.

'Not really Ezra. Thought you might be along. Iain saw you half a mile back. Have some tea.'

They sat in companionable silence for a spell, then Ezra sniffed.

'Well, that's me outa work. The son of a bitch paid well. I'll give him that.'

He chuckled. 'Left him more worried about you though. I doubt if he'll give you grief. He thought you might come along all polite like and challenge him to a duel. Thinks he's a gentleman 'coz he had a commission in some lousy militia regiment. Put him straight on that.

Told him how you'd do the business. He's a bully that's got a way with words. He ain't no soldier.'

'Lets hope so. There's enough bad feeling brewing up around the Otter. I just wanted to ensure he would think twice in case he had a mind to pay us a visit.' Jamie said. 'If you want some work Ezra, we could do with an extra hand.'

'Hell, Jamie…I appreciate it…but I ain't done an honest days' toil in years. Not sure if I could earn the cost of keepin' me.'

'We've not much time for hunting up fresh meat for the pot. We could do with someone to keep us supplied. How would that suit you?'

Ezra grinned delightedly. 'Sounds fine. Though it could be hard work if I'm keepin' Iain here fed.'

He choked on his tea as a ham like fist caught him in the back.

Chapter 23

In the summer of 1774 a letter arrived for Sarah from Albany. It was from a lawyer to inform her that Mistress Yonge had died and left her the house and it's contents in her will. Sarah had seen her only infrequently over the years but they had exchanged letters often, and it was with a heavy heart that she and Jamie travelled down to Albany to arrange the sale of the house.

Jonas greeted them on their arrival and they sat quietly in the familiar spacious parlour as he bustled around in the kitchen.

'We had some happy times here, did we not?' Jamie remarked.

'We did. After Mother and Father died I don't know what would have become of me without her.'

Jonas came back in with a tray and Sarah asked him. 'What of you, Jonas. What will you do now?

'Bless you Miss Sarah. Mistress Yonge, she left money for me. Enough to set up a stable maybe' he smiled.

'You be sure to spend it wisely then, Jonas.'

He nodded solemnly and left.

'Do you know. All these years I knew her, it was always Mistress Yonge,' Jamie said. 'I'm shamed to admit it, but I never knew her first name.'

'It was Berta,' Sarah smiled. 'Berta! And she hated it. I believe even her husband was obliged to call her Mistress Yonge.'

They decided to stay until the sale of the house was concluded, which the lawyer, a dry stick of a man, assured them would be in no more than ten days.

'We're overdue for a little leisure time,' Sarah said firmly. 'The bairns will be fine with Ilsa and your father. They're probably delighted to see the back of us for a while. You know how they can twist your father round their little fingers. Besides, I want to spend some of your hard-earned money.'

'You're a lady of means now,' Jamie growled. 'Spend your own!'

It had been some years since they had been in Albany and it was larger and busier than they remembered it.

Prosperous as the place seemed it was impossible to miss the underlying current of discontent that prevailed. Wherever they went they overheard a continual litany of criticism directed at the Government in London. A monologue of complaints against unjust taxes and the trampling under of perceived liberties. There was virulence in the dissatisfaction far removed from the usual mild disgruntlement of anyone obliged to pay tax of any kind. Fuelled by articles in newspapers and broadsheets it seemed to be a topic of heated debate wherever they went. Jamie took to buying newspapers, reading the articles avidly in an attempt to understand more clearly what the furore was about.

He had been concerned over the years by the sporadic periods of unrest and civil disobedience throughout the colonies that had occurred since the end of the war with France. The more cerebral arguments over the questions of sovereignty and the right of a London parliament to tax their colonies he thought best left to politicians and intellectuals.

That the British government should try to recoup a small portion of the vast amount spent on the defence of the colonies by some taxation he felt to be only fair. They had relieved the colonial assemblies of the burden of paying, equipping, and provisioning Provincial troops, adding greatly to the overall cost of the late war. To enforce laws against the smuggling and subsequent evasion of import taxes that had been endemic before and during the war was, in his eyes, right and proper. As an ex soldier used to the practice of quartering, the amount of hostility it had aroused within the colonies baffled him. If you wished for troops to be available for your defence, then in the absence of barracks where else could you house them but on the civilian population? It was unpopular in Britain, and private homes were exempt he knew, but it was the excepted custom where inns were scarce. A soldier needed somewhere to lay his head.

It seemed to him that much of the general unrest was brought on by the conduct of the colonists themselves. The ongoing and escalating situation of the New Hampshire Grants was a case in point. A situation created solely by the greed and envy of two colonial assemblies. He recalled the revolt of tenant farmers in the Hudson valley in 1766 brought on by the attempts of the great landowners of that region to impose a system of short tenancies. Landowners like Livingston and Van Ressellaer, themselves prominent in the Sons of Liberty movement calling on American rights and liberty to be preserved, but uncaring about fairness to the men who farmed their land. They had been grateful enough then for the presence of British redcoats to squash the revolt.

Who were the most voluble. Who were the most involved in this clamour to preserve these so called rights and liberties they complained the Government in London were trampling over? Many of the great landowners, certainly. Tight fisted assemblymen, suspicious and jealous of any interference by the London Government. Merchants and ship owners whose profits were endangered by the clampdown on smuggling. All had their own reasons and it occurred to him that these reasons had little to do with some high moral stance. He wished he'd listened more closely to Iain Mhor's observations on all that was happening around them.

When Sarah asked him how he stood on the argument he shrugged his shoulders.

'It's politics, Sarah. I don't profess to understand all the arguments. These taxes and new laws don't effect us to any great extent. I doubt if it effects the vast majority of folk. Let them that have the leisure talk it out. People like us have a living to make, families to care for. Parliament repealed the Stamp Tax after all the trouble it caused. I suppose this is just more of the same. It'll be resolved one way or the other.'

She looked at him quizzically. 'It's not like you to be so non-committal. You usually have an opinion on just about everything.'

'This time I'll reserve judgement,' he grinned. If it starts to effect us, you'll be the first to know how I feel about it.'

Despite his words he could not rid himself of a feeling of unease.

After the sale of the house they visited the lawyer again for Sarah to sign some documents. When he told her the amount the sale had raised she gave a little gasp and Jamie blinked.

'All that is required now Mistress Campbell, is your instructions regarding the monies,' the lawyer said.

Sarah looked at Jamie, and he answered for her.

'I think my wife would prefer it to be deposited somewhere safe at the moment,' he said. 'Somewhere really safe,' he added deliberately.

The lawyer looked up at him sharply, then coughed discreetly. 'I understand Mr Campbell. One cannot be too careful in these tumultuous times.'

It was agreed the money would be deposited with the same banking firm that had dealt with Jamie's draft from his father.

'What was that all about, Jamie Campbell,' Sarah asked as they left the lawyers office.

'A precaution, Sarah,' he smiled. 'Merely protecting your legacy. Now let's get home to the family. I'm heartily sick of Albany. Too many people.'

Chapter 24

The arguments rumbled on, both sides hardening their stance and by the late summer of 1774 they had reached a feverish pitch.

'I tell you Jamie, you have to watch what you say nowadays. There are things happening you wouldn't believe. Say the wrong thing in the wrong place and you could find yourself being ridden out on a rail or worse,' Iain complained. 'I've slipped up a couple of times myself and only got away with it because I'm bigger than most.' he added modestly.

Committees of Correspondence who liased with each other, planning some common strategy had sprung up in every large town and district. Crown appointed officials were being sidelined and in some cases driven from their homes, their places taken by men imbued with the Patriot cause. It had reached a stage where there was now an alternative government dictating affairs with the various assemblies putting aside their differences and forming a Continental Congress. A current of suspicion permeated the land. If you were not enthralled by the Patriot cause and loud in the championing of it, there was a good chance of being branded a Tory, a King's man.

Gathering the menfolk together one day, Jamie addressed them soberly.

'I don't know your feelings on all that's been happening and frankly I don't wish to know. Where you stand in this matter is for you alone to decide. I shall keep my own council and I would prefer you to do the same. You'll oblige me by refraining from any discussion on it. I don't intend to see friends falling out over any difference of opinion.' He paused. 'For all our sakes I would suggest you extend that to any dealings with others. I don't want to be losing any customers,' he grinned. 'We've rubbed along together happily for years now. I'd hate for that to change.'

There was a murmur of agreement from them and Ezra spoke up. 'No fears on that, Jamie. It's mostly gobbledegook and hot air. As for forming opinions, why, young Billy there can't even decide which to put on first of a morning. Shirt, britches, or shoes.'

Billy blushed and pulled a face at Ezra as the rest laughed at the teasing.

In the early spring he was preparing to sail down to Ticonderoga to repair some of the garrison's boats. He'd decided to take young James with him to help and they were loading lumber and tools into the whaleboat when three men came down the path to the jetty.

He didn't recognise any of them and greeted them courteously enough. A serious faced man wearing the sober dress of a minister of the cloth seemed to be their spokesman.

'Good day Mr Campbell. Your wife told us you were preparing to go off somewhere so I will be brief. We are all members of the district branch of the Committee of Correspondence. We are intending to raise militia in the district for our defence and we have heard you are an experienced military man. We would hope you could put that experience to good use. A commission perhaps.'

'I regret gentlemen, my soldiering days are long passed and I have little inclination to resume them,' Jamie said, striving to keep the coldness from his voice. 'Can I ask? Who would this militia be defending us from?'

'Why, the forces of tyranny that are attempting to impose their will on us of course.' the parson declared, severely.

'I see! Jamie said, his voice even. 'I'm sorry, gentlemen, but I hold to my decision. I have a trade other than soldiering that requires all of my time.'

'That is indeed regrettable,' the spokesman said coldly. 'You seem less than enthusiastic for our noble cause. Might I ask you how you stand in this matter?'

'You may not, sir!' Jamie snapped. 'My opinions are my own to keep and if I choose not to flaunt them then that is my business. Now, gentlemen, I have a living to make so I will bid you a good day.'

He watched them as they silently climbed the path, and cursed himself for his pride.

'You should have just lied,' he thought, bitterly.

It was only a few hours work to replace the odd rotten strake in the boats drawn up on the bank below the Fort. When he'd finished he and James made their way up to the gate. The sentry, an old soldier sheltering in the covered way leading to the interior quadrangle, grinned and nodded as they passed through.

Captain Delapace was leaning on the rail of the steps leading to his quarters and on seeing them enter the courtyard waved to them to come up, calling to his wife for some refreshments.

'Well Mr Campbell, will they float,' he asked cheerfully.

'Sink them for a few days to let the seams swell and they'll see you through another season,' Jamie smiled.

'I hope to be relieved before then. Two years as caretaker of this crumbling ruin is more than enough.'

The Fort was in a sad state from years of neglect and the hard frosts of northern winters that cracked the mortar of its walls. With a tiny garrison of twenty men, all invalids and fit only for garrison duty, there was little that could be done in the way of repairs.

They fell to talking about the current situation and Jamie told him of the visitors he had had.

'So! A militia to protect them from the forces of tyranny,' Delapace chuckled. 'That would be myself and my merry band of ancient warriors, plus the Sergeant and four men I have at what is left of Crown Point after the fire six years ago. Barely adequate numbers for imposing our will on anybody.' He turned grave. 'It sounds ludicrous if it weren't so damned serious. They appoint their own officials, form a Continental Congress, and are now planning to raise their own army. You would think they were looking toward some confrontation.'

He sighed and finished his glass of wine. 'Now! How much does King George owe you for the repairs?'

Jamie whistled up James who was prowling the ramparts inspecting the great guns that guarded the narrow lake passage and set off home.

On a fine afternoon in May, Ezra came skimming up to the jetty in his canoe his paddle digging deep.

'You aren't gonna believe this Jamie,' he bawled as he clambered ashore. 'That fool Ethan Allan and a crowd of his Green Mountain Boys has just gone and taken Fort Ti'. Him and some Connecticut feller' called Benedict Arnold.'

Jamie gaped in astonishment. 'Where did you hear this?'

'I went south lookin' for some duck to shoot and met a feller doin' the same. He said they just walked in during the night and Ethan called for its surrender in the name of the Great Jehovah and the Continental Congress. Loves them big words does Ethan.' He shook his head and his voice went quieter. 'That ain't the half of it. It appears there was a lot of shooting down towards Boston over three weeks ago. The Army went out to take the arsenals at Lexington and Concord and a whole crowd of folks turned out with guns to stop them. The troops got pushed back into Boston with a lot of casualties and now they're sort of penned in there.'

'So it's finally come to this,' Jamie murmured. 'Armed rebellion!'

Chapter 25

Young James Campbell sniffed the fragrant aroma drifting from the house and felt his stomach rumble in anticipation. He thought of sidling into the kitchen and looking wistful but decided against it. It had never succeeded before. He would be briskly told to remove himself while his sister smiled smugly at him in the knowledge that, as a female, she had free access on the pretence of assisting in the cooking. Wishing he had got up early enough to have gone off hunting with Ezra he went back to whittling at the mouthpiece of a whistle he was making.

He glanced up and saw the group of men making their way up the track toward the house and he rose and trotted to the kitchen window.

'There's some men coming to the house, Mama.'

Sarah appeared immediately, wiping her hands on her apron. She saw the men were carrying muskets and marching in file. She hurried anxiously down to the gate in the rail fence. For the past three weeks she had been seeing boatloads of armed men moving north on the lake and Ezra had reported numbers of them camped at Crown Point. Something momentous was happening and she dreaded what the presence of armed men on their land might mean.

'Go fetch your father, James,' she called over her shoulder.

She arrived at the gate just before them and recognised, with some relief, two neighbours from farms along the Shoreham road among them. The half dozen men appeared to be led by a man she knew by sight and repute, a tanner from Middlebury, named Jacob Buller. She had heard he was a rabid Patriot and a member of the recently styled Committee for Public Safety.

'Good day to you gentlemen,' she greeted them, forcing a pleasant smile. 'What brings you this way? Has your wife got over that terrible cold she was suffering the last time I saw her, Mr Slater?'

'She has indeed, Mistress Campbell...and thank you kindly for asking.' The neighbour she had addressed answered, doffing his wide brimmed hat sheepishly.

Jacob Buller gestured impatiently. 'Enough of the pleasantries,' he grunted irritably. 'Let's be about our business. We intend to search your house and outbuildings.'

'For what reason? And what gives you the right.'

'Reason enough. The Committee of Safety is charged with rooting out any that pose a threat to the Patriot cause. We suspect your husband to be a damned Tory. Now open the gate and let us pass.'

Sarah felt her anger rise. She stared at Buller, noting with distaste the man's heavy unshaven jowls and the ridiculous baldric of undressed cowhide that supported a rust pitted cutlass, without a sheath. She bit back the contemptuous words that boiled up and pressed herself firmly against the gate.

'If you would care to wait until my husband arrives, I'm sure he would be happy to conduct you round our property. We have nothing to hide. I've sent for him.'

'Damn you woman…get out of my way,' Buller roared and pushed hard against the gate.

Sarah stumbled back, then recovered and threw herself forward again, but the tanner had slipped through the gap. He lifted her bodily and carried her a few paces. She could smell the foul odour of his body and clothing and used her nails on his face and kicked with her feet. He cursed and threw her to the ground, the impact driving the breath from her.

She could hear some of the other men protesting at his actions.

Old James Campbell had seen the group at the gate from his little workshop and curiosity brought him limping down. When he saw Sarah manhandled he felt a rage he had never experienced before and uttering an inarticulate shout brought his cane down across the shoulders of Buller, in the first blow he had ever struck in anger.

Buller turned, twisted the cane from James's grasp and slashed it brutally across his face and as he fell beat him unmercifully until the cane shattered.

'For God's sake! Leave him be. He's an old man.' Slater shouted and pushed through the gate. Buller, blind with rage, ignored him and his heavy boots smashed into James's head twice before Slater and another man could haul him back.

Sarah screamed and threw herself over James's still body. His breath came in short gasps then ceased.

She looked up at Buller, dry eyed and cold.

'You've killed him,' she said quietly. 'If you wish to avoid more killing you had better leave now before my menfolk get here.' Then she sobbed and the tears flowed.

One of the Middlebury men dragged at Buller's sleeve. 'We'd best be gone from here Jacob,' he said nervously.

Buller looked dazed at all that had happened and wiped at the sweat on his face. 'Right! Right!' he stammered. 'Fall in men and we'll be off.'

Three of them glanced at each other and shook their heads.'

Slater spat at Buller's feet and looked at him in contempt. 'It will be a cold day in hell before I ever walk alongside you again, Jacob Buller. You murdered that old man.'

'You saw it. He attacked me. You're on militia duty. Now obey me!'

Another of the local farmers, a man named Pierce, spoke up. 'I didn't join no militia to treat folk's this way. The Campbell's have been good neighbours for years. You'd best take yourself off, Jacob Buller.'

Buller, his face twitching and eyes peering nervously about, spun round and beckoning to the other three men set off down the track, almost running in his haste.

Slater and Pierce carried the body of James Campbell up to the house and laid him on the porch. Ilsa, appeared and cried out in horror and incomprehension at the blood stained body, then rushed to comfort Sarah and little Bridget who had witnessed it all Then Jamie and the rest of the men arrived, staring with disbelieving eyes at the scene.

Callum called out when he saw his father unmoving. He rushed to his side and cradled his father's head, the silvery hair matted with blood.

Jamie went to his wife and held her close. 'Tell me what happened, Sarah,' he said, quietly.

She collected herself and told him in short precise sentences, and his features hardened.

He looked coldly over to where the militiamen stood. 'You came with Buller. Why are you still here?'

'He came by the farm. Told me to fetch my musket and that I was to accompany him on a duty. He didn't tell me for what.' Slater said. The others murmured their agreement. 'I'm sorry, Jamie. Your father was a good man.'

'Yet you stood and watched Buller do this thing. Beat an old man to death.' Jamie grated.

'No! They tried to stop him but it happened so quickly,' Sarah interjected.

'We're willing to stand witness when it comes to a trial.' Pierce said.

Jamie looked at him in disbelief. 'Trial? When will he ever come to trial. Who's to arrest him? All the sheriffs have been run off. Who will try him? Every damned Judge has left. Don't you see. Him and his ilk run this country now. Do you think any jury would find him guilty. Staunch Patriot that he is.'

He turned and walked into the house and reappeared with two muskets, shot bags, and powder horns. Iain grunted 'You're one short,' and strode off to his cabin. John MacKenzie turned and was about to collect his, but Jamie stopped him. 'Hold, John. No need for you to get involved...but oblige me by fetching a length of rope.'

Sarah gasped when she heard his words. 'Jamie, for God's sake, no. Leave it to the law. There are still fair-minded people around us.'

'No Sarah! I've held my tongue for two years and watched Buller and others like him strut around, bawling about liberty and freedom from tyranny, all the while harassing and cursing those who didn't agree with their opinions. Most folk are scared to open their mouths now or do anything that would draw attention to themselves. Like us, all they want is to be left in peace... but the Buller's of this world think different.' He patted Callum on the shoulder. 'Up Callum! We'll grieve later.' Iain joined them and Jamie pointed over at the high ground. 'We cut over the hill.' Without another word he set off at a loping run.

They crouched in the shadows of a copse screened by a fringe of bushes and watched the four men approaching. Buller was leading and kept glancing over his shoulder apprehensively. When they were feet away Jamie stepped out of cover, his musket levelled. The men stopped in shock and before they could recover Iain and Callum leapt out and snatched their weapons from them. Iain blew the powder from the pans and taking each by the barrel smashed them against a tree trunk.

Buller was the first to speak, the words tumbling out and his jowls quivering in terror.

'I swear, Campbell. It was an accident. He struck me and I defended myself.' When Jamie did not answer, he hurried on. 'Listen! I'm handing myself over for justice when we reach Middlebury. Take me there yourself.'

'I'll save you the journey, Jacob Buller,' Jamie said, softly, his face set like stone. 'You'll meet with justice here and now. Bind his hands, Iain.'

He walked over to a large oak tree, took the coil of rope off his shoulders and fashioned a noose on one end. He looked up and selecting a stout limb threw the noose over it.

'Bring him!'

One of the three others shouted out. 'My God, Campbell! You can't do this.'

Jamie ignored him and Buller was carried babbling and weeping to the noose. As it was slipped over his head and tightened round his neck his knees gave way and Jamie grasped him by the front of his coat and held him upright. He listened for a moment to the now hysterical pleas for mercy and forgiveness and shook his head in disgust.

'You're about to die Buller. At the very least you could try to do so with some dignity.'

He nodded to Iain and Callum who had grasped the end of the rope. They heaved and Iain's weight and strength held the choking man until Callum tied the end to another tree.

Buller's knees came up to his chest in spasm and he kicked and twisted until at last his legs straightened, the toes reaching down for the ground a foot below them. A thin trickle of urine pattered on the dead leaves.

Jamie turned to the dead man's companions, who had watched in horrified silence. He could hear Callum retching behind him.

'You can go. Take that carcass with you.' he said brutally.

'Bloody murdering Scotch bastards,' one shouted. 'You'll be hunted down for this.'

Jamie turned a cold eye on him. 'It may well be me who will do the hunting, my friend.'

'Canada then?' Iain asked as they headed back.

'Aye! Canada it is!'

Sarah, with some foresight, already had packs made up and food prepared by the time they arrived back. She saw the rope was missing and she looked at Jamie. He said nothing, merely nodded curtly in answer to the question in her eyes.

'What now?' she asked helplessly.

'We three go north tonight. We want you to stay here. You, Ilsa and the children. You'll come to no harm. They are not all like Buller. But if we all leave then we can lose our livelihood forever. You know what happened to the property of the folks the Patriots forced out.' He turned to the other menfolk. 'If you choose to leave I could hardly blame you. I suspect there will be few seeking our goods and it may be your association with us could lead to unpleasantness.'

'Unpleasantness I can handle. For myself, I'd feel a mite uncomfortable leavin' your families to look out for themselves,' drawled Ezra, who had returned from his hunting. 'I'll be staying!'

John MacKenzie spoke up. 'As will I. I'd go off to Canada with you but for this damned leg. They're going to need every man that can fight up there.'

'Ezra! John! Thank you!' He looked over to Liam and young Billy.

'Billy and me! We've talked it over. You've been good to us Mr Campbell. We'll stay!' Liam said, quietly.

'Thank you all. I don't know how long this sorry business is going to last, but depend on it, we'll be back just as soon as we can' .He turned to Sarah and took her by the shoulders. 'Whether I'd killed Buller or not it would still have come to this. I was a fool not to have seen it. It's not enough in these times to keep your opinions to yourself. Being silent is no protection. If you don't shout and bawl about liberties and rights then you're suspect. I'm sorry I've brought this on you, lass.'

'No! Don't be! You did what you thought was right. You always have, Jamie.' she said, her voice steady. 'I thought we were done with fighting and killing but it's come through no fault of ours. You wouldn't be the man I married if you had pretended to support a cause you had no belief in.'

They buried James Campbell at dusk in a makeshift coffin and a hastily dug grave. There were few words spoken as they made their way down to the lake. Only the quiet sobbing of the women and children. They loaded their muskets and gear into the canoe Ezra used for his hunting trips and pushed off onto the dark waters of the lake.

'Soon!' Sarah heard Jamie call in a low voice. 'We'll be back soon.'

Chapter 26

The snow was falling steadily, flurries whirling round as the wind gusted through the streets of Quebec's lower town. Jamie peered from the upstairs window of a house overlooking the Rue Sault au Matelot, the narrow thoroughfare lit eerily with the occasional rocket flare fired from the city walls behind them. To his right was a barricade blocking the street, behind which was ranged a company of the 7th Regiment along with a party of seamen. The houses forward of the barricade were manned by his detachment of Royal Highland Emigrants and Canadian Militia. He could hear the sound of artillery firing in the distance, but apart from the hiss and thud of the rocket flares the street remained quiet. A gust drove snow into his face and he drew back into the room partially closing the window

It had been a hectic four months since they had paddled off into the night.

Crown Point had been bright with the glow of hundreds of camp-fires, their gleam stretching across the narrows. They held close to the eastern shore, feeling vulnerable in the light, waiting for a challenge that never came. Then the long haul up the lake, moving by night and resting through the daylight hours. They watched as streams of bateaux passed them, all heading north carrying men and equipment The sight engendered a sense of urgency to their journey and they pushed on hard. At the head of Missisquoi Bay they cached the canoe and set off overland to St Johns but encountered a friendly Canadian who informed them that it was already invested by a rebel army. They swung north sighting columns of rebels heading for Chambly, slipped across the Richelieu River and finally over the St Lawrence to Montreal.

They viewed with dismay the broken down defences of the city as they passed them into the familiar streets.

Iain accosted the first redcoat he encountered. 'Excuse me friend. Who's enlisting men to fight and where would we find them?'

The man grinned. 'Scotch are you? At the end of this street there's the Royal Highland Emigrants recruiting.'

A tall sergeant dressed in a green jacket was seated behind a table at the door of a house and looked up sharply as Iain's voice boomed out. 'Long Rob Anderson, as I live and breath!'

Sgt Anderson, late of the 42nd and well known to them both, groaned in mock dismay. 'Oh God! Munro, of all people! Away down the street and you'll find the militia taking on men,' He rose and proffered his hand to them. 'How are you, Jamie? You look as if you've been doing some hard travelling.' He stuck his head in the door and called, 'Three recruits for you, Captain.'

An officer came out and looked them up and down approvingly. 'You know these men, Sergeant?

'I'm well acquainted with two of them sir. Sergeant Campbell and Corporal Munro of my old regiment, as was.'

'My brother has seen no service but he's a good piper,' Jamie said quickly.

The Captain rubbed his hands. 'Better and better. Two old hands and a piper and it's not yet ten of the clock. Sign them up Sergeant Anderson and I'll swear them in. I'll away and tell the Colonel he has another piper.'

'That was Captain Nairne, ex Fraser's Highlanders. Lt Colonel MacLean commands the regiment.' Anderson said, shuffling papers on the table. 'You'll be seeing a few familiar faces. With your service it's likely you'll be keeping your old ranks but your brother will have to go with the recruits for now. Fifty shillings bounty on swearing in. We're supposed to be uniformed in Highland dress but there's no plaiding to be had so it's britches for us for the time being. Right lads! Sign here.'

After swearing in, Lt Colonel Allan MacLean came out of his office and questioned them on their service. A brisk eager man, he nodded approvingly at their answers.

'Light Company, the pair of you. Ranked Sergeant and Corporal as of today. Mark them as such in the muster rolls, Sergeant Anderson.'

The Sergeant winked at them as he led them off to the quartermaster to draw uniforms, weapon and accoutrements.

Montreal was a city ill prepared for invasion. The defences were dilapidated and crumbling. One regular regiment was dispersed in penny packets garrisoning the distant posts to the west on the Great Lakes. The bulk of the only other regular formation was besieged in St Johns and Chambly, apart from one company in Quebec. Desperate efforts were being made to raise militias among the reluctant citizens of Quebec but the French Canadians were cannily awaiting developments, the bulk of recruits coming from the small number of British residents. The Royal Highland Emigrants formed the only disciplined unit, composed largely of old soldiers of the previous war.

As yet they numbered only two hundred and fifty with another hundred or so untrained recruits, mainly drawn from among other Scottish settlers.

The first rebel attempt on the city was a failure. Led by Colonel Ethan Allen, a small party of his adherents and some French Canadians, unsupported by the rest of the rebel army, had approached intending a surprise attack. Allen, acting on his own initiative, had decided he could take Montreal easily. Met by militia and Indians, who briskly killed and wounded some and captured the remainder, including Allen, it was by way of being a fiasco.

'The man's a glory hunting buffoon,' Jamie remarked in great satisfaction at the news. 'He probably thought he could stroll in here as he did at Ticonderoga. He likely had his speech all prepared. As Ezra said years ago, he's no soldier.'

The news that, first Chambly then St Johns had surrendered saw Lt Colonel MacLean leading his men in forced marches to bolster the skimpy garrison of Quebec. The only place strong enough to bear siege. They had reached it only days before a ragged rebel force commanded by Benedict Arnold arrived on the south bank of the St Lawrence after an arduous journey through the wilds of Maine.

'Stand to! They're coming,' Jamie whispered as he caught a glimpse of shadowy figures, their outlines blurred with the falling snow that muffled their approach.

They halted twenty yards short of the barricade and directly below him. The piquet gate in the wall of logs opened and a naval officer backed by some seamen emerged. Jamie heard him call. 'In the King's Name! Will you surrender your arms?'

A shot rang out and the officer fell back into the arms of the seamen who hurriedly withdrew and closed the gate. There was a yell and the column surged forward, scaling ladders poised to lay against the twelve foot high log barrier. A volley of musketry from the houses on either side of them shredded their ranks and Jamie saw them falter before he stepped aside to reload, allowing another man to fire. When he looked out again the mass of men had scattered, some retreating, others seeking cover from the fire in doorways.

He heard the door of their house splintering as desperate rebels tried to break in and he leapt for the stairs shouting at Iain to follow him. The door crashed open as he reached the bottom step. He shot the first man through. The next man squealed as Iain's bayonet took him in the stomach. He could see the white faces of others in the doorway but there was no return fire, their priming damp and useless from the snowstorm. Other Emigrants came down the stairs and a volley dispersed those rebels still outside.

Defenders were pouring out of the houses and the company of regulars emerged through the piquet gate and swept down the street, empty now but for the bodies and feebly moving wounded. Ahead of them rebels were throwing down their arms and calling for quarter as a column of Royal Highland Emigrants advanced, taking them from the rear and cutting off any retreat. More rebels were being rousted out of empty houses where they had taken shelter.

'That was quick,' Iain commented watching the prisoners prodded and pushed into ranks ready to march into the city they had attempted to assault.. 'We should have a bit of peace and quiet to enjoy a dram for New Year now.'

Jamie overheard a prisoner complain plaintively, 'Damnation! I was due to be discharged today.'

'Stop you're whining you rebel turd,' a Scottish voice said bitterly. 'But for the likes of you I'd still be working my farm on the Mohawk. Now move!' There was a yelp as the complaining prisoner received a prick from a bayonet. A voice from the rebel ranks shouted 'Parricide!'

'Poor souls,' Iain said. 'They look half starved and I've seen better clad crow scarers. It makes you feel almost sorry for them.'

'Why? Why should we feel sorry for them?' Jamie grated, an edge of anger in his voice. 'They chose to be here. We didn't. All that we worked for could be gone. We're separated from our wives and children, leaving them at the mercy of any vindictive bastard of a Patriot that can't bear to allow any other opinion but his own. You heard what they called us. Parricides! Killers of our family! What the hell do they mean? They learn these words from their lying newspapers and broadsheets or from the damned rabble-rousers. All manipulated by a gang of merchants, lawyers and landowners who have their own reasons for raising rebellion. Reasons that have nothing to do with liberty and equality. These men chose to believe the shit they're told. Spout words they don't know the meaning of. They get damn all sympathy from me…and never will.'

'Jamie! Jamie! Easy, man! They're only ordinary folk caught up in a war nobody wanted.'

'You're wrong, Iain. Somebody wanted this war. For all its faults and the blunders it's made it was not the British Government. It's been brewing for years, whipped up by people guarding their own interests. People like John Hancock who has a fine for smuggling hanging over him. So large it would bankrupt him if he had to pay it. All these land speculators like Livingston and Washington that have invested in the Indian lands on the Ohio. They can't get their hands on it as long as Parliament has a say.' Jamie wiped at his face wearily. 'Tell me Iain. In all the years since we left the regiment did you ever feel you'd lost your liberty? Ever feel oppressed?'

'Can't say I ever did, Jamie. Maybe just a little after I got married when Ilsa put her foot down on occasion.'

Jamie snorted with laughter. 'I should know better than to lecture you on politics Munro, Come on! Let's get in the warm.'

They followed the long column of prisoners heading for the Upper Town.

'What now Jamie? D'ye think we'll try a sally now we've whittled them down a piece?'

'I doubt it Iain. There are not enough of us. We're here until the ice clears and the first convoy of troops arrives.'

The first ships arrived in May and within days the British took the offensive, driving the rebels back and defeating them in sharp engagements at Trois Rivieres, and the Cedars. Pushing them back down the Richelieu River and out of Montreal until all that was left of the rebel army rotted in smallpox ridden camps on Isle aux Noix.

Chapter 27

'Sergeant Campbell! Could you report to headquarters straightaway. The Colonel wants you.'

'Do you know what it's about?' The orderly grinned and shook his head.

'Very well,' Jamie sighed, uneasy with the summons. 'Carry on please Corporal Munro.'

There was a collective but subdued groan from the squad of recruits he had been drilling. They would be sweating badly before they were dismissed.

The Colonel looked up from a mound of paper work as Jamie entered and doffed his hat. 'Ah! Sergeant Campbell! I believe you are well acquainted with this gentleman.'

James Grant turned from the window he had been looking out and strode forward, hand outstretched. 'A pleasure to see you again, Sergeant.'

'And I you, sir. I see you made Captain. Congratulations!'

'Right! Away out of my office the pair of you,' Lt Colonel MacLean said briskly. 'Come back when you've reached a decision.'

'Decision? What's all this sir?' Jamie asked as they left headquarters.

'All in good time. We'll discuss it over a beverage of some kind. Lead on Sergeant.'

James Grant eyed him speculatively over a mug of ale as they sat outside an inn with a view across the rapids of the St Lawrence.

'I heard of the circumstances that led you to come north. You appear to have no qualms about resolving matters in your own fashion.'

Jamie shrugged. 'We all have a story of how we ended up here! What of yourself?'

'I got out early before I was run off. I knew I was a marked man. I left two weeks after they took Ticonderoga. My wife and child are still at our farm near Ballstown. Right now I'm seconded to the Indian Department here in Lower Canada. You remember Captain John Campbell from the 42nd don't you? Well, he's now head of the Quebec Indian Department. Which brings me to the reason I looked for you.'

He took a long pull at his ale. 'Are you familiar with the workings of the Indian Department?'

'Only vaguely.'

'Mainly administering to their needs and keeping liaison with them. There are armourers to ensure their weapons are in order. Quartermasters to feed them when they're employed by the Army. Officers and rangers to accompany them in the field. They have their own leaders to command them though. They require no instruction from us in warfare...as we learned to our cost,' he grinned ruefully. 'Basically we accompany them to ensure they are not side-tracked or act in an excess of zeal.' He paused and took another drink 'The department is also tasked with the gathering of information.'

'Very soon, when we finish building the fleet at St Johns, the whole Army will be moving south down the Lake to finish this damned business. We need as much information as we can gather before we sail. There's a steady trickle of men making their way north, forced out as we were, looking to fight for what they believe. These men all carry information that's of use to us. A knowledge of their district. Who remains loyal, who the rabid patriots are. The names of those who sit on these damned Committees of Public Safety. Which of those gallant Sons of Liberty persecuted them.' His face hardened as he spoke. 'Oh yes! There's to be a reckoning, Sergeant. We'll serve them as they served us. Right now we need someone to speak to these men and gather that information. Someone who knows the Valley. Who's known and respected. Not least for a certain action he took. You are eminently suitable, Sergeant.'

'I'd be seconded to the Indian Department?' Jamie asked, thoughtfully.

'Oh, better than that. You would be commissioned and then seconded! I spoke to Colonel MacLean who told me he had already decided you warranted a commission. It's sitting right now in his desk drawer signed by Governor Carlton. A Provincial one, but a commission none the less.'

Jamie was silent for a minute as he took in the news. The implications of what James Grant had told him and the offer he had made. Foremost in his mind, it meant separation from Iain Mhor and he knew in his heart that he could not bring himself to take that step.

'I appreciate the offer, sir,' he said, slowly. However, before committing himself to an outright refusal he said casually. 'When you speak of knowledge of the Valley, I know a man who has travelled it length and breadth. Who knows everybody and who everybody knows...'

James Grant held up his hand and laughed. 'The greatest gossip in the old 42nd. The indomitable Iain Mhor Munro.'

'We've been together too many years. You know that.'

'When I heard you still served together I guessed there would be no David without his Jonathan. Or is it his Goliath?' he chuckled. 'That it would be both or neither. The Colonel was reluctant to lose two good soldiers but he is wise enough to recognise the pair of you will be more gainfully employed than merely shouldering a musket. So... Sergeant Munro will ably assist you.'

'Sergeant! My God he'll be insufferable,' Jamie chuckled, overjoyed at the news

'I want you down to St Johns as soon as possible.' James Grant's voice took on a serious tone. 'There will be nigh on six hundred Indians accompanying the Army. We need to know who our friends are so we can make sure they come to no harm. You understand what I'm inferring?'

Jamie nodded

'Congratulations Lieutenant Campbell, and to you, Sergeant Munro. Much as I hate to lose men of your experience, if it furthers the progress of this war I'm perfectly willing to make the odd sacrifice,' Lt Colonel MacLean said gruffly. 'You'll have heard by now the regiment will not be part of the Army going south. A severe disappointment to us all.' He sniffed disgustedly. 'At least I'll retain your brother, Lieutenant Campbell. He's a fine piper.' He rose from behind his desk and shook their hands.

'Good luck to you both. You may be seconded, but you're still Royal Highland Emigrants. Don't forget it!'

Iain paused outside the headquarters building and brushed self consciously at his sergeants' chevrons.

'Jamie, sir. Would I have time to take a wee stroll around the lines and maybe have a few drams to wet the stripes, as it were?'

'No, Sergeant Munro. As soon as we say our goodbyes to Callum, we're off to St Johns.'

'Damn! There it is again. Always the hurry and rush. What's the point of promotion if there's no time to enjoy it.'

Chapter 28

'Look who I found wandering about the docks!'

Jamie looked up from his paperwork to see Iain Mhor in the doorway with his arm over the shoulder of a slight, bedraggled figure.

'My God! Billy!' He felt a jolt of alarm. 'What's happened? The women and children…are they safe?'

'It's all right Mr Campbell. They're well!' Billy stammered, swaying with tiredness. 'Mistress Sarah asked me to find you. I didn't know where to start looking… then Mr Munro found me.'

'Here Billy, sit down. You're worn out. Iain, find him some food and drink.'

Impatient for the news as he was, he forced himself to wait until the youth had eaten voraciously.

'It's three days since I had a morsel, Mr Campbell,' the lad said apologetically.

'That's all right, Billy. Now! Tell us how you come to be here. All that's happened since we left'

'Well! They came searching for you the day after. They arrived looking pretty angry, but Mistress Sarah, she stood up to them, cool as you like. Showed them your father's grave first off. Mr Slater and Mr Pierce were there too and they told them what they'd seen that day. They searched all around for a while then left, but from then on there was always militia patrols sniffing round. We didn't do much trade after that. I guess folk had been warned off buying from us. The winter was pretty peaceful. We cut more timber and planked it ready for you all coming home. Then spring came and it started to get bad, especially when word spread about how things were progressing up here. Folks wouldn't sell provisions less we paid hard money and even then they overcharged. We didn't starve! Ezra saw to that.'

He grinned ruefully. 'Never thought I'd sicken of fresh game. Then finally they refused to sell us anything. Liam and I, we went up to Shoreham to see if we could get some flour and salt. They whipped us out of the village with branches.' He shifted uncomfortably at the memory. 'I was pretty scared. They said they'd tar and feather us if they saw us again. Called us Tory scum.' A tear trickled down his cheek and he sniffed. 'Why would they do that, Mr Campbell? I don't even know what a Tory is.'

Jamie and Iain exchanged grim looks. 'I can't explain why folks behave as they do, Billy,' Jamie said quietly. 'It's a madness that's been festering for years and now it's all boiling out.'

Billy looked at him blankly, then continued. 'Mr Slater gave us what he could in the way of necessary's but somebody reported him and they locked him up for five days. Then they came and took away the horses. Said they were needed for military use and gave us some useless piece of paper saying so. Finally Ezra got us together and said he couldn't keep us all supplied in food on account of running short of game to shoot. He thought it best us menfolk moved on so he had enough for the women and children. Liam and I had already decided to go north. We knew they'd be enlisting us in the militia soon and. we weren't about to fight for the same folk that had treated us so bad. John Mackenzie, he crossed the Lake and headed for the Mohawk. Said he had a cousin who farmed there. Ezra took to spending most of his time in the woods especially when patrols were about.'

The youth paused for breath and his head went down as if he had reached a part of the account that hurt him to tell.

'Liam and me, we started north and met up with three other men who were doing the same. We were all down by the shoreline just north of the Onion River and sat in a little bay cooking up a mess of fish we'd caught when a whaleboat came round the point. The men in it shouted at us and we took off running… Then they started shooting. I never saw Liam again. I think they might have killed him.'

His shoulders heaved and he gave a hiccuping sob. Iain patted him clumsily on the shoulder. 'It's likely you just got separated son. Why, he could turn up any day.'

Billy brightened a little at his words. 'I hope so Mr Munro. I liked Liam.' He thought for a few moments then continued.

'I split up with the other three men a couple of days ago. They were heading for Montreal, but I thought I'd best start looking for you here in St Johns. I'm glad I did!'

'Thank you, Billy,' Jamie said. 'We're indebted to you. You brought us the first news of our families we've had in almost a year. I can't tell you how much that means, knowing they're well. Now you get some rest.'

'I want to fight them Mr Campbell. Pay them back for what they did to Liam and me,' the boy gritted.

'Of course you do, Billy…but you need to learn how to fight first. You stay with us for a few days and get your strength back. I'll write you a letter you can take to the Royal Highland Emigrants in Montreal. Callum's there, so you'll have a friend in that regiment. They'll teach you to fight.'

As the summer passed Jamie found himself with less to do. Iain still trolled the town looking for men who had newly arrived from the south and finding fewer and fewer.

'They'll have guessed we're coming soon and decided to sit tight and wait for us,' Iain commented.

The information they had been gathering had been of huge value. Information that Jamie had collated and sent back in weekly reports to Headquarters in Montreal.

Of a rebel army riddled with smallpox and deserting in droves, but with fresh men arriving daily. A frantic building of gundelo's and galleys to increase the size of the small fleet that gave them control of the Lake, preventing the British forces from advancing until they had built their own fleet to match them. Of Patriot shipwrights who had to be bribed with a wage of five dollars a day before they would agree to build them. The work on strengthening the fortifications at Ticonderoga and how far it had advanced.

Gathered also was the information of a more sensitive nature which Jamie kept secure and sent off in separate reports to another department in Montreal. Lists of names and locations of those that remained loyal and could be depended on to assist when the army advanced. Another list was of the key Patriots and of those most zealous in the persecution of Loyalist sympathisers.

They watched the activity by the river as teams of carpenters pieced together sections of ships prefabricated in Quebec and transported to St Johns. Gunboats were swiftly rigged and armed by seamen from the fleet. Three schooners mounting fourteen 12 pound cannon apiece joined the growing fleet, then a three masted ship of eighteen guns slid sideways into the river. Regiments came marching up from Montreal. Hessians in dark blue or the bottle green of the Jager battalions and the familiar red coats of the British infantry filled the town with the music of their bands as they tramped through on their way to the vast tented camps that sprang up.

James Grant arrived on the first day of September along with a French Canadian officer. They had brought a large contingent of warriors with them, mostly tribesmen from the west.

'We left them a couple of miles up river putting their canoes to order. This is Lieutenant Francois Geurlac. Francois has been working with the tribes since he was a boy. He was one of the laddies who gave us such trouble in the last war. Is that not so Francois?'

'I had that honour,' the Frenchman smiled with a slight bow of his head, his English good, although heavily accented. He was short and barrelchested, his face scarred and weather-beaten, but his dark eyes were warm and friendly.

'Francois, this is Lieutenant Campbell and Sergeant Munro. They will be accompanying you when we go south.' He smiled at the expression of relief on the pair's faces.

'I thought you'd be pleased to hear that news, Jamie.'

'More than you'd know, James. It's hard, as you can appreciate, sitting here with our families only two or three days sail from us. We had some news of them last month and it was worrying.'

James Grant nodded sympathetically. 'We shall be on our way very soon. No more paperwork for you, Jamie. You'll be returning with us to our camp where Francois will endeavour to educate you in how we operate with our native allies.'

He produced a bottle of brandy from his knapsack. 'A drink to it, gentlemen,' he said, splashing the liquor into mugs. 'Confusion to our enemies and a reunion with our loved ones.'

Their talk turned to the news of a Declaration of Independence by the Continental Congress.

'What else is left to them. They gambled that by taking and holding Canada they had a strong bargaining chip. They failed. They can't hope to defeat us militarily now and when the Crown reasserts its authority they are all ruined men. Traitors!' James Grant spat the word out vehemently. 'They declare Independence in the hope that by clever lawyers arguments they can avoid hanging.'

'How so?' Jamie asked.

'Why, by claiming that as an independent state they owe no allegiance to the Crown and therefore cannot, in law, be rebels and traitors. A year ago they were insisting that despite being in armed rebellion, their argument was only with Parliament's policies and their loyalty to the Crown remained.' James laughed scornfully. 'They use fine words as a matter of expediency to save their miserable skins.'

Some days later, they travelled downstream to join their Indian allies.

Francois led them to a campfire where a tall Indian upon seeing him approaching, leapt up and embraced him. Others gathered round, calling out to him in cheerful voices.

'This is my brother in law, Catahecassa. He leads the Shawnee warriors.'

He spoke fluently and at length in Algouquian to the war leader who smiled and answered, waving toward the campfire.

'I told him you were both old and wise in the way of war and although we had been enemies many years ago we are now friends who will fight together. He welcomes you to his fire.'

Some hours later, sprawled by the fire, sipping tea heavily laced with rum, Jamie asked Francois why he had decided to offer his services.

'Surely you have little reason to support us in this quarrel, given all that's happened previously? Seven years of war. The occupation of your country.'

'You are wrong, my friend,' Francois smiled. 'I have many reasons. True, after the defeat, we Canadians felt as all people do who have lost a war. Anger, shame, much resentment. But for most people these feelings pass. Life goes on,' he said, reaching out and patting Jamie's knee with a grin.

'In some ways life changed for the better. Your government's rule is hardly tyrannical. We retain our religion and customs. We pay less tax now than we did under the old regime. Corruption, which helped to lose us the war, is a thing of the past.' He gave a Gallic shrug of the shoulders. We would rather have won...but such is life.'

'That doesn't explain why you are here,' Jamie persisted. 'You could sit back and let your old enemies kill themselves off.'

'Do you recall the Proclamation of 1763, when your government pronounced that all lands west of the Allegheny Mountains were Indian lands. That no colonial settlements would be allowed and those already there were to return to behind the Proclamation Line. It was a wise act. Almost impossible to enforce perhaps, but nevertheless it gave some hope and reassurance to the western tribes of the Ohio and beyond. I for one applauded it, married into the Shawnee Nation as I am.'

He kicked moodily at a log on the fire, his face sombre in the flare of light.

'Two years ago I was down the Ohio trading for furs. Matters were becoming worse. Settlers were coming over in ever-greater numbers and your soldiers were too few to prevent them. There were unwarranted killings of Indian families. I spoke to a commandant at one of your forts and he told me that the Colonial Assemblies did little to stop the numbers coming over. Indeed, they encouraged it by turning a blind eye. Many of the most prominent landowners had speculated on land in the Ohio Valley, and were doing everything in their power to overturn the Proclamation Act by lobbying the parliament in London. Land hunger, my friend. Land hunger and greed! The Ohio Valley is a powder keg ready to explode.'

Pausing to pour more rum in his cup, he continued. 'When I returned to Montreal the Americans were already there. Oh, at first they wooed us with fine words. Join us! Let us drive the British out together and be free of the tyranny.' He laughed scornfully. 'Jamie! We Canadians are not stupid. First we ask ourselves. Then what?

Francois spat in the fire. 'Soon we find out. Their General Wooster does not like Catholics so he bans the Mass at Christmas. They run out of hard money and they begin just to take what they want without payment when our people refuse to accept their worthless paper notes. They even began to levy a tax. What has been their rallying cry? No taxation without representation, was it not? Strange they should tax us without any consultation. Then again…maybe not. They say one thing and do another when it suits them. The Quebec Act was announced in 1774. Quebec province to include the Great Lakes and to the banks of the Mississippi. Freedom of religion and a reinstatement of French civil law. A confirmation of the ban on settlement in Indian lands or at least to limit it by proper treaties and fair purchases..' He raised an enquiring eyebrow at them. 'Strange is it not that their Congress should declare it another of the Coercive Acts, as if Quebec was some part of the thirteen colonies, then one year later be in rebellion?'

'You're saying the Quebec Act is the main reason for the rebellion?' Jamie asked.

'Yes, my friend! I'm saying it is the main reason. Pennsylvania and Virginia claim all the land from their western borders to the Pacific. Ridiculous is it not…but true. The men who sit in their Congress know that as long the Quebec Act stands they are denied the free hand they would dearly love. They discovered their power to change policy when they caused the British Government to repeal the Stamp Tax by civil disobedience. They took it one step further by armed rebellion, but it is going badly for them. Now they have taken the final step and declared themselves independent. So…I will fight alongside you. For my Shawnee family and for myself. Because if the Americans have their way there will be no protection for the tribal lands.'

The warriors they found themselves among were largely from the Great Lakes and Ohio valley area. Wyandots, Mingos, Delaware and Shawnees, among whom Francois was highly regarded. They found many could speak some French through long dealings with traders and voyageurs. With the French they had acquired in the months spent in Montreal after the surrender, their memories jogged during the winter in Quebec, they could converse after a fashion and their vocabulary increased with each passing week as Francois patiently taught them the native language.

They went out with them on sweeps to the south searching for rebel parties attempting to discover how powerful was the fleet assembling at St Johns, twice clashing with scouts and killing, capturing or dispersing them. A diversion that kept them occupied, until at last, in the autumn, the fleet sailed.

Chapter 29

The North canoe drove it's thirty foot length through the chop raised by a cold northerly wind, the ten warriors grunting in unison at each thrust of their paddles. Francois, on the steering paddle, nudged Jamie and pointed over to the whaleback shape of an island close to the western shore.

'Valcour Island,' he grunted. 'There's a sail showing at its south end.'

Beyond them stretching westward of the fleet of canoes and whaleboats were the gunboats and two schooners, with the larger ships a mile behind. Stretching back up the Lake was a swarm of bateau's carrying the infantry and supplies.

They had been waiting over a month for the final preparations to be made and a favourable wind to carry them up the Lake in search of the rebel fleet and now they had found them.

The sail they had sighted cleared the tip of the island and headed toward the gunboats. The two British schooners changed course to intercept it and they saw a puff of smoke from one of them and a few seconds later the sound of the cannon.

'If they're where I think they are we'll have trouble beating back into this wind to get at them.' Francois grinned. 'Clever!'

'In the channel between the island and the mainland you think? If so, it also means they are trapped,' Jamie said dryly. 'Not so clever!

The gunfire increased and they saw the American schooner turn away and head back to the island pursued by the two British ships.. The clumsy gunboats, now under oars, followed behind slowly

James Grant pulled close to them in a whaleboat manned by a mix of Indian Department rangers and Indians and yelled. 'Head for the island. If they're in the channel we'll have some sport with muskets.' He waved cheerfully and swung away westward.

Francois shouted instructions to the paddlers who whooped excitedly and dug their paddles in, the canoe hissing through the water with their eager thrusts. They passed close under the stern of the flagship 'Inflexible', the seamen aboard pausing in their preparations for action to give them a cheer, the Indians answering with more war whoops.

'By God, they've run her aground!' Iain shouted from the bows.

The rebel ship had missed stays in its change of tack and struck the shoals at the point of the island. Her topmast had come down in a tangle of cordage. The British ships stood off and pounded her. Before the canoes had closed the shore of the island the gunboats had began to form a line across the passage between the mainland and the shoals where the enemy schooner lay grounded. They began firing at an enemy fleet still hidden by the bulk of the island to the swarm of small craft.

Once ashore the three white men followed their party of Indians up the thickly wooded slope to the height of land. Trees masked their vision but they found a granite outcrop, which afforded a view. Below them, anchored in a crescent, their guns belching smoke and shot, lay the rebel's fleet. Fountains of water rose from the return fire of the gunboats, the noise magnified in the narrow confines of the channel. The vessels below had a ragged look until Jamie realised they had nailed a breastwork of small spruce trees to their gunwales to protect the men working the guns from the musketry James Grant had proposed.

He joined them on the outcrop, took the scene in at a glance and shrugged.

'Let them have their fun. We may not kill many but we can make it little more unpleasant.' A sputter of musketry could already be heard below them between the crash of the heavier weapons. 'Gather a few, Francois. I intend to head down to where that schooner ran aground. We may pick up some prisoners if the crew abandoned her.'

They moved down the spine of the island until they reached the headland that ended in low cliffs and peered through the trees at the schooner grounded fifty yards off shore. Most of their party moved off to scour the woods for the schooner's crew.

'Now there's a sight I never thought to see. A naval battle,' Jamie said, admiringly.

The British schooner, 'Carleton', lay anchored a hundred yards off shore and no more than three hundred yards from the nearest enemy vessel, her guns belching fire. She was taking punishment, splinters flying from her hull, the water around her spouting up in near misses. A cannonball skipped over the water and they heard it crash into the rocks below them.

Further off there was a muffled thud as a British gunboat exploded in a fiery ball leaving only a circle of disturbed water littered with boat fragments and the heads of a few surviving crewmembers.

More guns were hammering the 'Carlton' now and her upper works were gaping, her fire lessening as guns were overturned and gun crews decimated.

'Get out of there,' Jamie heard Iain say aloud, echoing his own thoughts.

Men ran up to her bows and a single foresail rose and flapped uselessly, the wind blowing from dead ahead A slight figure of a young officer raced daringly on to the bowsprit and leaned his weight on the foot of the sail. The wind caught it and reluctantly the ship's bows swung as the anchor cable was cut and she sheered away from the island and slowly back through the line of gunboats.

'Inflexible' had finally worked back against the wind and was adding her heavy broadside.

The rebel fleet was suffering now, one gundola heeling over and sinking and other craft listing, their masts, yards and rigging damaged. Darkness was falling fast, the flash of the discharges lurid in the gloom until finally the firing died away.

There was a burst of flames from the abandoned schooner and in it's light they could see a small boat rowing back toward the British line, it's crew having boarded the enemy vessel and set her alight. A mist rose from the surface of the lake and an uneasy silence settled in.

They watched until the schooner burnt down to the waterline then pulled back off the headland, lit a small fire and ate their rations. There was very little conversation before they rolled into their blankets and slept

Jamie woke to a misty first light and heard Francois calling. He and James Grant scrambled to join him on the headland.

The channel was empty. There was no trace left of the rebel fleet apart from some shattered timbers floating and the charred ribs of the schooner protruding. The rebel fleet had somehow slipped away aided by the mist.

'Damn me!' Captain Grant murmured. 'That, gentlemen, is downright embarrassing.'

They caught up with the rebel fleet the morning of the following day while they were still thirty miles from the protection of the guns of Ticonderoga. It was a running fight that saw the bulk of it destroyed. One vessel hauled down its colours and surrendered, others were run ashore and set afire. The last, Arnold's flagship, less than eight miles from Crown Point Canoe loads of Indians landed beside the burning wrecks and set off in pursuit of the crews. As the rest of the flotilla neared Crown Point there was a huge explosion inside the fortress and a thick column of smoke rose. A column of men could be seen hurrying up the road toward Ticonderoga.

'Our families will have heard that. They'll know we're coming Iain,' Jamie called jubilantly.

Passed the narrows of Chimney Point, James Grant's whaler drew up to them.

'I think I can spare you for a few hours,' James shouted. 'Off with you! Go see these families of yours.'

Francois called out to the paddlers and they dug deep and sent the canoe speeding along.

As they approached the familiar landing place Jamie could see the sawmill and workshops still stood but the piles of lumber and sawn planks were gone. He could see the roof and upstairs windows of his house on the hill above. He stood up in the stern of the canoe and removing his bonnet waved both arms.

'Can you keep them in the canoe while we go up to the house, Francois.'

Francois nodded and as the canoe glided alongside the wharf, Jamie and Iain leapt ashore and ran up the path.

The house looked deserted and Jamie's heart gave a lurch of fear. Then the door opened and Ezra appeared, a smile on his face but a musket cradled in his arms.

'Thought it was you wavin' but wasn't about to take chances with a canoe full of Indians.' He stood aside. 'There you go, ladies. Your menfolk are here,' and the families poured out the door.

Sarah managed to kiss him before the flying bodies of young James and little Bridget, alternately laughing and crying swamped him.

Sarah looked tired and thin faced but her brown eyes were sparkling and warm.

'You took your time, didn't you?' she murmured, teasingly.

Ezra went quiet as Francois and the warriors filed up from the lakeside at Jamie's call. He merely nodded curtly when introduced to Francois. Sarah and Ilsa set about preparing a meal for all with rations brought up from the canoe and the children excitedly mingled with the Indians, chattering away unintelligibly to them. They in turn grinned and nodded in good nature, allowing the children to peer into their medicine pouches and hold mirrors for them while they renewed the war paint on their faces.

'Iain and I, we can't thank you enough for what you've done Ezra. But for you....' Jamie left the rest unsaid.

'No need for thanks, Jamie. I hadn't anything special to do anyway,' Ezra grinned. 'I sorta enjoyed it. The responsibility I mean. Also it was a sport dodging them militia patrols. Reminded me of the old days. I'm sorry I couldn't stop them hauling away all your seasoned lumber and your saw blade. Took your tools as well. Needed them for that fleet they built. Sarah gave them a goodly earful, but they paid no heed '

He glanced over to the Indians and his mood sobered. 'I ain't overjoyed with the company you're keeping, mind.'

'It's a war, Ezra. You know how it is. You do all that it takes to win it. The rebels would do the same if they could find a tribe willing to fight for them.'

'Maybe! It don't make it right though.'

It was in Jamie's mind to say that hounding folk off their land because they didn't agree with what was happening was hardly right either, but he bit back the words.

'Can I ask you to play nursemaid for a while longer, Ezra. We need to rejoin the rest of the army. I'll get back just as soon as I can.'

Ezra nodded. 'You take care, y'hear.'

It was hard to leave after the all too short reunion but as the canoe headed over to the western shore Jamie felt the burden of worry that had plagued his thoughts for more than a year leave him. He looked back at the figures on the jetty waving and as he did so he felt a snowflake land on his cheek.

Chapter 30

'Fort Ticonderoga is too strong and we've no time for a regular siege,
what with winter coming on so early,' Captain Grant announced
bitterly to the assembled officers and rangers. 'It's hard enough keeping the army fed right now and once the Lake freezes it'll be nigh
impossible. Governor Carleton has decided we've done all we can
this year. I have to say I think he's right.' He looked round the disappointed faces. 'We begin pulling back soon. I suggest those of you
who have families and friends in the area should consider bringing
them back with you. The other Loyalist units are doing the same. I've
procured some bateaux's for your use. You have lists of people
friendly to us. I intend to warn those we can reach and advise them
to leave with us. It may go hard for them if they stay and we've no
way of protecting them.'

'Sir! That means the damned rebels will take over the farms of
whoever abandons them,' a ranger called, his voice distraught.

'No, they wont. Tomorrow we go out to bring in our friends and
families. While we're doing that we also burn every rebel gristmill,
farm, barn, and outhouse we can. We kill their animals and cut down
the trees in their orchards. We spare those of Loyalists. We teach them
the lesson they preached to us. If you're not for us then you're against
us and must take the consequences. Most rebels have run off when
we came. When they come back after we've gone they'll find a smoking wilderness.'

Plumes of smoke were rising as the loyalist families gathered. The
Slater's and the Pierce's arrived with squalling children and frightened
bewildered wives, carrying a few meagre belongings. Both men were
obviously torn between the agony of leaving their farms and the relief
of being free of the persecution that had dogged them since that fate-
ful day in the yard they now huddled in.

Iain called to Jamie. 'One more family coming in then we should
be ready to leave.'

'Ezra! Are you coming with us,' Jamie asked quietly, knowing as
he did so what the answer would be.

'Can't do it, Jamie. I ain't got no quarrel with you and I don't understand how it all came to this.' He jerked his head in the direction of

the pillars of smoke. 'All I can see is folk losing their livelihoods and these red hellions running riot. No! I cant be party to that.'

'You've no regard for the rebel cause. If you'd been around when my father was killed you'd have come along with us and pulled on the rope with Iain and Callum.'

'Probably would have. I tend to act first and think after. Been a failing of mine. And you're right. Them Boston lawyers and clever thinkers are full of cow manure. They've talked folk into a war, but you can lay money on it you wont see them pick up a musket to defend their liberties. They're clever enough to let ordinary folk do the killing and dying. I'm sorry, Jamie. You and Iain and all your folks have been good friends. You still are, but I'm heading back to New Hampshire to make sure my kin don't come to any hurt.' He grinned sheepishly. 'I guess that makes me a rebel, don't it?'

'No Ezra. Just a decent man caught up in something that's not of your making. Whichever way this sorry business turns out there'll always be a place at my table for you.'

Sarah wiped at her eyes as the bateaux pulled away from the jetty. The children, Ilsa and herself had made a tearful goodbye to the lone figure watching them from the shore.

'We would never have managed without him. I don't understand why he chose not to come with us. He dislikes the rebels as much as we do,' she said quietly.

'Perhaps! Ezra may hate all that's happened and have contempt for those who brought it on but he knows there's many people who owe no particular allegiance to either side of the argument. Who wish only to get on with their lives. He's fought Indians for most of his life and he sees our side using them. So he'll go off and help protect those he thinks will need it. The same way he helped protect you all. The politics of it means nothing to him.'

She bit her lip to hold back more tears as the roof of her home came into view. 'Do you think we'll ever live here again?'

'I don't know, lass. I think this war has a fair way to run and the longer it goes on the more hate it'll create. Things will never be the same. I'm not sure I could ever forgive what's been done and live among people who treated us the way they did. And I doubt if we'd be welcome back here after what I did,' he said, his voice tinged with bitterness.

More plumes of smoke marked the army's return passage north. Raiding parties peeled off to devastate a swathe of the valley, miles inland from the shores of the lake, the raiders returning with plundered goods, a few frightened captives, and more loyalist families, unwilling to face another winter of suspicion and persecution.

Chapter 31

He blew hurriedly on the embers of the fire, waited till flames crept up the sides of the logs he had placed on it, then, shivering in the icy cold leapt gratefully back into bed. Sarah stirred, complaining sleepily as his cold limbs touched hers. He felt the heat of her body warm him and he relaxed with a groan of pleasure as the chill left him. There was a faint gleam of light through the iced up glass of the window in the small bedroom they shared with the children. He could just make out their bed, bodies hidden by the bulky bearskin that covered them.

He lay awake waiting until the fire built up enough heat to drive the chill from the room.

The officer's quarters in the Fort at St Johns were small two roomed affairs, but warm enough with the fires burning all day. With only a small garrison left to man it while the bulk of the Army was in winter quarters the Fort was not overly crowded,. Most of the regiments were in Montreal but there were detachments in every village around the city. With the influx of Loyalist refugees, accommodation was at a premium and Jamie was thankful they had remained in St. Johns. Even Iain had succeeded, by making friends with the sergeant who allocated accommodation, of finding a room for Ilsa, young Iain, and himself, instead of some blanketed corner of a barrack room. Ilsa and the boy spent most of the day with Sarah and his children in their reasonably spacious parlour next door, while he and Iain went about their duties.

Despite the harshness of the winter Loyalists were still making their way into Canada. Men would trickle in, singly or in small groups, exhausted and hungry, often frostbitten, and all with stories to tell. Jamie recorded so many of the harrowing tales that the anger and bitterness he had felt when his father had been killed swelled into a deep hatred of the people who had brought about so much misery.

He was aware of the change in himself and it concerned him. For all the years of fighting the French he had never grown to hate them. He had respected them as soldiers, admired them on occasion and had admittedly feared them and their Indian allies at times, but had never felt as he felt now. He knew that others felt the same. To a man the Loyalists who had come north through the depths of that winter had one question on their lips. 'Where can I enlist to fight?'

He understood how they felt. The long months of harassment and suspicion. The ever present fear that at any time they would be arrested and shipped of to the dreaded Simsbury Mines where Loyalist prisoners were held. The helplessness of being unable to retaliate. When it became too much they left wives and children, the farms and businesses they had toiled to make a success of, and risked everything to reach Canada and hit back at their persecutors.

He knew it was happening all over the colonies. Wherever British troops were, Loyalists would come flooding in. New Loyalist regiments were being formed monthly. All this despite the fact that Congress had declared independence from Britain and all Loyalists who fought against the embryonic nation were now proscribed and their property to be confiscated. It was a civil war and had been, from its beginning.

The British response was gaining momentum. While they had been waging last year's campaign on the Lake, an army under Lord Howe had landed on Long Island, defeated Washington's army on Harlem Heights, then again at White Plains, before capturing New York. Jamie had heard the 42nd were back in America with Howe's army and had felt a surge of nostalgia at the news.

The army in Canada would sail south again this year and a determined drive from Howe's forces up the Hudson could see the two armies join and the United States would be split neatly in half.

The room having warmed sufficiently he rose reluctantly and dressed ready to begin another day of paperwork. There was impatience in him to be free of it. To record no more of the misery that fuelled his hate. An impatience to be on campaign again, carrying out the role that he was better equipped to deal with. The straightforwardness of soldiering.

Chapter 32

'It brings back memories does it not?' James Grant murmured, as they stood on the slopes of Mount Hope watching the light troops skirmishing forward to drive back the rebel pickets, the red of their coats, flecks of brilliance amongst the grass and scattered trees.

'None too pleasant memories, either,' Jamie said with a grimace. 'You took a wound here also?'

'A mere scratch that required no tedious stay in hospital.' James waved his arm at the panorama below them. 'It looks different since last we viewed it. They've been busy since last year,' he commented.

Fort Ticonderoga still loomed in the distance but the main defences surrounding it were the raw earth of redoubts and solidly built blockhouses linked by trenches. The hill on the opposite shore had also been fortified, connected by a pontoon bridge across the narrows. A massive boom spanned the lake barring the way south to ships and small craft.

'Onc thing hasn't changed. D'ye see the hill to the south of the fort on the other side of the river mouth. It used to be called Rattlesnake Hill, but now it has a grander title. Mount Defiance. Can you see any fortifications on it?

Jamie trained his eyeglass on the mountain, its tree-clad sides falling steeply into the lake and the mouth of the river. He scanned its rocky and sparsely wooded summit but could see no sign of defences. He shook his head. 'Nothing I can see.'

'No! And yet it's the key to Ticonderoga. I was up there once on a scout with Rogers. From the top you've a rare view and if you could get an artillery piece up there. Ticonderoga would be untenable. Neither the French nor the rebels ever bothered about it because it's deemed impossible to get cannon up there. Well, I've climbed it and steep as it is I've climbed steeper and we've got something other armies attacking this place never had.'

'And that would be?' Jamie asked, intrigued.

'Why, seamen from the fleet, Jamie. These sailors can hoist and rig a topmast in a full gale. Give them enough blocks and tackle and they'll move any damned weight.'

He glanced round and grinned. 'The very people we're waiting for. A few hours from now we'll know if it's possible or not.'

A small group of officers were approaching led by a major of artillery. Two of them were engineers and another was a lieutenant of the Royal Navy.

'Captain Grant?' the major asked.

'At your service, sir,' James replied.

'A warm day for what we have in mind, Captain. Let us hope it will be well worth the effort,' the major smiled. 'If you'd care to lead on.'

The escort of Indians and Department rangers rose on James Grant's signal and the party headed toward the crossing at the Chute river.

'Good Lord Almighty,' the major exclaimed excitedly, mopping the sweat from his face. 'There's a sight to gladden the heart of any gunner.'

They stood on the rocky summit of Mount Defiance Jamie had scanned with his spyglass three hours before and almost the whole of the rebel works lay below them. Across the narrows spanned by the bridge the new defences on Mount Independence looked so close he felt he could throw a stone and hit one of the tiny figures of men moving among the huts and cabins.

'Twelve pounders could reach, but eighteen pounders would be my choice. What do you say gentlemen?' the major said, turning to his companions. 'Is it feasible?'

'Level a few of the rock outcrops. Leave enough stout trees for purchase, and with blocks and tackle, my Jacks will haul up any size guns you wish,' the naval lieutenant grinned.

The engineer officers nodded in agreement. 'A hundred good axemen, crowbars and picks and we'll have something resembling a road in a day,' one of them commented

The major clapped his hands in satisfaction. 'Excellent. Back we go then. In two days time we'll have that ant's nest in a rare upheaval.

True to the major's prediction, within hours of the first shot being fired from Mount Defiance the rebels began retreating from the fort. A fire in one of the cabins on Independence that night lit up the sight of men streaming across the bridge in disorganised retreat. The surviving vessels of Arnold's fleet cast off and headed for Skenesborough. By morning Ticonderoga was deserted and units of British and Hessian troops were pressing hard on the heels of a demoralised American army. There were sharp fights with their rearguard at Hubbardton, Skenesborough and Fort Anne that allowed the bulk of their army the time to reach Fort Edward, but the way to Albany and the Hudson River was open.

It took almost a month for the army to reach the Hudson, advancing only about a mile a day as the Americans used the axe as a weapon. Hundreds of trees were felled across the road. Streams were diverted and the land, flat and boggy as it was, became a quagmire. The problems of re-supply increased and more troops were bled off to protect the routes. It was a much diminished and exhausted army that finally reached Fort Edward, then pushed down to Saratoga.

The news had been good from other quarters. A force composed mainly of Indians and Loyalists had heavily defeated the militias of the Mohawk valley in a particularly bloody battle at a place called Oriskany and were now besieging Fort Stanwix prior to marching to join Burgoyne. Worryingly though, there was no word of Howe forcing his way up the Hudson for a juncture of the armies at Albany.

Chapter 33

'Here, take a look at that,' Jamie said, passing the telescope to Iain. 'I can't even guess how many that encampment holds, but it's a big one.'

They were on a rise that gave them a good view of the stretch of open ground a mile off where tents and campfires filled the space.

'I can see smoke above the trees over to the right of it.' Iain grunted. 'Another camp I would say. There has to be at least a couple of thousand men in that near one.'

The Indians in the small party Jamie led were scattered along the front of the rise at the edge of the tree line, their painted bodies merging with the shadows.

'Go call them in, Iain. We'll pull back a mile or so, then take a swing round to see if your right about another camp.'

Iain slipped down through the trees and had almost reached the nearest Indian when the warrior glanced round and made a hurried hand signal. Iain froze and cautiously went into a crouch, peering through the trees at the open space beyond.

He could see a file of men approaching. There seemed to be no more than eight or nine of them. They seemed relaxed, muskets carelessly draped over shoulders or carried at the trail. He could hear them talking to each other and there was a burst of laughter.

The volley came as the first of them reached the tree line and it cut down the leading men. Warriors broke from cover, with spine chilling whoops and leapt at the four stunned and terrified survivors of the ambush, pulling the weapons from them, and threatening them with hatchets. Others lifted the scalps of the dead and dying militiamen.

The captives were quickly hustled back up to the ridge where Jamie was scanning the ground before them with the telescope.

He spoke hurriedly to the Indian war leader who nodded in agreement. The captives were roped together and the warriors slipped on the packs they had left on the ridge and began moving swiftly off to the north.

'We're heading back Iain. That shooting was bound to have been heard.'

They donned their packs and joined the file of warriors and prisoners, now loping along at a steady pace.

Jamie and Iain walked over to the huddle of prisoners tied together and guarded by a single Indian. The militiamen looked up at them, slack faced and apprehensive.

'Have you been fed,' Jamie asked, and one of them nodded sullenly.

'That was a big camp you came out of. Three or four regiments in it, at least,' Jamie said, his voice friendly. 'Where are you men from?'

'New Hampshire!' one growled. 'What's going to happen to us, mister?'

'That depends!' Iain grinned. 'All New Hampshire militia then was it?'

'In our camp, yes. There was New York troops further west.'

'Quite an army you're collecting,' Jamie remarked casually. 'I'm surprised you have New England men rubbing shoulders with Yorkers. I thought you couldn't abide them. How many would you say you've got in this army?'

'A damned sight more than you think,' the man shouted with a flash of spirit that quickly subsided when the Indian guard scowled and raised his hatchet menacingly.

'How many would you say, roughly?'

'I don't know. Twelve, maybe fourteen thousand I've heard,' the man muttered.

'Hell!' Iain laughed. 'Congress must be paying out some hefty bounties to raise that number. Come away man, stop exaggerating.'

'We don't need bounty money to come out against Burgoyne and these red hellions you're running with. We know what happened to Jane McCrae and we know what'll happen if we don't stop you. There's men pouring in from all over,' the man spat hatefully.

'Jane McCrae?' Jamie said in puzzlement. 'Do you mean the Loyalist girl who was killed on her way to join her fiancé? What has this to do with her?'

'If you can't protect your own people from these murdering savages, what does that mean for our women and children?'

'Hold on, friend,' Iain snapped. 'She was being escorted back to our lines and ran into a rebel party. They fired and she was killed. By Americans!'

'That's a damned lie. The Indians that were escorting her butchered and scalped her.'

'Why would they do that? And if there were no Americans around how the hell do you know what happened to the girl?'

'I read about it in the broadsheets. They told how the Indians got arguing about something, then one of them just upped and killed her for no reason. Everybody knows about it. That's why folk are gathering to beat the tar out of you. We don't want it happening to our womenfolk,' the man snarled, his faced flushed with anger.

'Now look...' Iain began, but Jamie touched him on the arm and jerked his head in the direction of their cooking fire.

'As they walked away the man called after them. 'You ain't told us yet what's to become of us, mister.'

Jamie turned. 'The Indians captured you so you're their prisoners. When they get you back to Canada they'll sell you to the Army for a few bottles of rum. Then you become regular prisoners of war. If they take a fancy to you, you could end up in their village and be adopted into the tribe. Personally, that would be what I'd prefer. They treat you pretty good compared to conditions in the prison hulks.'

He smiled without humour. 'What you'd better hope for is that these broadsheets were lying. I wouldn't want you to be worrying every time an Indian raises his voice.'

'Why didn't you let me put them right about Jane McCrae,' Iain grumbled as they settled in their blankets. 'Hell, her own friend who was with her when it happened told Burgoyne that the rebels shot at them. She said the lassie was on a horse and that was why she got hit.'

'A waste of breath; Iain. They read it in their broadsheets so it must be right. They've got so they'll believe anything bad they're told about us. Whatever happened to that girl, the rebels used it to their advantage. Nothing you or I say is likely to change these men's minds. What concerns me is if the prisoner is right about the numbers they've assembled we're getting to be badly outnumbered, what with losing all these Hessians at Bennington.'

A force of fifteen hundred Hessians had been sent to Bennington to take a supply depot there and been heavily defeated by men from the Grants and New Hampshire under Rogers's old captain, John Stark. Francois Geurlac had been killed there leading a native contingent. With the casualties from the earlier actions and the need to protect the supply route, Burgoyne's army was down to strength of less than seven thousand. And now, as autumn was setting in the Indians were beginning to leave.

'That ties in with other reports, Jamie. They seem to be gathering quite an army,' James Grant said. He dug moodily at a small field desk with a penknife. 'The other bad news is St Leger won't be joining us from the Mohawk. He's back at Niagara. A force of rebels lifted the siege of Fort Stanwix. And it appears Howe has gone off to take

Philadelphia. There'll be no army coming up the Hudson. We're on our own with at best a couple of week's supplies.

'Burgoyne will have to attack soon then.'

'He will! It's all he can do. And it'll be no easy task. You've seen these works the rebels have thrown up.' He reached behind his tent flap and produced a bottle of rum, and poured each of them a mugful. 'Your Indians gone?'

Jamie nodded and James gave a short bark of laughter. 'That makes us supernumeraries then. Surplus to requirement. You want to head back,' he asked seriously. 'You can if you wish.'

'Thank you, but no. I'll stay around and see what happens.'

'I thought you might feel that way.' James chuckled.

Three days later the army marched from Saratoga heading to the west of the rebel works on the Bemis heights to near a place called Freeman's Farm. The intention was to seize the high ground there and bring up artillery to bombard the American positions from the flank. James Grant with his Indian Department rangers and the few Indians that remained attached themselves to the right wing. Crossing a deep ravine with the light companies and grenadiers of the British regiments they formed up in the woods and waited for the centre to come up in line.

The rangers and Indians pushed forward as a screen along with a company of light infantry and before they had gone fifty yards there was a crackle of shots and a ranger beside Jamie grunted and folded over.

Iain threw himself down cursing. 'Of all the folk we had to meet it had to be riflemen,' he called to Jamie

Long-range shots were dropping men all around and the Indians were beginning to fall back in confusion as the white smocked figures of the riflemen moved closer, but still out of effective range of the muskets. A whistle blew and Jamie could see James Grant waving his arm to the rear. As men broke and ran the riflemen surged forward.

Jamie was only yards from the main line of redcoats when he felt a ball sear across his thigh. He stumbled slightly then threw himself through and behind the files of grim faced infantrymen.

Men were twisting and falling in their ranks long before the first return volley rang out. Then bayonets were fixed and the line advanced at the double toward the slow loading riflemen who fell back and scattered as the redcoats closed on them.

A regiment of Continentals recognisable by their white cross belts marched forward and exchanged volleys with the light companies, to be thrown back as the grenadiers came into line and added their fire.

Iain came through the trees peering worriedly at the scattered bodies of redcoats until Jamie saw him and called out. He came up looking relieved.

He grinned. 'Hot stuff!' he said jovially, then the smile vanished. 'What's wrong with your leg. You're bleeding.'

'It's only grazed. I've had a look. It's deep but not serious. What's happening?'

'The fight's moved to the centre. It sounds heavy. Come on! Lets get you back and have that leg seen to.'

Jamie stood up and winced as the weight came on the leg. 'Damn! That hurts.'

As they made their way back across the ravine the volume of fire from the centre rose to a crescendo as American units pushed into the gap between the centre and the right wing.

By the time Jamie was bandaged up by a surgeon, the battle was over as Hessian regiments came up from the east, taking the Americans in the flank and driving them back in disorder. An exhausted and battered British army retired back over the ravine having lost another six hundred dead and wounded they could ill afford. The next day they retired back some two miles and fortified their camp.

Chapter 34

'That's the last of the tea,' Iain said, passing a mugful of the steaming liquid to Jamie.

He sipped the bitter brew then looked up as James Grant approached wearily.

Iain poured another mug as the Captain sat down heavily.

'Thank you, Sergeant. Most welcome,' James said, then sat staring at it's contents for a time.

'Are you fit to travel?' he asked finally.

Jamie nodded. 'I'm fine. Why do you ask?'

'We're leaving the army tomorrow. Heading back north on Burgoyne's orders All the Loyalists.'

Jamie's heart sank, fearing what was to come next.

'He feels that as things stand it would be for the best. He said the rebels might well act vindictively toward us if the worst were to happen and we were captured. Particularly us Indian Department people.'

'He's surrendering the Army?'

James Grant shook his head. 'Tomorrow when we leave he intends to have one more stab at their positions. Try for the heights near Freeman's Farm again.' He rubbed at his face irritably. 'We have around four thousand men fit to fight. From what we've gathered from rebel prisoners they have upwards of fourteen thousand men and more coming in, and I believe them. Over three to one is pretty heavy odds. It'll take a miracle.'

Iain spat into the fire in disgust. 'Fourteen thousand men and they sit behind earthworks waiting for us to do something. It strikes me they're being a trifle cautious.'

'Their general over there,' James smiled, mirthlessly. 'His men call him 'Granny' Gates. While he's in command they'll do nothing but sit. I doubt if we'd still be sitting here if Arnold were in charge. We'd have succeeded at Freeman's Farm if Arnold hadn't led his division out and stopped us. We'd have been in Albany last year if he hadn't built just enough ships to delay us. We should be grateful they have generals like Gates leading them. God help us if they ever promote Arnold to a position where he can really use his talents.'

They crossed to the east bank of the Hudson by the pontoon bridge a few miles south of Saratoga. In the distance they could hear the sounds of battle and see a cloud of powder smoke rising above the tree line from far off. Men glanced behind them every few paces as they marched until at last the contours of the land hid the pall of smoke and the sound died to a sullen mutter.

Reaching Ticonderoga they waited for news of the fate of the army they had left behind, until at last those detachments left protecting the supply route began marching in.

It was news that had been half expected but all had hoped they would never hear.

The attack had failed. The numbers ranged against them having proved too much. A retirement to Saratoga followed with the Americans at their heels. Surrounded and with only a few days food, Burgoyne had asked for terms and surrendered his army. He had less than three thousand five hundred men left fit for duty.

The terms of surrender he signed were generous. He was to march his army to New York and there take ship for Britain, pledged never to take part in the conflict again.

His soldiers were never to be returned to Britain, as Congress overturned the signed Convention of surrender and gave orders for the British troops to be marched into the hinterland. Out of reach of any hope of rescue and moved from camp to barren camp, poorly fed and harshly treated, only a pitiful remnant survived the five years of captivity.

Chapter 35

He threw the newspaper down and stared dully at the weed-infested yard from the porch of the house they had rented in Montreal. He picked up the paper again and re read the news that Congress had signed a treaty with France.

'How could they do that?' he thought angrily. 'How could they bring themselves to go cap in hand to a nation they've been at odds with for so long? They rejoiced at France's defeat, yet a mere fifteen years later invite them back to fight against us. Do they hate us that much?'

He threw the paper down again and wondered what he could find to do today. Iain Mhor was off doing a stint as orderly sergeant at Headquarters and Ilsa had taken the children for a long walk to use up some of their excess energy.

The winter had been spent in an enforced idleness, the losses sustained in last year's campaign curtailing any hope of offensive operations until the St Lawrence was again free from ice and reinforcements and supplies could come pouring in.

A horse and rider splashed down the muddy roadway and James Grant dismounted. Tying his horse to the rickety fence bordering the property he made his way up to the house.

Jamie called inside, warning Sarah they had a visitor and stood thankfully to welcome him.

'I see you've read the news,' James said, nodding at the newspaper. They both sat down on the steps of the porch.

'They must be pretty desperate to sign a treaty with the French of all people. Either that or they have particularly short memories.'

'Oh, they're desperate all right. They know they can't win the war without outside help and who better than the French, itching to get back at us. Their economy is in tatters. Their money is worthless. They can barely keep an army in the field.' James chuckled in amusement at a thought. 'Do you remember how they regarded the army when we arrived all these years back. Godless scum who drank too much, was forever taking the Lord's name in vain, and could only be kept in order by the lash. They had a point, mind! Most of our army was like that. What I find amusing is the way they've suddenly discovered that if you want an army that'll stand in line and match British regulars volley for volley then that's the kind of men you need. Their Continental Line is made up of men like that.. Mostly the poorest and the landless. Immigrants straight off a ship or deserters from our army. Washington has introduced the whipping post to keep them in order.'

Sarah came out with mugs of tea. 'Good day, James. Why the amusement? I thought you'd be sitting with glum faces now we're at war with France again.'

'Just meditating on how reality rapidly overcomes ideals, Sarah,' James smiled. 'You're right though. We should be worried. When France goes to war with us, Spain normally follows. It's us against the world all over again.'

'How do you think the Canadians will react,' Jamie asked.

'Hard to tell. I think that their experience when the Americans were here soured them for any more of the same. Personally, I doubt if the majority wants to see Americans lording it over them even if France is involved.'

They sat making small talk for a while until James finished his tea and threw the dregs into the yard.

'I actually came with other news. I'll be leaving for Niagara shortly. I have just recently had word that my wife and child arrived there. I've arranged a transfer to Butler's Rangers. I've been promised a company.'

Jamie clapped his friend on the back. 'I'm delighted for you, James. How long has it been since you last saw them.'

'Nigh on three years.' He wiped at his face with his hand. 'God! Has it been that long.'

He rose and shook hands with Jamie and kissed Sarah on the brow.

'I saw Sergeant Munro at headquarters and said farewell to him there. I shall miss you all. With our service in the old 42nd and this latest stramash, we've shared some interesting times together.'

They watched as he walked toward his horse. Mounting, he grinned back at them.

'Keep fighting the good fight, Jamie Campbell,' he called and with a wave off his hand, rode off.

France's declaration of war changed the nature and scale of the warfare on the northern frontier. There would be no more invasions by large armies, ponderous in their movements and plagued by the problems of re-supply. Instead, the new Governor of Canada, Haldimand, uneasy at how the French Canadians might react at France's involvement, and experienced in the difficulties of warfare in America, instituted a campaign of raids intended to destroy the American's wherewithal to mount any invasion of their own. The farms and settlements of the frontier were to be the targets. Devastate these and they would be deprived of the food, without which an army could not function. Throughout that year, parties of Loyalist rangers and their Indian allies mounted destructive raids into the Mohawk, Wyoming and Champlain valleys.

The house and cabins still stood, windows shattered, doors drooping on broken hinges, their roofs gaping in places. His father's lean-to workshop, where he had puttered around lovingly constructing his fiddles, ever striving to create one with the sweetest sound, had collapsed. Sarah's vegetable garden was a wilderness of weeds, his party of Caughnawaga Indians cooking a meal where her neat rows of beans had stretched. He stood for a moment over the mound where his father was buried, the wooden marker long since burned as firewood by parties of militia who had camped there.

He walked up to the headland where Iain was standing.

The schooners and smaller craft that had brought the raiding parties of Rangers, Indians and Regulars down from St Johns were moored south of Chimney Point, the lines of their rigging clear in the crisp brightness of a November day. To the north and east, plumes of smoke climbed into the still air as Otter Creek burnt.

'I was forgetting how bonnie a view we had from here, Jamie,' Iain said, his arm sweeping across the vista of blue lake, its waters reflecting the vibrant colours of the trees in their autumn hues, with the blue grey ramparts of the Adirondack mountains looming away to the west.

'It's a black shame is it not? A grander place you'd be hard put to find anywhere on God's earth, yet this valley has seen more than its share of war and killing,' he continued. 'And we've played our part in it,' he added, soberly.

'Aye! It's a mercy the land has no memory. She has a way of renewing herself whatever we men do to her or each other. I think sometimes she'd be better off without us.'

Iain laughed. 'A world without men. There's a thought. And a damned boring place it would be, for sure.'

They stood quietly for a few minutes.

'Time we were gone,' Jamie said, and they walked back to where the Indians sat patiently waiting.

Their cooking fire still burned and Jamie reached down and lifted a blazing log. He turned to Iain with a question in his eyes. Iain nodded and he went up to the door of the house and threw the burning brand into a pile of litter and dried leaves that had blown in. Once the heap was well ablaze and flames were taking hold on the surrounding woodwork he walked back slowly, the Indians watching curiously, then he gestured to them to burn the rest of the buildings.

They did not look back as they marched north to where the ships lay at anchor, their home just another plume of smoke among the many.

Chapter 36

They hurried back through a deserted land after delivering yet another pinprick of a raid in the early hours of the morning, firing a sawmill and a couple of cabins near Pittsford. Targets were few and far between that autumn of 1779, the whole Champlain valley emptied of its people. Only the stone chimneys of burnt out farms and cabins were left standing as mute monuments to the effectiveness of the ruthless strategy.

The party Jamie led was small. Himself, Iain, another Indian Department ranger, who himself had originally come from Pittsford, and twelve Caughnawaga Indians. The old Military Road they padded along was overgrown now, the forest encroaching quickly in its disuse. After a few miles they left the road striking east of north toward the lakeshore and the canoe they had cached two days earlier after paddling down from Crown Point where the raiding parties would rendezvous when they had completed their tasks.

'A lot of effort for all we finally did,' Iain commented, groaning as he stretched out on his blanket after they had halted for the night.

'It reminds them we're still about.' Jamie said, brusquely

'I suppose!' Iain said half-heartedly.

'I heard rumours before we left St Johns that the rebels had sent an army up the Mohawk into Indian territory and were burning out the Indian Townships. You know if there's any truth to it, Lieutenant?' Sherrat, the other ranger, asked.

Jamie shook his head. 'You know as much as I do. It's probably true. From all the reports our raids have hit the Northwest hard. There's no food coming out of the area and that's hurting their army. I read that they're finding it difficult to keep them supplied. They were bound to try something of the sort. Not a particularly clever thing to do if it's true. The Indians will come back at them twice as hard.'

'All this burning each other out! Things were nicer when it was a real war like the last one,' Iain, said drowsily.

'Nice? I seem to remember a place called St Francis,' Jamie laughed.

'Oh, that!' Iain murmured. There was silence, then a loud snore.

They were only a couple of miles from the lakeshore, following an old track and about to cross a wide but shallow stream when the two Indians scouting ahead came splashing back with the news that they had sighted a party of Americans ahead of them and coming this way. They reported only six.

Signalling to the others, Jamie pulled them back from the stream and they took up positions along the top of the low bank.

'Where the hell did they come from,' Iain whispered. 'A follow up party from the raid who got ahead of us somehow, d'ye think.

'Too small a group. They send scouts out to watch the lake. It's probably one of these.'

Waiting tensely they saw the group approaching through the sparse trees. They moved steadily but appeared alert, a leading scout ten yards ahead of them. As he approached the stream he paused and scanned the far bank intently. Jamie held his breath, praying none of the Indians would spring the ambush prematurely.

The man turned and waved his companions on, stepped into the water and splashed forward. Jamie lost sight of him, the tree he was lying behind blocking his view, but as the rest of the party began to cross, he shot the lead man of that group.

The volley that followed threw down two other men and the Indians surged forward out of cover, whooping triumphantly, to claim the scalps. A half dozen of them set off in pursuit of the two survivors of the volley who had fled.

'Jamie! Over here, quickly,' he heard Iain shout and he scrambled over the bank in the direction of his voice.

When he reached the streambed he saw Iain standing over the body of a man he took to be the lead scout, Iain was holding the arm of an irate Indian brandishing a scalping knife. Jamie rapped an order at the Indian who looked at him sullenly but stepped back.

He knelt beside the crumpled figure and the man looked up and drawled in a husky but familiar voice. 'You caught us fair to rights there, Jamie.'

'Oh Christ! Ezra!'

Iain lifted Ezra's shoulders and propped him against a boulder and Jamie pawed frantically at the bloodstained shirt to look at the wound to the chest. A trickle of blood flowed from Ezra's mouth.

'Lung shot!' Ezra wheezed. 'Just like that elk I downed. D'ye remember that day, boys?'

'Not likely to forget it, Ezra,' Iain mumbled.

'You said you were going back to New Hampshire,' Jamie choked.

'Did, but my family had moved to the Grants. How's your families' doin?'

'They're well, Ezra. Don't talk!

'Wont make no difference talkin' or not talkin'. Tell them I said hello.' He grinned up at them. 'It's comforting to die among friends. Let that red skunk take my scalp when I go. For all the hair I've left he's welcome to it. He's just fair itchin' for it.'

He opened his mouth to say more and blood poured out. He looked down in surprise as it soaked his shirt and stained the water. Then he sighed and his head fell to one side.

Jamie stood up, his face expressionless. Then his shoulders sagged as if with a great weariness. He looked over at the Indian and gave a curt nod.

'Christ no, Jamie! You can't let him. Ezra was our friend,' Iain protested.

'Stop him now and he'll sneak back later and take it anyway. Don't you see Iain? It doesn't matter. Ezra's dead and we killed him. It can't get worse than that.' He turned and walked away, blowing his whistle to recall his party.

Sitting by a campfire at Crown Point, waiting for morning and the schooner 'Carlton' to take the raiding parties back to St Johns, Iain was quiet and subdued. He kept glancing over to Jamie, his gaze concerned and questioning. Sherrat had gone off to another fire to speak to friends.

Jamie sat nursing his rum and staring into the flickering flames.

'I know what you're thinking, Iain,' he said, without looking up. 'That I've become a cold-hearted bastard.'

'No! You're wrong. I know your hurting as much as I am. It's just we react in different ways. You hide it. You always have when something bad has happened. Me! Well, I tend to let the world know. You were right back there. It made no difference to Ezra. He was past hurting.'

He buried his head in his hands

'Who shot him Iain?' Jamie asked quietly.

'I don't know and I never want to know,' Iain mumbled, the anguish plain in his voice. 'It could have been Sherrat, the Indian, or me. We all fired at the same time. I keep telling myself that even if I'd recognised him it wouldn't have changed what happened. Ezra was a dead man as soon as he crossed the stream.'

Jamie reached out and squeezed his friend's shoulder. 'It's best our wives and children don't know he's dead. They loved Ezra. Let them think of him as just an absent friend.'

He took a swig of his rum, and as if finally coming to a decision, said firmly, 'I'm done with all this. What happened today finished me, Iain. There's been too much hate in me and I can't live with it any longer. I'm all burnt out, just like this valley. I'll see it through to the end, but when we reach Montreal I'm transferring back to the Emigrants. Get back to what passes as normal soldiering in this damned war. Are you coming with me?'

Iain looked up, his eyes wet 'I normally do,' he sniffed. He blew his nose noisily on his grubby kerchief. 'I'm glad! The truth is you were beginning to worry me. I had the feeling you sort of enjoyed what we've been doing this past year'

'You're right! I did…. And I'm not proud of it. You're the lucky man, Iain. I envy you. I don't think there's an ounce of hate in you. I've had too much of it bottled up inside me. I should have reserved that hate for those who had earned it. The ones who brought about this whole sorry business…. But I didn't. I began to hate everyone I perceived as not being on our side.' He paused and stared into the fire for a long moment. 'Jacob Buller! He was like that. Did I become like him?'

Iain shook his head. 'Buller! He was a natural born hater. Being a Patriot just gave him the opportunity to indulge himself. The fact you feel guilty about how you felt just shows how different you are from what he was. It's this war, Jamie. When we fought the French it was simple. Straightforward! This one's become too personal. We're burning the farms of people we did business with. There's hardly a farmhouse between here and Rutland where I haven't sat and had a dram with the man of the house. We're shooting at folk we would say hello to in the passing five years ago. Today we killed a good friend.' He breathed out heavily and took a gulp of his rum.

'When you say I don't have an ounce of hate in me, you're wrong,' Iain said quietly. 'If I could lay hands on the men who persuaded folk to turn against each other I'd kill them without hesitation…. But they're out of reach. I'll never find them standing in the battle line. These people fight with their mouths and fancy words. So I put it from my mind. I refuse to let how I feel about them change me.'

'You won't change Iain Mhor. You're the best of men and I bless the day we became friends,' Jamie said affectionately. He reached for the rum bottle and poured more in their mugs. 'If I were more like you I'd be easier in my mind. I can take life a little too seriously.'

Iain Mhor snorted. 'Now, haven't I just been telling you that for years.'

They drank their rum and rolled into their blankets.

Jamie was drifting into sleep when he was nudged awake.

'Had you heard the news before we left St Johns?' Iain whispered hoarsely. 'The Emigrants have finally had an issue of plaiding and red coats. It'll be rare to look like real soldiers again, Jamie.'

Chapter 37

Sarah looked up as they entered, her face flushed with the heat of the kitchen where she and Bridget had been preparing a meal since rushing back from the parade in Montreal.

She looked at her husband and son resplendent in their full regimentals of a Captain and Ensign in the 84th Regiment of Foot, Royal Highland Emigrants. The belted plaids of the familiar dark Government tartan, the blue facings and laced trim of their red coats, and the broadswords hanging by their sides. Her eyes prickled with tears of pride and she hurriedly wiped at them.

'The last parade!' she said, softly.

'Aye, lass,' Jamie smiled. 'The last parade. How did we look?'

She recalled the hollow square of companies facing the colours, the men listening to the address of their Colonel reading the orders for their disbandment and thanking them for their service. The cheer that rang out as his speech ended, then the companies wheeling away to the sound of the pipes leading them in their final march back to barracks.

'Fine! You looked just fine.'

He winked at his son. 'Did you hear that, James? Your mother thinks we looked fine. High praise indeed from a soldier's daughter.'

She laughed and punched his shoulder, then helped him remove his broadsword.

Bridget came through from the kitchen, an image of her mother when first they'd married. She kissed her father, then mischievously accused her brother of being out of step during the march off.

Jamie and Sarah left them squabbling and walked out to the shaded porch.

'It's a pity Iain was not there to share it,' she said.

Iain was already discharged and far to the west with Ilsa and young Iain, preparing for their arrival on the land they had been allocated by the shores of Lake Ontario.

'We'll be seeing him soon enough once we settle our affairs here. With the Government compensation for our loss of land and property and what's left of your legacy from Mistress Yonge we'll have more than the wherewithal to start over. That last letter from Iain was encouraging. Prime plots on the lakeshore and between us all, more acreage than we can handle.'

He saw Callum with his French Canadian wife turning into the gate, carrying their two children,

'He's arrived at last. Now we can eat. I'm starving!'

The men left the womenfolk cooing over Callum's infants and moved out to the porch with their glasses of wine.

'I can't persuade you to change your mind then, Callum?'

'I'm sorry Jamie. My mind is made up. The offer Yvette's father has proposed is far too good. I can do what I do best and that is make fine furniture. Besides, I love Montreal,' he laughed. 'I'm practically French now.'

'We've fairly chosen a rare mix of womenfolk between us. An Irish lass for me, French for Callum, and Dutch for Iain. What of you, James? Might you have any particular preference of country?'

'Don't be daft, Father! You know fine I've been too busy these last two years to even speak to a lass.'

'You should ask Bridget if she has any eligible friends,' Callum grinned.

'I'd not ask her the time of day in the certainty she'd lie about it. Do you know Uncle Callum, she had the impudence to accuse me of being out of step when we marched off.'

Jamie shook his head in bemusement as his son proceeded to list all the tricks his sister had played on him over the years. For all that he'd been an Ensign of the 84th from the age of seventeen and had two years of hard service behind him, he could still react to his sister's teasing.

He left the pair of them and leaned on the porch rail sipping his wine and savouring the cool night air.

The last parade! Today has seen an end and a beginning, he mused. Eight years we've fought and now it's over, but we have to start rebuilding our lives again. We are in our middle years yet we're back where we were twenty years ago. Breaking new ground with all the hard toil that'll go with it. All because of a difference of opinion!

His thoughts turned to those he had known and who had died because of that difference of opinion. His father, a gentle old man, incapable of hate. Liam shot down because he ran. Young Billy, who had wanted to fight so badly, drowned in a river crossing on his way to what would have been his first engagement with the enemy. Francois Geurlac, fighting in a war he saw as crucial to his Indian kinfolk. James Grant killed leading his company of rangers in one of the last skirmishes before war's end. And Ezra!

For a moment that bitterness he kept locked inside, overflowed.

How many people in that new country, he wondered, now look back on the last eight years and reflect if what they had gone through was worth it These years of killing and hardship in the name of liberty and equality. High sounding words, used by men who would jealously guard the right to decide just how much liberty and equality they would allow the people they purported to serve. Perhaps some future generation might value these words and ensure they really meant something.

We lost to a Congress that cannot pay its army or even feed them on a regular basis. Who ran bleating to the one country that they knew would help them. Not out of sympathy for their cause, but from the desire to revenge a defeat. A Congress, who denounced monarchy as tyrannical and rejected it, but became wholly dependent for their very survival on a country with an absolute monarch.

He was startled from his thoughts as Sarah touched him on the hand.

'You're brooding,' she said in mock severity. 'I can tell by that look on your face. I won't have it. Not tonight!'

'You're right as usual. It's over and I should accept it. Just give me a little time.'

She stretched up and kissed him on the lips then took his hand.

'The instruments are out and we're tuning up. Callum has borrowed your spare fiddle. Yvette has forbidden him to play the pipes, as the children are asleep upstairs. So come away in. You've always said music was the best way to forget your troubles.'

He put an arm over her shoulder and together they joined their family who were already playing the first bars of a lively reel

Chapter 38

The families gathered in the dappled shade of the orchard, the women carrying succulent smelling baskets of food, the younger children running riot, excited by the unexpected holiday from school lessons and chores. The menfolk gathered round a keg of cider pressed the previous year from the fruit of the trees around them, the boughs heavy with another crop.

Jamie filled his mug and wandered down to the stile in the fence and sat on its top step, looking out over the tranquil expanse of Lake Ontario, its surface shimmering with myriad points of light. To the east he could make out the first of the many islands that studded the lake where it narrowed and emptied into the St Lawrence River. South of them, lost in a heat haze, lay the United States. They had only recently declared war on Britain and already the young men were leaving the settlements in droves to protect the land from their neighbours to the south.

'So it all begins again. They want Canada and they think they can take it this time,' he thought angrily. 'With Britain fighting Napoleon we're stretched as usual. Two regiments of regulars and some units of untried militia is all we have.' He scowled at the unseen shores across the lake and slapped the flat of his hand on the wood of the style. 'You drove me out once. You'll not do it again, damn you,' he vowed angrily.

'Ach! Here you are.'

He moved over on the stile to make room for Iain Mhor.

'Jamie! I've been thinking,' Iain said after a long pull at his tankard.

'Och! God preserve us,' Jamie groaned, rolling his eyes to the sky.

'Ach, listen now. Hear me out. Do you remember a man named Donald…or was it Duncan…No! Donald Cattenach. Served in Three company. Got himself wounded at Fort Ti in 58. Lost an arm…or was it a leg? Whatever! Do you mind him?'

'I do. He went by the nickname of Father Abraham.'

'The very man…and they called him that because of his great age. Why… he would have been all of sixty five when he…'

'You can stop right there for I know where this is leading. You're about to suggest it would be a rare ploy if we went off and joined the Militia with our grandsons.'

'Man, but you're sharp. What do you think yourself?'

'That you've finally lost what wits you had. We're way past our three score and ten. I can barely raise my arms above my shoulder for the rheumatism, and the noises you make when you put on your brogues has to be heard to be believed.'

'Now Jamie! It was just a thought. The merest of notions.' Iain took a gulp of cider and sighed. 'Mind! It would be a fine thing to go with the lads. Keep an eye on them. Teach them a trick or two. Aye! It would be a fine, fine thing.' he said wistfully.

Jamie snorted. 'Two damned wars we've come through and you're hinting we up and enlist for another one. You're as daft as the day I met you. The trouble with you Munro is you think you're indestructible…and there were times you almost had me convinced. The biggest damned target in the Americas' and you never took so much as a scratch. Half an army dying of fever and you've never been ill… apart from when you ate too much. I'll remind you it was myself took enough wounds for the pair of us…and near died of the fever. We almost starved to death in 59 because I let you talk me into going off with Rogers on account of how you were bored. It's all been a game for you. Just an amusement.' He paused for breath.

'So! You're not exactly in favour of the idea, then,' Iain said, mildly.

Jamie spluttered with laughter, spraying cider. 'Look at the pair of us. Can you imagine us turning up with our lads to enlist. Why the two of them would be black affronted with their grandfathers trailing along to act as their nursemaids.' He clapped an arm round his friend's still massive shoulders. 'Tell you what though. If the Yankees come near here…providing they're within easy walking distance…you and I can always sneak off and try a few shots at them. Long range, mind! Wouldn't do to get too close on account we're little use at the running these days.'

Iain beamed. 'Aye! We could always do that. Find out how good these rifled guns of ours really are.' They both chuckled at the prospect.

'You're like two great bairns hatching up mischief,' Sarah said from behind them. She had heard most of the conversation. 'The boys will be leaving soon, so come and say your goodbyes.'

She watched them climb down from the stile stiffly and carefully with a half smile on her face. Both carried themselves erect as befitted old soldiers. Jamie still lean, his hair snow white and neatly clubbed, framing the lined weather-beaten features, contrasting with Iain's bald pate fringed with grey, his form as bulky as it had always been, although added to by the stomach hanging over his belt. They spent a lot of time with each other these days, Iain's wife Ilsa having died three years previously. She was well used to the sight of them sitting together, reminiscing, arguing, and laughing about some event in the past...and it gladdened her heart to hear them.

Her own house had been quiet for years. Bridget had married a Scottish farmer in Glengarry County and was now a matronly figure with children of her own. James had long been wed to a Mohawk girl from Cateraqui a few miles away. She bit her lip thinking of him already off to Fort York with a contingent of warriors from the settlement where he served as a captain in the Indian Agency. Now the grandsons were off to enlist.

It had been her idea to have a farewell meal for the lads who were leaving. Five from the village were off today.

'It's little point in being miserable about it,' she had commented to Jamie. 'Let them leave knowing we're proud of them and care for them.'

Alex, Jamie's oldest grandson, stood beside his mother Beth, a tall slim woman, half Mohawk, half Scottish, her sleek black hair belying her fifty years Her father, Simon McDonald had been killed serving with Butler's Rangers in the last year of the war. Despite a husband already off to fight and a son about to do the same she looked calm and composed. Alex had inherited the dark hair and looks of his mother and grandfather.

Iain Mhor's grandson, another Iain, stood close by with his mother and father, large boned and blond-haired.

'Will you just look at the two of them,' Sarah said, as they approached their grandsons. 'Dress them in kilted plaids, with a red coat on their backs and a broadsword at their hip, I'd swear I was looking at the pair of you fifty years back.'

'Aye, we were brisk handsome lads then,' Iain Mhor chuckled, looking down ruefully at his sagging waistline.

Alex smiled as his grandparents joined them. 'Well, grandfather! Have you any words of advice for us before we go?'

Jamie shook his head. 'None that I can bring to mind, lad. Ach! You'll be fine, the pair of you.'

The families were coalescing around the young men who were leaving, saying their goodbyes, many of the women in tears. Then the groups made their way to the road and watched as the young men set off. They halted a short distance away at a bend in the road and turned, raising their bonnets in farewell.

A memory came to Jamie of a time long gone. Of an old blind man standing by the side of a road, his cheeks wet with tears, as a column of his countrymen tramped passed him on their way to an almost forgotten war, the sound of the pipes preceding them.

The Gaelic words came to his mind in clear remembrance and he cupped hands to mouth and shouted.

'*Cuimhnich gniomhan ur sinnsearan!* Remember the deeds of your ancestors!

Historical notes.

The opinions expressed, particularly in the latter part of the book, are those of the characters, inasmuch as they were written from what I imagined would be their point of view. These opinions may sound partisan and prejudiced to some, but the perceptions of men and women caught up in the events of that time were dependent on, then as now, which side of the argument they took. That some of the opinions and perceptions held by my characters were justifiable and contain elements of truth is a matter of historical record.

The early history of any nation, as taught to the children of that nation, is normally a sanitised and often romanticised version of the events. A sweet smelling potpourri, where the heroes are lily-white, the villains are… well…villainous, and the more unpalatable facts ignored or very quickly brushed over.

For the majority of people this picture of how it was is sufficient. Few have the inclination to delve deeper into the sometimes murky depths of factual history and they happily retain the over simplified version of what they were taught. And why should they not! These events happened a long time ago.

Chapter 1

General Braddock has often been labelled as a blunderer, when, in fact, he was a brave and capable general by European standards. Ambushed in his advance toward Fort Duquesne, he found himself embroiled in the type of battle his redcoats were not trained to fight. His dying words were, 'We shall do better next time.'

The philamhor, or belted plaid, was a length of tartan cloth around twelve yards long. The bottom part was laid in pleats, the edges passed over and secured with a broad belt. The remaining cloth was secured at the shoulder or in inclement weather, worn shawl like. The philabeg or little kilt was the bottom part only, the excess material cut off.

Drummossie Moor! Better known as the Battle of Culloden

Chapter 2

Fontenoy was the first battle the 42nd fought. Their conduct was highly praised.

Am Freiceadan Dubh. The Gaelic nickname given to the regiment. The Black Watch. Deriving from the dark tartan and their origins as Independent Highland Watch companies. The nickname was incorporated into their title when the system of referring to regiments by their number ceased, and finally became the regiment's sole name

The three-year enlistment option was actually brought in more than a year after Jamie took the shilling.

Chapter 4

Englishmen made up less than 30% of officers and men in the army of the Americas. The Celtic fringes supplied the bulk of serving officers and soldiers.

Chapter 5

It is fact that the officers of the Provincial forces gathered at Fort Edward informed the Commander in Chief that they would resign and their troops would desert en masse if joined by Regular Army regiments

Lord Louden amended the ruling regarding the seniority of Crown officers over Provincials less than a year later, although if of equal rank, the Crown officer was the senior.

Martin McConnell's views on Provincials were widely held among regular soldiers. Their poor camp discipline was a recurring complaint in military records of the time.

Curling was introduced around this time to America and later to Canada by the influx of Scots.

Chapter 6

The events at Fort William Henry happened much as the Corporal related it. The Indians carried off over 500 captives, most of whom were subsequently bought back by the French.

Chapter 7

As troops became accustomed to the nature of the warfare, most ranger operations contained substantial numbers of volunteers, officers and men, from the regular and provincial regiments.

Chapter 8

The Ranger's 'Battle on Snowshoes' gives an indication of the savage nature of the warfare, particularly in the vicious minor clashes that were a continual feature of it. Of the 187 men in Rogers' command, only 52 survived. Ensign Andrew Ross was the only man from the 42nd recorded as having taken part and was listed among the dead.

Chapter 9

If any battle deserves special mention in the annals of the Black Watch then surely Carillon, or Ticonderoga, is one. From a strength of around 1300, they had almost 300 killed among their 603 casualties. They continued to attack despite being ordered to retire three times. An officer of another regiment wrote.

'With a mixture of extreme grief and envy I consider the great loss and immortal glory acquired by the Scots Highlanders in the late bloody affair. Impatient for orders they rushed forward to the entrenchments, which many of them actually mounted. They appeared like lions breaking loose from their chains.'

Chapter 10

The 42nd had been designated a Royal Regiment before the news of their conduct at Ticonderoga had arrived in Britain.

Chapters 12, 13 & 14

The events in the St Francis Raid occurred much as I have described them and based on Major Rogers' own journals.

Opinions differ on the number of casualties inflicted on the St Francis Indians. That many women and children were killed is highly likely, given the suddenness and timing of the attack. Rogers' estimate of around 200 killed does not give any indication of how many were warriors. His figure is generally regarded as an over estimation.

Lieutenant Stephens, a Ranger officer, was court marshalled and cashiered for failing to remain at the Wells River rendezvous with the badly needed food for Rogers' men. It appears he heard shots and assuming it was Indians, departed with the food, literally hours before Rogers' men began arriving.

Rogers and Ogden's journey down the Connecticut River by raft to secure food for the starving men was and is, an extraordinary example of human endurance and determination.

Chapters 16 & 17

The 1/42nd was so reduced by the sickness and fever of the West Indies expedition that only 200 were fit for duty on their arrival back in America. Every other regiment suffered the same or worse.

Chapter 21

Charles Hutchinson, described in records as an ex NCO of the Highlanders did not, in fact, go to Canada after Ethan Allan burned him out. The records of Hebron, New York State show he relocated there. The records also mention that he would often talk of that night.

Lt Colonel Reid's acquisition of 7000 acres north of Otter Creek led to Ethan Allen and ninety of his Green Mountain Boys driving off the Scottish settlers and burning their farms and gristmill. The settlers were told to inform Colonel Reid that if he set foot on the land again 'his head would be cut off.'

Chapter 22

The words used to describe Ethan Allen's character are echoed by many of his contemporaries. An oft repeated comment used by his admirers in defence of his tactics is that, despite the campaign of fear and intimidation he instituted, the beatings of Yorkers and the burnings of their farms by he and his Green Mountain Boys…they never once killed anyone. So… that's all right then!

Yet, he is a hero of the Revolution. It may be understandable his being somewhat of an icon in Vermont, a state he was instrumental in creating, but his record of loyalty to the Patriot cause he so eagerly espoused in the first year of war bears scrutiny.

By 1780, Vermont, now an independent republic and angered at having been refused recognition as a state by Congress was virtually neutral, refusing to supply food or manpower to the Continental Army. The British were more than happy to exploit the rift. A letter to Governor Haldimand of Canada from Allen, who had been exchanged after his capture at Montreal, assured the Governor that there would be no interference from Vermont to British military activities on Lake Champlain. With a secure left flank, the way was open for a huge raid that devastated the farms and settlements of upper New York as far down as Saratoga. Vermont also served as a useful conduit for Loyalists making their way to Canada.

Later, negotiations were opened on the possibility of a return of Vermont to it's allegiance to the Crown. They came to nothing as Allen was probably only attempting to force a change of heart on

Congress. Vermont took no further part in the war, and did not achieve statehood until 1791

It is difficult not to compare Allen's inflated place in American history to that of Benedict Arnold's. A name that to young Americans is a byword for treachery, yet whose drive and energy did more to save the Patriot cause in its early years than any other of their military leaders.

Chapter 24

The taking of Ticonderoga has often been referred to as a battle, whereas the tiny garrison, unaware that armed rebellion had taken place near Boston fired not a shot. It is probable the idea to take Ticonderoga was Benedict Arnold's. Why else would he have been there? As the Green Mountain Boys refused to follow anyone but Allen, it was he who reaped the glory. The guns taken from Ticonderoga were instrumental in driving the British out of Boston

In his memoirs, Ethan Allen claims his actual words to Captain Delapace were 'Come out of there you old rat!'

Chapter 26

The Royal Highland Emigrants were raised from among the Scots veterans of the previous war augmented by other Scottish settlers. The 1st Battalion under Lt Colonel MacLean served in the northern theatre throughout the war. A 2nd Battalion known as the 'Young Emigrants' was raised in Nova Scotia by Major Small, an ex 42nd officer, and served in the eastern and southern campaigns

The New Years Eve attack on Quebec in a snowstorm was forced on the commander of the rebel force, General Montgomery, as many of his soldiers enlistment's were up the following day. He was killed in the attack and Benedict Arnold was wounded.

Chapter 28

The Coercive or Intolerable Acts was the name given by the colonists to a series of laws passed by Parliament in response to the destruction of cargoes of tea, famously known as the Boston Tea Party. Largely directed against Boston and the colony of Massachusetts, regarded as the hotbed of sedition, they included the closure of the port of Boston until such time as reparation had been made for the tea.

The Massachusetts Government Act sought to bring that Colonial Assembly under more direct control. A law that the other colonial assemblies feared could be eventually applied to them.

The Quartering Act permitted troops to be quartered in uninhabited houses, barns or other buildings, but not on civilian families.

The Quebec Act aroused the anger of many of the interest groups in the colonies, particularly those speculating in land across the Proclamation line and others who held a strong anti Catholic view. Unrelated to events in Massachusetts it was still labelled a Coercive Act.

Chapter 31

The popular conception of an entire people in arms driving out the forces of tyranny is appealing, but totally incorrect. Only around 23% of a population numbering two and a half million actively supported the Patriot Cause. However, they possessed a powerful political organisation. An estimated 30-40% was Loyalist at the onset of the Revolution. Many of those may have disagreed with the British government's handling of colonial affairs but hoped matters would be solved by dialogue. They had no wish to break ties with Britain. The remainder of the population was largely apolitical. It was America's first civil war and was regarded in Britain as such. British regiments do not carry on their colours the names of any of the many battles they fought during the Revolution for this reason.

Thousands of Loyalists fled the country or were forced to take an oath of allegiance to the new state. Over 160 Loyalist regiments or militia units were raised during the course of the war.

At the end of the war, over 100,000 Loyalists abandoned their ties with the United States and re settled elsewhere, most of them in Canada.

Chapter 33

Jane McRae is an unusual heroine of the Revolution given that she was a staunch Loyalist and at the time of her death on her way to join her fiancé, a Loyalist officer in Burgoyne's army. The argument as to how she met her death and at whose hands still rages. Iain Mhor is correct in stating her female companion, also travelling with the Indians, but delivered unharmed, told Burgoyne they had been pursued and shot at by Americans. Whatever the circumstances of her death, it was used to great advantage by the Americans. Their version of how she was killed helped raise the numbers who fought against Burgoyne.

Burgoyne understood that the 1777 campaign plan was for Howe's army to advance up the Hudson Valley in conjunction with his thrust from the north, thus splitting New England from the rest of the colonies.

Unfortunately the planners in London failed to inform Howe, who pushed down toward Philadelphia. By the time realisation had set in and a force under General Clinton was dispatched up the Hudson it was too late for Burgoyne's army. His surrender encouraged the French to enter the war on America's side and was probably the greatest single factor in deciding the final outcome.

Chapter 35

James Grant's observations on the Continental Army were correct. After the initial zeal of the first eighteen months of the war, fewer and fewer citizens wished to have anything to do with service in the Continental Army, most of the better off paying to hire substitutes.

A French officer, Louis Duportail, who became the chief engineer of the Continental army, reported to his Government, 'There is a hundred times more enthusiasm for the Revolution in any Paris café than in all the colonies together.'

Washington's Army was soon composed of only the poorest in that society, many of them recent immigrants. The discipline imposed on them was as harsh as that of their counterparts in the British Army, who at least were paid on a regular basis and fed adequately. A situation that resulted in the Continental Line suffering high desertion rates and causing regiments to mutiny. The manpower crisis became so bad that Washington contemplated invading the Republic of Vermont to retrieve the large numbers of deserters who had taken refuge there. His Continental Army never numbered more than eight thousand men.

Governor Haldimand, convinced, as he was, that the rebel colonies would again attempt to take Canada with the help of their French allies had just 4000 men at his disposal and a border stretching from the Atlantic to the Great Lakes. His strategy of destroying the sources of supply was a legitimate military operation, but regarded by the rebels as purely vengeance attacks by spiteful Tories. Some of the smaller raids undoubtedly were. The hugely destructive raids of 1780 known as the 'Burning of the Valleys' seriously worried Congress, concerned that people would begin looking to the British for a protection that they themselves could not provide and the effect it was having on the provision of Washington's army.

Chapter 38

The War of 1812 was ostensibly caused by the impressment of American seamen into the British Navy but had other causes, including a suspicion that Britain was arming the native tribes in their ongoing struggle with American expansionism. The majority of Canadians saw these as excuses for the true reason. The conquest of Canada!

Former American President, Thomas Jefferson wrote,

'The acquisition of Canada this year (1812) will be merely a matter of marching and will give us the experience for the attack on Halifax, the next and final expulsion of England from the American Continent.'

. The invasion of Canada by American troops was thrown back in a series of battles around Detroit and Niagara in the west, and on the St Lawrence and in Lower Canada. The Americans themselves were divided on the need to go to war, the New England states opting out of any participation

A small glossary of Scots words and expressions used.

Wheeching...Flicking or slicing.
Dab hand... Expert, clever at.
Hurdies...   Thighs and buttocks
Stramash......A fight or brawl
Rickle......... A heap or scattering of.

LaVergne, TN USA
06 June 2010
185046LV00005B/309/P